Praise for

Hooked on Murder

"Hooks the reader from the onset with likable characters . . . Readers will admire the feisty, caring Molly."
—*Genre Go Round Reviews*

"Readers who enjoy craft-and-hobby-related cozies will find lots to like in *Hooked on Murder* . . . Betty Hechtman does it all so well: writing, plotting, and character development."
—*Cozy Library*

"Hechtman's writing is fun and introspective, and Molly is a likable character."
—*Romantic Times*

"A great start to a new mystery series."
—MyShelf.com

"A gentle and charming novel that will warm the reader like a favorite afghan. Its quirky and likable characters are appealing and real."
—Earlene Fowler, author of *Tumbling Blocks*

"Betty Hechtman has written a charming mystery. Who can resist a sleuth named Pink, a slew of interesting minor characters, and a fun fringe-of-Hollywood setting?"
—Monica Ferris, author of *Thai Die*

Berkley Prime Crime titles by Betty Hechtman

HOOKED ON MURDER
DEAD MEN DON'T CROCHET
BY HOOK OR BY CROOK

By HooK or
By CrooK

BETTY HECHTMAN

BERKLEY PRIME CRIME, NEW YORK

THE BERKLEY PUBLISHING GROUP
Published by the Penguin Group
Penguin Group (USA) Inc.
375 Hudson Street, New York, New York 10014, USA
Penguin Group (Canada), 90 Eglinton Avenue East, Suite 700, Toronto, Ontario M4P 2Y3, Canada
(a division of Pearson Penguin Canada Inc.)
Penguin Books Ltd., 80 Strand, London WC2R 0RL, England
Penguin Group Ireland, 25 St. Stephen's Green, Dublin 2, Ireland (a division of Penguin Books Ltd.)
Penguin Group (Australia), 250 Camberwell Road, Camberwell, Victoria 3124, Australia
(a division of Pearson Australia Group Pty. Ltd.)
Penguin Books India Pvt. Ltd., 11 Community Centre, Panchsheel Park, New Delhi—110 017, India
Penguin Group (NZ), 67 Apollo Drive, Rosedale, North Shore 0632, New Zealand
(a division of Pearson New Zealand Ltd.)
Penguin Books (South Africa) (Pty.) Ltd., 24 Sturdee Avenue, Rosebank, Johannesburg 2196,
South Africa

Penguin Books Ltd., Registered Offices: 80 Strand, London WC2R 0RL, England

This is a work of fiction. Names, characters, places, and incidents either are the product of the author's imagination or are used fictitiously, and any resemblance to actual persons, living or dead, business establishments, events, or locales is entirely coincidental. The publisher does not have any control over and does not assume any responsibility for author or third-party websites or their content.

PUBLISHER'S NOTE: The recipes contained in this book are to be followed exactly as written. The publisher is not responsible for your specific health or allergy needs that may require medical supervision. The publisher is not responsible for any adverse reactions to the recipes contained in this book.

BY HOOK OR BY CROOK

A Berkley Prime Crime Book / published by arrangement with the author

PRINTING HISTORY
Berkley Prime Crime mass-market edition / June 2009

Copyright © 2009 by Betty Hechtman.
Cover illustration by Cathy Gendron.
Cover design by Rita Frangie.
Interior text design by Kristin del Rosario.

ISBN: 978-0-425-22838-8

BERKLEY® PRIME CRIME
Berkley Prime Crime Books are published by The Berkley Publishing Group,
a division of Penguin Group (USA) Inc.,
375 Hudson Street, New York, New York 10014.
BERKLEY® PRIME CRIME and the PRIME CRIME logo are trademarks of Penguin Group (USA) Inc.

PRINTED IN THE UNITED STATES OF AMERICA

10 9 8 7 6 5 4 3 2 1

Acknowledgments

I didn't know filet crochet existed until Sue Meyer of the Lace Museum in Sunnyvale, California, pointed out a sample of it on the wall. It opened my eyes to all kinds of possibilities.

Thanks to Paula Tesler for the Thursday crochet and knit group and all the crochet advice. Thanks to Roberta Martia for her enthusiasm and friendship, and for trying out the crochet patterns.

Appellate Defender and friend Judy Libby always comes through with answers, even if I keep asking the same question over and over just to make sure.

I want to thank everyone at Berkley Prime Crime for all their efforts and particularly my editor, Sandy Harding, who continues to be great to work with.

I will always be grateful to my agent, Jessica Faust. The crochet mysteries wouldn't have happened without her.

Thanks to Spike Tretsky for being the inspiration for Mason's dog.

And a special thank-you to Burl and Max for not thinking I'm nuts when I talk about my characters like they're real people and for always being available any time of the day or night to taste test recipes.

CHAPTER 1

NOBODY NOTICED THE BAG AT FIRST.

It was just a plain brown grocery bag sitting on the end of our table at the fund-raiser for Los Encinos State Park. I must have moved it at least once during the day and never given it a thought. The park was really what was left of a rancho and had an old house and some outbuildings, along with either a small lake or a big pond, depending on how you look at things. The pond attracted all different kinds of ducks and geese, and they were already looking for places to roost as the sun faded on the February afternoon.

We were packing up the few things we hadn't sold. The *we* were the Tarzana Hookers—that's hookers as in crochet. We had made a bunch of scarves, along with some teddy bears and baby blankets for the fund-raiser and were donating all the proceeds to the park to help keep it afloat.

Well, most of us were clearing up the table. CeeCee Collins was posing for a photo with the park ranger and at the same time eyeing the brownies left on the bake sale table. Actually, her name was Connie Collins, but everybody called her CeeCee. Up until just recently, she'd been re-ferred to as a "veteran actress" because her old TV series, *The CeeCee Collins Show*, was practically ancient history. But ever since she started hosting *Making Amends* things had changed. Every week the reality show gave another "guest" a chance to right some old wrong. There was al-ways lots of embarrassment, usually some tears and hope-fully some laughs. The program was a big hit, and CeeCee was enjoying being referred to as simply an actress once again.

"Look what I got," CeeCee said when she rejoined us. She held up a white bag that had telltale grease stains and a strong chocolate scent. "There are still some goodies left over at the bake sale table."

"Oh no, I'm late," Ali Stewart said as she caught sight of the time. "I have to go. I promised to help my mother with something."

Ali Stewart was our newest member. Adele Abrams liked to think of herself as Ali's mentor, though from what I'd seen of her crochet work, Ali didn't need any help. The crocheted pink miniskirt she'd worn over leggings was adorable and expertly made. She had topped it with a white mohair poncho and finished the look with a dainty choker of tiny crocheted pink flowers. She was in her early twen-ties, tall and slender, and carried off the look with ease.

"That girl has a problem with time," Dinah Lyons said. "She's always late and then has to leave early because she's already late for something else."

Adele glared as if Dinah's comment were a personal af-front to her. I wondered if she was identifying too much with Ali. Adele was in her late thirties with a generous build and a voice that carried over a crowd. Her outfit almost matched the one Ali had worn, only the effect was different. Ali looked cute and Adele looked silly.

Sheila Altman, another of the younger Hookers, re-mained speechless as she put several small teddy bears into the box. She kept looking at the darkening sky with a tense expression. Even though she tried to control it, Sheila tensed up about most things. I could understand why: She didn't have much money and was working a bunch of jobs while trying to go to school at night to become a costume designer. Lately she'd been making exquisite scarves and blankets with gorgeous color combinations that she had begun selling in some local boutiques. "We better hurry up," she said anxiously. "The park closes in a few minutes."

"Don't worry, they're not going to lock us in," CeeCee said. "Besides, we're almost done anyway. Brownie anyone?" She held out the bag. "Wouldn't you know just when I went to the bake sale table I ran into the executive producer of my show and his wife. They asked me a bunch of questions about the crochet group, but I think it was just a cover to see if I was going to buy any baked goods."

CeeCee's sweet tooth was legendary, but being the host of a show made staying trim important. "I don't know what they're concerned about. The stylist I hired is a wonder," she said, laying the white paper sack with her purse. "She's a wiz at making an extra five pounds disappear with a long tunic."

CeeCee's attention turned back to helping us clear up, though there wasn't much left. She absently picked up a red fuzzy scarf and started to fold it.

"Watch how you're folding that," Adele said, taking it from CeeCee. Adele and CeeCee were still trying to work out who was in charge of the group.

"Dear, I can handle folding a scarf," CeeCee said, taking it back and rolling it into a tube. "It seems to be the only one left." She checked the items still on the table. "No wonder—it's so cold." As if to punctuate her comment, she shivered.

Dinah rolled her eyes. "Cold?" she said with a laugh.

"Yes, cold," CeeCee repeated. "It *is* winter. For once everybody was buying scarves for warmth instead of style."

Dinah rolled her eyes again. She was my best friend and

taught English at Walter Beasley Community College. She claimed teaching English to rowdy freshmen had prepared her to deal with anything, including the Hookers' personalities.

Dinah pointed to the green grass and the orange trees loaded with fruit still visible in the low light. "Yes, it is February, but this is Southern California. What is it—maybe fifty-five degrees?"

"Yes, dear, but you have to factor in the windchill," CeeCee said, wrapping her charcoal gray shawl around her shoulders. "And look, the sun's setting. You know how the temperature drops in the evening."

Adele stepped between them and turned toward CeeCee. "Are you kidding? Windchill factor?" Adele nodded toward me. "Pink, I can't believe you're not saying anything."

I tried to keep my smile intact even though it grated on me that Adele insisted on calling me by my last name. She only called me Molly by mistake. Adele and I had had a problem since day one, when I'd been hired for the position at Shedd & Royal Books and More that she wanted. She couldn't seem to see that I was more qualified to be the event coordinator–community relations person. I had experience in public relations thanks to my late husband Charlie's business. True, I hadn't really been a salaried employee for Charlie, but I had arranged launch parties at hotels and set up TV interviews for clients. Adele had just been a clerk at the bookstore.

As a consolation, Mrs. Shedd had given Adele kids' story time. Adele hadn't taken it well or given up. I'm not sure how it happened, but Adele had ended up working with me on some store events.

"Yes, but this is the Valley, and the temperature is always extreme compared to the other side of the hill," CeeCee was saying. There was some truth to that. We did bake in the summer and sometimes got frost in the middle of the night in winter. Technically both sides of "the hill," as the Santa Monica Mountains were referred to, were part of the city of Los Angeles, but the Valley was considered a bunch of suburbs with all that it implied.

Attempting to bring the debate to an end, I suggested we adjourn to the café at the bookstore.

"Wait. You can't forget this," Sheila said, pointing at a brown paper grocery sack as CeeCee started to close the box of leftovers. Sheila spoke so fast, she choked on her words, and she began to tap the fingers of her nonpointing hand on the table. Then she took the pointing hand and used it to stop her moving fingers.

"What's in that bag? I don't remember putting anything in a bag," Adele said, glancing at the rest of us. We all shrugged in reply and eyed it ominously.

"Pink, why don't you check it out?" Adele suggested. She stepped away from it as she pulled on a long denim coat over her leggings and miniskirt. Adele had adorned the coat with doilies. She hadn't said anything, but I knew she thought it was a walking advertisement for the wonders of crochet.

Sheila had edged down the table and was standing next to me. I felt her hand grab onto my arm.

"Too bad Eduardo isn't here," CeeCee said, referring to our other member. Eduardo Linnares was a hunky cover model/poet/expert crocheter. He was also a gentleman and would certainly have dealt with the bag that was creeping us all out if he hadn't had to skip the fund-raiser do some of his cover-model work.

"Stop being so silly," Dinah said, moving along the table toward the sack. Dinah was a gutsy ball of energy. She flipped her long, intertwined purple and orange scarves over her shoulder and out of the way, and grabbed the bag. She opened it with abandon and looked inside. She seemed perplexed but not horrified, which I took as a good sign. What were we expecting? Maybe something dangerous like a gun or a bomb? Or something furry and dead? Or something forgotten like a dirty diaper? Everyone had moved to the other end of the table to distance themselves from the threatening bag, and Sheila was gripping her purse with white knuckles. We held our breath as Dinah dumped the contents on the table. Nothing exploded nor did anything disgusting spill out. Just something colorful and some papers. Dinah started to sort through them, but CeeCee stopped her.

"We can't do anything about this here. Let's just take everything with us." The park ranger was locking up the buildings, and all the other people were gone.

"Yes, yes," Sheila said quickly. "The ranger is going to lock the gate any minute." Between concern over the bag's contents and the ranger shutting things up, Sheila had started to hyperventilate. Adele took the empty grocery bag and handed it to her. Sheila began breathing into it in an effort to calm down. Meanwhile, Dinah gathered up the contents; she waited until Sheila was finished and then reloaded the stuff in the bag.

A few minutes later, we all walked into the bookstore café. It felt warm and cozy after the chilly evening air and smelled of fresh brewed coffee and hot chocolate chip cookies. This aspect of the modern bookstore still amused me: It used to be that bookstores didn't want patrons to come in with drinks or food, but now, realizing that selling refreshments was a good income source, they practically pushed snacks on their customers. Shedd & Royal Books and More went the extra distance: The café's onsite baking sent the smell of freshly baked cookies wafting into the bookstore, which made the customers salivate.

We all ordered drinks and were soon seated around a small table, onto which Dinah poured out the contents of the grocery bag. CeeCee picked up the colorful piece and spread it out, while Adele picked up what appeared to be a note and read it out loud:

"I did something a long time ago that I now regret and would like to make right. I'm not sure everyone

*involved will agree. I'm leaving the enclosed for
safekeeping with you. If I don't come back for them,
I trust you will know what to do. Please—"*

"And?" CeeCee said impatiently.

"And, nothing," Adele said with a snort as she looked at
the back of the sheet and showed us it was blank. "That's
it."

"Since it ends in midsentence," Dinah said, "I would
guess the writer got interrupted. Just a wild guess, but I'd
bet it is a she. I don't see a guy writing a note like this."

"Here we go again." CeeCee shook her head and sighed.
"Ever since my show became a hit, people have started acting like I am the go-to person to fix their mistakes. Mostly,
I get e-mails with their dark secrets, or regular mail. Sometimes they're confessions and sometimes they want me to
be the middleman between them and their Aunt Sara to
help patch things up." She looked at the small pile of stuff.
"Chances are the person who wrote the note will come
back looking for her things. We had enough signs on the
table saying who we were and where our group meets. But
in any case—" She pushed the pile toward me. "Molly,
you're the one who deals with mysteries."

Was that my rep now? It was a long way from my old
life. Before my husband Charlie had died, I'd been a wife,
mother and occasional helper with his public relations
business. My only dealings with murder were distant, like
reading about it in a book or a newspaper article. I'd never
seen an actual dead body, and certainly had never been
considered a murder suspect. But all that had changed and
I'd begun a whole new chapter in my life.

If Charlie could see me now, I wondered if he'd be surprised. I had a regular job, belonged to the crochet group
and had been in the middle of several murder investigations. My two sons were having trouble with the new me. I
suppose it is uncomfortable having your middle-aged
mother change, but what choice did I have?

I had assumed the colorful thing in the bag was some kind of scarf, but now, as it lay spread out on the table, I realized it didn't look like something you'd wear around your neck. It was shaped like a scarf—long and rectangular—but something was off.

"Anybody have an idea what it is?" I asked.

"I don't know what it's supposed to be, but the style is called filet crochet, Pink," Adele said with a generous amount of attitude.

"I know what kind of crochet it is," I said. CeeCee had told me about the particular kind of thread crochet and shown me samples once when I was at her house. "I meant what is it supposed to be? Maybe a table runner?"

"Filet crochet—what's that?" Dinah asked. Right, Dinah hadn't been with me at CeeCee's. I was about to explain the method of crochet when Adele stepped in and pointed to the open mesh and areas that were blocks of solid stitches. By now I'd begun to see that the filled in areas formed images. I recognized one as that of a cat, though because it was formed by squares, it had a slightly awkward geometric shape.

Adele was in full form now. There was nothing she liked better than to lord her superior crochet knowledge over someone. "The open spaces are made with double crochets and a chain stitch, and the solid areas are continuous double crochets."

Dinah picked the piece up and held it at distance for all of us to see. It seemed to have ten or so panels that had been joined together, and viewed from afar, the images became more apparent. Or some of them did.

"What's that?" Dinah said, pointing to what looked like a big ring.

I shrugged and indicated another panel. "This looks like a guy with a bow and arrow," I said.

"This looks like a house of some sort." Dinah pointed to an adjacent area. "And here's a vase of flowers."

"Isn't that another cat?" Sheila said. The one I'd recognized had been sitting down facing front. This one appeared to be walking.

"Well, that looks like a bath-powder box I have on my dresser," CeeCee said. She'd obviously tried to keep out of it but ultimately couldn't help herself. "And that looks like the Arc de Triomphe."

"Molly, you better come quickly," a voice said, interrupting. When I looked up I saw that our main cashier, Rayaad, had come in from the store and appeared troubled. "There are some people doing strange things in the bookstore."

Out of the corner of my eye, I noticed Adele retreating into the corner. Typical. Adele liked to be in the midst of book signings and the bookstore's other notable events, but when trouble surfaced, she made herself scarce.

Dinah, on the other hand, got up as I did and followed me into the store. She was my backup even if she wasn't an employee.

I watched as a man and woman I didn't recognize walked around the main area of the store. They pushed on bookcases to see if they moved. They looked at the ceiling and periodically stopped to talk to each other, at which point one of them would write something in a notebook. They pushed two display tables together and started rearranging the books. They dragged over two comfortable chairs and appraised them quickly. Then they both got on their cell phones. I had heard of takeover robberies, but makeover robberies?

They were definitely up to something. They moved on to the best-seller table and put all the books on the floor before pulling the table off to the side. Then they took photos of the empty area from different angles.

Rayaad had rushed back to her station. She stuck the cordless phone under her arm and held up nine fingers, then one twice and looked at me with a question. I was about to signal her to go ahead when the phone rang. She jumped in surprise and the receiver fell.

When she recovered, she put it to her ear. A moment later, she began waving me over, mouthing that it was Mrs. Shedd. Dinah moved closer to the duo to keep tabs on them while I went to the phone.

"I'm glad you called," I said. "There's a couple doing weird stuff. They're moving things around and taking pictures. I was just about to call the cops."

"Don't," Mrs. Shedd yelled. "Or you'll ruin our big chance for fame. I'm sure they're from the show."

"What are they doing?" I asked.

"Don't worry about it. Just be helpful, Molly," Mrs. Shedd said.

"Show?" I asked. "Are they going to televise one of our book signings on that cable program?"

"Thank heavens, no. Who can stay awake to see the end of *that*? Somebody could make a fortune taping those shows and then selling them to people with insomnia. I'm talking about a hot show. A show that millions of people watch. I wish I knew how to get in touch with Mr. Royal," she said. The bookstore was called Shedd & Royal, but Mr. Royal seemed to be a silent partner. None of us had ever met him.

"We have to make sure the place looks perfect," Mrs. Shedd continued. "Too bad there isn't smellovision—we could pump out the smell of Bob's cookies." Mrs. Shedd found that funny and chuckled at her own joke. Then she urged me to get off the phone and help the couple.

I hung up, joined Dinah and the two of us approached them.

As soon as I confirmed they were from the show I tried to be friendly. "You television people work a lot. Here you are and it's Sunday evening."

"This is nothing. We're just in preproduction. When we're actually in production we're 24/7," the man said, explaining he and the woman were set directors. I introduced myself and said I was the event coordinator–community relations person. The woman handed me her card and shook my hand. They assured me they didn't need any help and mentioned the filming date in a few weeks.

In all the excitement I'd never found out the name of the program. I quickly asked.

"*Making Amends*," the man responded as they got ready to leave.

I did a double take. That was CeeCee's show! I was about to mention she was in the café, but they were already walking toward the door.

I turned to Dinah. "I wonder why CeeCee didn't say anything about them taping an episode here."

There was no chance to ask CeeCee about it. When Dinah and I returned to the café, the table was empty. Bob waved from the counter and held up the paper sack. It looked like the ball was stuck in my court.

CHAPTER 2

THE PHONE WAS RINGING WHEN I FINALLY unlocked my back door. I put down the bag on the kitchen table and grabbed for the cordless as two fur balls danced around my feet and then rushed out into the yard. They raced around the perimeter and disappeared in the bushes. Thinking that CeeCee was probably right about the owner showing up for the package, I'd decided to just hold onto it. I had given Rayaad instructions to call me if anyone came looking for it.

"Molly, why did you take so long to answer?" the caller demanded. She didn't have to identify herself. Did anyone not recognize their mother's voice and the emotional buttons she could immediately push with her intonation?

I started to explain, but after a moment she was obviously bored with my description of the fund-raiser at the park. Even the mention of the mystery package didn't capture her attention. I could tell by the sound of her breath and the fact that she started to talk before I finished.

"Daddy and I are coming to visit." She paused to let the information sink in, then continued. "Lana got a call from an agent. He wants to put us on tour. On a national tour," she said.

My mother had been part of a girl group, the She La Las, who'd basically had one hit—"My Man Dan." But it had been a *big* hit and still got played on the radio, though mostly on oldies stations. The group had gone their separate ways, and my mother spent the rest of her career as a backup singer for various artists. In her own mind, though, my mother remained a star. In my father's mind, too, I guess. He was a dermatologist with a quiet, even temperament that never threatened her center stage persona.

My brother had developed his own life early and as a kid practically lived at his various friends' houses. He never wanted her to come for parents' day. I could see his point after what she did at mine. Do you know what it's like to have your mother come to a school assembly and insist on putting some attitude into "My Country, 'Tis of Thee"? Her voice rose above everybody else's, too, which led to everyone in my class staring at me as though I were some kind of a freak.

My parents had moved to Santa Fe years ago supposedly to retire, but all that sun meant a lot of business for a dermatologist, so my father was still doctoring. My mother kept her fingers in things, too. She had joined some group that toured senior centers putting on shows.

"They'd put you on a tour with just one hit?" I asked. I detected a slight groan of annoyance in my mother's breathing.

"We might do some covers for other groups that have passed on or can't travel anymore," she said.

"And how does that relate to you coming here?" When my mother got excited she often left out important details unless prompted. Now it came out that the tour wasn't exactly set yet.

"The agent wants to see us in action. So, the girls and I need to practice before the audi—I mean, meeting. You're all alone in that big house now. It would be ridiculous for Daddy and me to stay in a hotel."

I wanted to suggest that it wasn't, but of course I didn't. I was in my late forties, and I should be able to handle a visit from my mother. We were both adults now, so it should be okay. Shouldn't it? They say mothers never retire from their jobs, and well, I didn't think daughters ever graduated from theirs, either.

"Honey, there are a few things I need. I'm sure you wouldn't mind picking them up before we get there. I'll just grab the list." She put my father on the phone while she went to find it. I'd always wished he'd called me some sweet nickname like Princess or Bunnykins, but he was too matter-of-fact and just called me Molly.

"How's your skin?" he asked after the basic hellos. "I'll bring you a bunch of samples of sunblock and some new antiwrinkle cream. It'll be good to see you and the boys," he said, referring to my two sons, Peter and Samuel. My mother grabbed the phone back.

"Here's the list of things I need. Do you have a pencil and paper?" she said in her upbeat voice. An uh-oh went off in my head concerning the length of the list.

But the "sure" was out of my mouth before I could stop it. You never said "sure" to Liza Aronson without knowing what you were agreeing to.

The list went on and on. A humidifier, some exotic concoction of essential oils that stimulated her voice, one hundred percent organic cotton sheets that were washed three times in lavender-scented natural laundry detergent, a purple silk meditation pillow, some exotic tea that was good to bathe her vocal cords in, a particular brand of dark chocolate with raisins and cashew nuts and a bunch of other things that were going to keep me running all over the area to find.

"Oh, and Daddy's a vegetarian now. Won't it be fun us all being together again? Just like old times," my mother chirped. "And we'll finally get to meet your boyfriend."

What? I'd never told her about Barry Greenberg. And *boyfriend* wasn't exactly what I'd call him—he was in his fifties for heaven's sake. I hadn't planned on mentioning anything about him ever unless we got married. I could read my mother's breathing, but she could read mine, too.

"Did you think I wouldn't find out? Samuel told me all about him, including the fact that he's some kind of cop and you picked him up in the grocery store."

Was that story going to haunt me forever? You'd think I was some desperate woman who'd been hanging out in a singles' bar that catered to twenty-somethings instead of someone who simply happened to strike up a conversation in the grocery checkout line. I explained to my mother that I'd already known him, slightly anyway since he taught the traffic school I'd had to attend when I'd gotten my ticket. We just fell into conversation in line at the store, and I'd invited him to the dinner party I was shopping for.

My mother's breathing said she wasn't impressed. "Samuel said something about a nice lawyer who helped him get some gigs. Personally, he sounds more promising than your boyfriend in blue."

"He doesn't wear blue. He's a homicide detective and wears a suit, and he's not my boyfriend."

"Then what is he?"

That was a good question. Recently our relationship had gone through somewhat of a change. All along I had tried keeping it casual, while he was always pushing for something with a name like engaged or married. I'd reluctantly given in and started thinking of us as a couple. But now that we were supposedly a couple, I was beginning to wonder if I could live with his job.

Was this what I really wanted? How many times had I been left sitting alone at a restaurant because he got a call and had to go? Then with no warning, he'd show up and want to do something. The unpredictable nature of his work dictated our relationship. Sometimes days would go by and I wouldn't even hear from him because he was so

entrenched in a case he forgot about everything and everyone. But then he always made up for it when he did show
up—I blushed at the thought.

While I was thinking all this, my mother had answered
her own question and said she'd decide when she met him
whether *boyfriend* described him, and then she got back
on the topic of the tour and where it was going. She barely
took a breath during her recitation of details, and although
my call-waiting was beeping, she didn't pause long enough
for me to excuse myself to see who it was. The call ended
when she was ready. Some things just never changed.

When I checked the phone for messages, I saw the call-
waiting had been Barry. Short phone calls and messages
had been the extent of our conversation lately. He'd bounced
from one case to another with barely a night's sleep. He
sounded rushed as he explained he wasn't going to make it
to take care of Cosmo—his dog currently in residence at
my house. He said something about missing me, but I could
tell by his voice he was already looking away from the
phone.

As I hung up, the two flying fur balls came back inside.
Cosmo and Blondie—my dog—stopped short and sat down
at my feet. Two sets of dogs' eyes let me know it was time to
eat.

I was relieved Samuel hadn't told my mother about
Cosmo.

The black mutt really belonged to Barry *and* his son.
When they'd adopted him, I'd cosigned as backup care. I
could personally vouch for Barry's undependability. I could
get by if he called at the last minute and canceled dinner
plans. A sweet little mutt couldn't. And, Barry's son was
almost fourteen. Need I say more? So, Cosmo started out as
a visitor but quickly became a permanent resident. And er-
ratic as Barry's dog care was, he really loved that dog and
did try, which was why I gave him the key to my house. But
it was supposed to be for dog care only. I still needed my
boundaries.

Actually, Cosmo was great for Blondie. My terrier mix had been in a shelter too long by the time I adopted her, and the experience had left her with a catlike, aloof personality. Cosmo had turned her back into a dog.

"Okay, guys, you're in for a treat," I said as I put food in their bowls. "You're going to get to meet the parents." The dogs didn't look impressed.

I changed into my around-the-house outfit. It was another reason I liked living alone. No one looked askance at my gray sweatpants that felt warm and snuggly on the chilly night or my pink and green fuzzy socks. I'd topped the outfit with an ancient periwinkle blue long-sleeve tee shirt. There were a few holes in it, but it was so soft from endless washing that I didn't care.

I popped some leftover noodle pudding in the oven, took out the paper sack and spread the contents on my dining room table. The three copper and green hanging fixtures bathed the items in bright light.

I folded out the filet crochet piece first and looked it over. It was made of two rows of loosely shaped square panels. Whoever made it was obviously an accomplished crocheter. The stitches were even and well done. A lot of time had probably gone into making it, too. But why put all that time into such an odd piece? And what was it for? Though it was sort of shaped like a scarf, I didn't think it was meant to be worn. And if someone tried to hang it on a wall, the middle would droop. It wasn't even that attractive, although I did like the colors of the thread, particularly the aqua.

I wondered if the panels that had nonsensical images were deliberate or mistakes. I ran my finger over the two panels with big rings. One ring looked like a donut that was all hole, and the other had a bar across the middle. Another panel depicted a cylinder on stilts attached to a trapezoid; this seemed too planned to be a mistake. Even the recognizable things were strange. Why would somebody stick a bath-powder box, an oddly shaped house, a sitting cat, something that resembled the Arc de Triomphe, a walking cat and a vase of flowers together in one piece?

And what about the last panel? It was twice the size of the others and was a solid aqua rectangle with a window in the middle. What could it mean?

I was getting dizzy trying to figure it out. I reread the note to see if maybe there was something I'd missed when Adele had read it out loud. I looked inside the bag and saw that something white had gotten stuck on the side. I pulled it out and took it to the light. It was a piece of paper, dated at the top, and appeared to have been torn from a book. The position of the date and the kind of paper made me think it was a diary entry. I sat down in one of the chairs and looked at the handwriting. My handwriting always went every which way and had gotten worse as I got older. This was done in fountain pen with clear, even letters. It was dated December 20, twenty-three years ago. The same year Samuel was born.

There was no salutation. It just began.

The island is decorated for Christmas. All the colorful lights brighten up the short, cold days, but it doesn't help me feel any less sad. I hate to have to say good-bye even for a short time. I know things will work out and we will be back together again for keeps. Tomorrow I go back as if nothing has changed. I know I am doing the right thing.

"Nicely vague," I said out loud. "A few specific details like who she was and who she was talking about might have helped." The only effect of my solo conversation was that the two dogs came in and looked around to see if I had company. I was going to have to watch the talking out loud once my parents arrived. It might make me come across as a widow who spent too much time alone.

While I waited for my food to heat, I reread the note that had come in the bag. I even read it out loud thinking hearing it might offer some new meaning, but nothing new struck me. And it still ended with a cliff-hanger.

"What's the rest of the story?" I said, letting the paper fall back on the table. "And why couldn't you have just taken another minute to add your name."

Oh, dear, I was doing it again. Did all this talking out loud to myself mean that I *was* lonely?

The buttery smell coming from the oven made my mouth water, so I took out my noodle pudding, but then my thoughts returned to the puzzle.

The Average Joe's Guide to Criminal Investigation, my own personal go-to book, said everything has clues, you just had to know how to pick them out. After reading over the note and the diary entry countless times, I started to think the crochet piece was some kind of code for the secret the note writer was planning to disclose. But no matter how long I looked at all those panels, they didn't make any more sense.

Sometimes a fresh point of view helped, so I called Dinah. Besides, I thought, I need to talk to a real person.

CHAPTER 3

"LYONS RESIDENCE," A TINY VOICE SAID. "ASHLEY-Angela speaking."

It was hard not to laugh at how serious she sounded, but I knew if I did I would hurt her feelings. Was this really the same wild child from a few months ago?

I was the only one who knew the truth about why Ashley-Angela and her brother E. Conner, four-year-old fraternal twins, were staying with Dinah. Everyone else assumed they were her grandkids on an extended visit. But they weren't even really related to her, unless you counted that they were her children's half siblings.

Dinah's ex-husband, Jeremy, was their father and the new ex-Mrs. Lyons was their mother. She'd dropped out of sight, and Dinah had taken the kids in while Jeremy adjusted to a new job out of state. It was only supposed to be for a few weeks, but that was months ago.

Dinah was somewhere in her fifties. She wouldn't divulge exactly where even to me, her best friend. She was convinced that people judged you when they knew your age. I couldn't imagine anyone thinking she was old. She was practically bursting with energy, and she was always up for an adventure.

"Hello," Dinah said taking the phone. I complimented her on Ashley-Angela's phone manners, and I could hear the pride in her voice when she thanked me. No matter how much Dinah said she couldn't wait for their father to come pick them up, I knew she'd gotten attached to them.

"There was something else in the bag. It seems like a diary entry." Then I described how I'd been staring at the crochet piece and finally decided it was somehow the key to the secret mentioned in the aborted note.

"Read me the diary piece," Dinah said.

My noodle pudding was getting cold and I took a bite. Dinah heard me chewing and wanted to know what I was eating. When I mentioned I had enough to share, she sighed.

"I love your California Noodle Pudding," she said. "It is times like this I wish I wasn't tied down."

I promised to save her a piece and then took out the diary entry and started to read. I heard Dinah say "uh-huh" when I read the part about saying good-bye.

"It's obvious she was having an affair and was upset about having to say good-bye. She said something about them being together eventually. Maybe that didn't happen and that's what she wanted to change." Dinah stopped for a moment. "Hmm, it mentioned an island. I wonder what island it is."

"There's Balboa Island near Newport Beach, there's the Hawaiian Islands. And there's always Alcatraz," I said with a laugh.

"But the entry doesn't even indicate a state. It could be Bainbridge Island near Seattle, or St. Thomas in the Caribbean."

"If the secret has something to do with an affair on an island, you'd sure never guess it by the crochet piece. I've been staring at it until my eyes are blurry and I still don't get what a lot of the images are, let alone what they mean," I said.

"Maybe the best thing to do is just wait and see if some-one comes looking for it. It also might be the only thing to do," Dinah suggested.

"I suppose you're right. It's odd, though, the way it was left on our table and the way the note breaks off—why just stop writing like that in the middle?"

"I can answer that one," Dinah said. "Ever since Ashley-Angela and E. Conner have come to stay with me, I do things like that all the time. It's called getting interrupted. I have to be really careful with comments on students' papers and remember to go back and finish what I started. Telling someone, 'Your paper has a powerful beginning,' and tell-ing someone, 'Your paper has a powerful beginning but the rest doesn't make sense,' are a little different." Dinah punc-tuated her comment with a chuckle. "What did the note say again?"

I pulled it out of the bag and read it to Dinah:

"I did something a long time ago that I now regret and would like to make right. I'm not sure everyone involved will agree. I'm leaving the enclosed for safekeeping with you. If I don't come back for them, I trust you will know what to do. Please—"

"Hmm," I said, looking at the diary entry and the note side by side. "The note seems different after reading the diary entry. Obviously whatever she did a long time ago is what she was talking about in the diary entry. Whatever she wants to fix probably has to do with the person she said good-bye to."

"The diary page says something about the note writer getting back together with someone. Maybe they didn't and she wants to make that happen now," Dinah said. "The most obvious scenario is the writer had an affair with some guy on an island and maybe they were both married and the plan was they would go home and get divorces and then live happily ever after—but it didn't happen. And now all these years later, the writer still wants her happily ever after."

I pushed my plate of food away and held up the crochet piece. "All that makes sense, but what do all these weird images have to do with it?"

"Who knows? Maybe they represent lyrics to—" Dinah's voice came in and out, and I could tell she was looking away from the phone. I heard kids' noises and Dinah sighed. "See what I mean about getting interrupted? The end of that thought is lyrics to their song." She sighed again. "I promised to read them a story. Why don't you bring the bag to the crochet group. Maybe with all of our brains storming together we'll come up with something."

I agreed to bring it and then told Dinah about my impending houseguests. She laughed.

"Batten down the hatches! Liza Aronson is coming to town."

I WENT INTO THE BOOKSTORE EARLY THE NEXT morning. Mrs. Shedd generally did her work when the store was closed, so I was surprised to see her sitting in her office. But there was no mistaking her hair. Although she was in her late sixties, she didn't have even a lock of gray hair. The dark blond color was all natural, and the page-boy style reminded me of an old shampoo commercial. Her clothes were kind of old-school, too. She didn't wear pants, she wore trousers along with feminine big-collared blouses. Everybody called her Mrs. Shedd. I had only recently learned her first name was Pamela. She was leaning back in her desk chair and waved me in as I passed.

"Tell me again about the couple who came in. Did they seem happy with the way the bookstore looked? Did they make any comments about the arrangement?" Mrs. Shedd sounded unusually nervous. "You know, Molly, the way the bookstore looks on TV is really important. It's national television. Millions of viewers. This is the ultimate event for our little place. It will put us on the map, and we could become a tourist stop or at least *the place* in the Valley to visit for your book needs," she said in an excited voice.

I nodded to show I was listening as she began to talk about how impressed Mr. Royal would be if he knew. I continued nodding and hoped my disbelief that he existed didn't show. "So be sure and offer any assistance to anyone involved with the show," Mrs. Shedd finished.

After assuring her I would do my best, I went back onto the bookstore floor. We'd just opened so there were barely any customers. Bob, our main barista, was brewing fresh coffee, and the pungent fragrance mixed with the sweet scent of his homemade butterscotch oatmeal cookie bars cooling on the counter. It was too much to resist; I went into the café, grabbed a cup of fresh coffee and some hot cookie bars and then headed back into the main store.

A man had come in and was standing at the front counter talking to Rayaad. When she saw me, she waved me over. The man's slightly long gray-streaked hair, intelligent face and rimless glasses made me think he might be a college professor. But the manicured nails and designer tennis whites complete with a sweater made me think not.

The man nodded to me and held out his hand. "Hunter Katz."

I balanced the cookie bars and coffee mug in one hand and shook his.

"I'm the executive vice president of Rhead Productions. We produce *Making Amends*. I don't usually get involved with locations or the details of any of our shows, but since this is my neighborhood . . ." He pointed toward the view of the hills and Santa Monica Mountains dotted with homes, implying one of them was his. "So I thought I'd drop by and make sure the ball has started rolling."

I mentioned meeting the set designers the previous day, and then I asked him the question I'd thought of after they'd left. Why were they filming at the bookstore?

Hunter laughed. "That's because someone in the bookstore is the subject of the show. They're the one someone is making amends with."

"Oh really. Who is it?" I asked.

He winked. "Sorry, but the whole emotional arc of the show is based on it being a surprise." He handed me his card. "If there are any problems with the setups or anything, give my office a call. Like I said, I don't usually get involved with the nitty-gritty of any of our shows, but since it's my local bookstore, I have a personal interest in things going smoothly."

Which really meant he didn't want anything to go wrong. Oh dear, the pressure was on. Let's just say that some of my author events have had a certain unpredictable quality to them, like the time a cooking demonstration led to the fire department showing up. I put on a confident smile and told him I was sure everything would go perfectly. "So, I guess you're CeeCee Collins's boss."

"I've never quite thought of it in those terms, but yes," he said, preparing to depart. "You have some kind of crochet group here that makes things for charity, don't you?"

"Yes," I said tentatively, wondering why he was asking. "Does that have something to do with the show?"

He took a step backward while still looking at me and winked. "Sorry, I can't give out that information." Then with a wave, he was gone.

A busy morning already and it wasn't even ten yet. I headed to the event area to do setup for the crochet group. The morning sun poured in the window that faced Ventura Boulevard. A city maintenance worker was giving a shot of water to the giraffe topiary that stood guard by the window. The ivy was finally beginning to cover the metal frame and mossy stuff in the middle.

Someone had decided a while back that the Valley communities along Ventura Boulevard should each have some kind of identity. Because we were located in Tarzana, there was the obvious Tarzan connection, and hence, we got the designation of Safari Walk. What that amounted to was a street sign announcing it, garbage cans with animal cut-outs, an occasional sidewalk square made of red tiles with a big rock on it and topiary animals sprinkled down the boulevard.

Turning my back on the ivy giraffe and his keeper, I began to prepare for the group. I pulled out the long table and unfolded the legs. Dinah came in before I finished setting up the chairs. Actually, I heard the tinkle of her long earrings before I saw her. As usual, she had several scarves twined around her neck, but no kids with her.

"Thank heavens for preschool," she said when I asked. "They've started going every day." She dropped her craft bag on a chair and undid her sweater coat. She picked up one of my cookie bars and took a nibble, then said she was going for her own treats.

While she was gone, I took out the filet crochet piece and the note and diary entry.

"Wow, it's different than I remember it," Dinah said, glancing toward my display as she returned with a latte and more cookie bars. She set down her café purchases and gave all her attention to the stitched item. "I see what you mean. Who knows what most of this stuff is supposed to be? Cancel what I said about song lyrics." She pointed at the aqua rectangle with the window in the middle. "It's as if she decided to mix abstract things with recognizable ones. Like that." Dinah pointed at the man with the bow and arrow.

Dinah took a sip of her latte and with a thoughtful look picked up the diary entry. She read it over several times, frequently glancing back toward the panel piece. Her eyes suddenly brightened. "I think I've found a connection." She pointed to December 20 on the paper and then to the bow-and-arrow figure. "The zodiac sign for that date is Sagittarius." She stared at me, apparently waiting for some kind of reaction. When it didn't come, she continued. "Don't you get it? You know, the ram is for Aries, the lion for Leo and the archer for Sagittarius."

"Oh," I said, letting it sink in. "You're right. Wow, that's impressive."

"What's impressive, dear?" CeeCee moved past me, pulling her craft case on wheels to the head of the table and positioning it next to her chair. The production company had hired a stylist to work with her when the show took off, and the new look suited her well. Gone were the reddish blond bubble hairstyle and the jewel-colored velour warm-up suits she'd worn before. Now her hair was a soft brown with natural-looking highlights. The soft bangs knocked years off her face, her outfit—slacks, shirt and long vest—hid any hint of extra curves.

Before I could answer her question, CeeCee had spied my last cookie bar. "Does that belong to anyone?" she said, reaching for it. When I told her it was hers, she closed her eyes and savored the flavor.

"Dinah just figured out something about the crochet piece," I said, showing CeeCee the date and the archer.

"Oh dear, no one showed up for it, did they?" She threw up her hands, appearing upset. "I just can't deal with this. You'll take care of it won't you?" Without waiting for an answer, she pushed the items down the table toward me. "Besides, it's distracting us from our real purpose."

The purpose of the group was to crochet things either to give to those in need, or to sell to raise money for some worthy cause. Our current project was making blankets for the police or social service organizations to offer to trau-matized older kids.

At that moment Eduardo and Sheila came in together. They weren't a couple or anything, they just arrived at the same time.

"I finished a blanket," Sheila said. She held up a small throw the same beige color as Dinah's drink and then draped it on the edge of the table. We all praised her fine work, but the look of strain across her forehead remained. Fitting in the crochet group around her job at the gym, her costume design classes and assorted odd jobs was an

ongoing struggle for her. I felt nervous just thinking of all
she had to do. As usual, she was wearing the black suit she
was required to wear as receptionist at the gym. I thought
it an odd clothing choice for a place where the members all
wore sweats or spandex.

"Lovely," CeeCee said one final time before folding up
the blanket and setting it at the end of the table.

"Sorry I had to miss the park fund-raiser," Eduardo
said, setting his leather shopping bag on the table. His
shoulder-length black hair was loose, and he was wearing
jeans and a soft blue tee shirt. Everything looked good on
him—that was probably why he was such a successful cover
model.

Eduardo was also a master crocheter. He'd learned the
craft from his grandmother, and he did it as though it were
second nature. Reaching into his bag, Eduardo pulled out
the child-size blanket he'd completed. It was moss green
and so soft to the touch I wanted to cuddle it. But wasn't
that the point? We hoped these coverlets would provide
warmth and the comfort of something to hang onto.

"Eduardo, that's beautiful," CeeCee said, taking it and
putting it next to Sheila's. "I have three now. I'll drop these
off at the West Valley Police Station." CeeCee pointed to
the bags of yarn the bookstore provided and encouraged
them both to start another.

Eduardo saw the filet crochet piece and his brow wrin-
kled. "Where did that come from?"

Dinah told him the story, and he examined it. "Nice
stitch work, but what's the point?" He spread it out on the
table. "Is it some kind of tablecloth?" We all studied it and
shook our heads. It was too wide for a table runner but too
narrow for a tablecloth.

"I don't think it has a practical purpose," I said, straight-
ening it. "I still have a hard time thinking this is really
crochet."

Eduardo had a deep hypnotic voice. He could read the
phone book and make it sound like poetry, so we were all

rapt listeners when he started to talk about filet crochet. Even CeeCee.

"I understand your dilemma," he said. "Filet crochet looks quite different than the blankets we're making. I learned from my Gran Maeve that it was developed to make trimming that looked like lace for dresses and household items." Eduardo grinned. "Not that I was interested in trimming anything." Eduardo had told us how he was Irish on his mother's side and, being the youngest in a family of boys, had been chosen by his grandmother to carry on the family tradition of Irish crochet. "But she made me learn filet crochet anyway. By the way, *filet* means 'net' in French." He took out a hook and some yarn and proceeded to make a foundation row and then began a row of mesh spaces. "She said it was like drawing with thread because you could make pictures with it." His fingers were nimble, and the yarn made the stitches easy to see. In the next row he made several open meshes with blocks, followed by more open meshes.

"If I was going to make a pattern or a picture, I'd make up a chart first. You can use graph paper, and then you mark in the blocks and leave the meshes open."

Somehow when he said it, it all made sense. "Now, I get it," I said as he handed me the little swatch he'd made. I compared it with the panel piece and was able to pick out the tiny double crochets and chains.

"Ah, but if you look so closely, then you lose the picture." He took the panel piece from me and stepped away, holding it up. Sure enough, it was easier to see the pictures in each panel when I viewed the piece from a distance. It did not, however, make the meaning of the pictures any easier to figure out.

"Where's Adele?" Eduardo asked, glancing up and down the table.

"No wonder it's so quiet," Dinah said.

"She called me early this morning to say she was going to be late," I said. "She and her new best friend Ali went to some special yarn store this morning."

"Oh dear," CeeCee said suddenly, glancing toward the window. We all followed her gaze, but when she saw what we were doing she became agitated. "Don't look. Keep your eyes on your work and maybe she'll go away."

"Who?" Sheila asked. She had looked up from the new blanket she was starting. She'd picked up on CeeCee's upset, and consequently, her stitches were growing tighter and tighter. CeeCee and Adele had helped her deal with her too-tight stitches so many times, she now knew what to do herself. She pulled out a smaller hook, took some deep breaths and started the mantra of "keep it loose" as she slowly poked the hook into each stitch.

"Her name's Camille Rhead Katz," CeeCee said between her teeth.

"There was some man named Katz in here a little while ago. He said he was involved with your show. Are they connected?" I asked, nodding toward the window as I looked at CeeCee.

"Yes, he's her husband." CeeCee said, forcing her gaze away from the window.

"Why didn't you tell me they were going to tape a show at the bookstore?"

"They are?" CeeCee said. "Someone should have told me." She sounded perturbed. "I can't believe I don't know what's going on at my own show. Whatever anyone says, I *am* the show. Why else would people be leaving me their problems to fix?" Her voice had grown a little shrill, and it wasn't clear who exactly she was talking to, but it didn't seem to be any of us.

When I glanced back toward the window, no one was there. Maybe CeeCee had gotten her wish.

Or maybe not.

The woman was standing next to the table.

CHAPTER 4

"HELLO, CEECEE. I DIDN'T KNOW YOU WERE part of the Tarzana Hookers," the tallish dark-haired woman said. One glance at her face was enough to figure she must have a charge account with her plastic surgeon. She looked as though she'd been lasered, Botoxed and injected with fills until her face had the too-smooth shape of a doll's. Her most distinctive feature was her lips, which were big and puffy, but I didn't think it was the work of injections. They were just imperfect enough to be natural.

"Camille, so nice to see you," CeeCee said in an authentic-sounding sweet voice. CeeCee was certainly a good actress. If I hadn't heard her comments about Camille just a few minutes earlier, I would have totally believed CeeCee was thrilled to see her.

CeeCee introduced her to everyone at the table in the same friendly sounding voice.

I tried not to stare at Camille's clothes. If you threw in the Rinny Fooh shoes, I bet the jeans, loose-fitting top and cropped jacket cost as much as some people's monthly mortgage payment. Though Camille seemed indifferent to her outfit. To her, wearing designer stuff was probably the same as wearing an old bathrobe.

"Well, thanks for stopping by. It was nice to see you," CeeCee said in a tone of dismissal, but Camille made no move to leave.

"I don't think you understand," Camille said, turning toward CeeCee. "I'm here to join you." Then she turned back to all of us. When she got to Eduardo, she seemed uneasy. "He's not a member, is he?"

"Yes, he is. In fact he's one of our best crocheters," Cee-Cee said with just the slightest edge to her voice. "Obviously you have a problem with that, which is why I'm sure you wouldn't be happy in our group."

"Oh, I'm sorry, that probably didn't come out right. My life coach has been telling me I have to watch how I speak. I was just surprised that you had a male member."

Eduardo sighed. "It's okay, I get that a lot, and no, I'm not gay."

Camille looked embarrassed. "I wasn't implying you were anything. Oh no, I'm talking myself into a corner again." She took a deep breath. "Maybe if I explain . . . I'm trying to turn over a new leaf. I have always been on committees for fund-raiser dinners and charity events of all kinds. I've arranged countless silent auctions. My life coach says I ought to try being on the other side of the auction table. You know, actually making something." She saw the blankets at the end of the table. "Are you making these for poor people?"

There was a collective cringe at the table. Camille's life coach probably wouldn't have been happy with her, either. She said *poor people* as though they were aliens from another planet who had cooties besides. She caught herself again and apologized.

"Oh dear, my life coach said I needed to try being like a regular person, but I have no experience at it." She slid into a chair. "My father is Alexander Rhead—of Rhead Productions." She left it hanging, clearly expecting we would understand what that meant. When no one reacted, she continued. "We do CeeCee's show, and a lot of others."

"Then maybe you know who's the subject of the episode they're taping here," I said.

Camille's mouth fell open as if I'd asked her an inappropriate question. "My father is the head of the production company, and my husband is the executive vice president. We don't deal with what goes on with the shows. We have people for that." She slouched when she finished. "That sounded haughty, didn't it? You see, I really need to be in this group. I need to be around regular people so I can get in touch with the regular part of myself."

"Is that what your life coach said?" Dinah asked, holding back a smile.

Camille brightened. "Why yes. How did you know?"

"A lucky guess," Dinah said.

"You don't know how to crochet, do you?" CeeCee said. Her acting ability was falling by the wayside, the edge in her voice growing more obvious.

"Well, no," Camille said.

"We only take members who at least know the basics. You really need to know what you're doing if you're going to make the blankets."

I regarded CeeCee with surprise. New people showed up all the time and most of them were clueless. She or Adele were always happy to teach them. Why was she trying to scare off Camille?

"Maybe I can find somebody to give me some private lessons first," Camille said.

CeeCee was shaking her head and about to speak when Adele made her entrance.

"Somebody needs crochet lessons?" she asked Camille brightly. CeeCee gave Adele a dark look, which had no effect. "I'd be happy to teach you."

Adele took the opportunity to show off her latest project. Burgundy and gold striped mohair leg warmers. "Ali and I made these together," she said to the group. "We met at the Yarnatorium this morning. They're having a huge sale. She was going to come to the group, but she had to go to work."

"Work?" Sheila said. "What does she do?"

"Why don't you ask her next time she's here," Adele said, clearly not interested in talking about it.

Camille had started tapping her finger against the table in annoyance. This unnerved Sheila, who began tapping her fingers as well. The noise made the rest of us tense. Even the usually unflappable Eduardo seemed unsettled.

I had the feeling Camille wasn't used to being kept waiting. And even though I insisted I wanted no part in running the group, I felt a responsibility for keeping Shedd & Royal's customers happy. "Adele, why don't you show us what you made later. If you're going to give Camille crochet lessons, you ought to arrange it."

It was a toss-up who appeared more annoyed: Adele for being interrupted or Camille for having to wait. CeeCee didn't look too happy, either.

Camille moved down the table toward the filet piece and with her perfectly manicured fingers picked it up. She looked at it oddly for a moment, then let it flutter back to the table. "I'm not going to have to make something like that, am I?"

CeeCee saw her moment. "You might. You know, crochet isn't for everyone. You might like knitting better."

I could hear Adele sputtering behind me. She stepped between CeeCee and Camille. "Don't listen to her. You don't want to knit."

I traded looks with Dinah. Uh-oh. Adele went ballistic whenever anyone brought up knitting. We all thought crochet was superior, but Adele was rabid about it. Her voice rose as she started her crochet rant, and Camille took a step backward.

"Crochet is more portable. Just one nice little hook instead of two poky needles. And there are so many things you can do with crochet." Adele started to pick up the panel piece but apparently suddenly remembered Camille's reaction to it and let it drop. Instead, she pointed to the yellow and white yarn daisy attached to her jean jacket. "You can make flowers like this, and granny squares, and afghans like you wouldn't believe, and—"

Camille interrupted and said she had to go. I wondered if despite her life coach's suggestion she had changed her mind about joining us. Not that I could blame her. CeeCee had been anything but cordial, and Adele had been, well, just plain weird.

"Okay, what was that about?" I asked after Camille left. Adele had written down her phone number and pushed it on her just before she walked away.

CeeCee sighed and glanced around the table. "It is just a waste of time having her join. Do you understand who her family is? Besides my show, Rhead Productions does *Squirrels in Space*, that animated series all the kids are crazy for, and *Malibu Beach Watch*, or as I call it, an excuse to broadcast a lot of good-looking people in tight bathing suits, and *The Highlands*, probably the most successful glitzy nighttime series ever. And there's one more. *Hercules Crawford, PI.* Only Alexander Rhead would figure out the public was ready for an old-fashioned detective series."

"I love that show," Eduardo interjected, and CeeCee threw him an annoyed look. Undaunted, Eduardo said his agent was trying to get him a part on it. "Playing myself, of course. A cover model who ends up in the middle of a murder."

"And the list goes on. It's the most successful production company around," CeeCee said. "Camille has been brought up like a princess. No matter what she says about wanting to be a regular person, she's the kind who'd bring her maid with her to the group and have the maid do the crocheting for her. Besides, I don't think her showing up has anything to do with wanting to make blankets for needy children."

I shook my head at CeeCee. I'd never seen her react to anyone like this. "Is there something else you're not telling us?"

CeeCee groaned and started to run her fingers through her hair, but must have realized it would muss it and stopped herself. "Okay, the real reason is I think's she's a spy."

"What?" Dinah said. "A spy for what?"

"I haven't mentioned it because I hoped it would be re-solved by now," CeeCee began. "But my agent is having some problems with my new contract. The Rhead Produc-tions people are trying to say it's the show that's the hit and that my being host doesn't matter. I think it's all negotiat-ing, but who knows?" CeeCee sighed. Of course she was worried. Before she'd gotten the job hosting *Making Amends*, she'd been reduced to doing occasional guest shots on series or cameos in movies. People knew who she was and the paparazzi had still snapped her picture, but finan-cially she had been struggling. Her late husband had blown all the money she'd made over the years and she'd had to start from scratch.

CeeCee picked up a skein of iridescent white yarn and began to make a foundation row of chain stitches. "I've always been able to relax at our group get-togethers, but if Camille joined, I'd have to watch everything I said—or ate. When they were downplaying my importance to the show, they also made some comment about my not being as trim as they'd like." CeeCee sighed again and glanced around at all of us. "I mean if you can't have an occasional creme brulee, life just isn't worth living. And I'm sure she can't understand the hypnotic lure of a cream puff. If I were to take even a bite of one of Bob's extraordinary cookie bars, Camille would go running to her husband and daddy and tattle on me." CeeCee stopped talking and cro-cheting, clearly contemplating something.

She turned toward me. "Dear, didn't you say Camille's husband was in here right before we started?" When I nodded, CeeCee's eyes grew bright. "Aha, I bet it was his idea she join us."

"But we can't keep anyone out," I said. "Mrs. Shedd would have a fit, and I don't like the idea anyway."

Sheila touched CeeCee's arm in support. If anyone knew about feeling upset, it was Sheila.

"I know, dear," CeeCee said in resignation. "That's why I did my best to try to make Camille not want to join."

"Good work," Adele said with a snort, holding up her cell phone. "She's already texting me, wanting to set up her lesson."

"Oh dear," CeeCee said with a worried expression. We all assured her it would be okay and we finally got down to serious crocheting. But by now, most of the time for the group was over. Sheila had to rush back to her job at the gym. CeeCee had a lunch engagement, and Dinah had to get to the college for her office hours.

Adele was the only one left at the table. She finished off a row on the blanket she was making. Her creations usually incorporated wildly vivid colors, but for this one she had chosen a soft butterscotch and snowy white and was following CeeCee's pattern of stripes with a border.

As I rose to clear off the filet crochet piece, she said, "So, Pink, CeeCee really did leave it up to you to deal with that." Then she kind of *harrumphed* as if she weren't impressed.

Well, we were even there—I wasn't too impressed with her, either. Especially her clothes. Since she'd started hanging out with Ali, her outfits had gotten several notches more ridiculous. Ali had the figure and style to pull off the miniskirts and odd combinations. Adele didn't have either. Not that it stopped her. Today Adele wore a winter concoction with sheepskin boots that made her shuffle when she walked. She had tucked her black pants in and they puffed out, giving her a gaucho look. On top she had a short orange vest over a white tunic and about ten necklaces and a long yellow and black striped scarf. She'd added some highlights to her hair, but they were too regular and they made her hair look striped. Knowing Adele, I suspected it had been intentional.

I informed Adele I'd made some progress and told her about the diary entry and the astrological sign. "Though I still don't have a clue who the things belong to."

Adele held it up to examine it and then appeared way too pleased with herself.

"Maybe I should change my name to Adele Drew," she said, flipping the hair off her shoulder. "I know how you can find out who made it."

Okay, she had my attention and she knew it. She paused and kept looking at the piece, her self-satisfied smile widening.

"Are you going to tell me or are you just going to keep it to yourself?"

"I wish I had a drumroll or something," Adele said, looking around as if some kind of musical flourish would appear. "It's simple, Pink. See the aqua thread in this panel. It's not your typical Super Craft Mart ball of yarn. I know because I made something out of it. There's only one store around here that carries it—Yarnie's. And they keep meticulous records."

Adele began to gather up her things, putting them into her patent leather tote bag. "Sorry I can't stay and chat. I have an important meeting in the children's department."

"Is it Koo Koo?" I called after her. She turned back and glared.

"His name is William," she said with a hiss of annoyance.

Okay, his name really was William Bearly, but his nom de plume was Koo Koo the Clown. He wrote books about common childhood traumas from a clown's point of view. He was also Adele's boyfriend, but I suspected her important meeting was more about his upcoming event. Mrs. Shedd had started to let Adele handle the children's authors programs. I'd seen the signage in the office. Apparently, this time, Koo Koo had taken to the skies. His current of-fering was *Koo Koo Goes on a Plane Trip.* I bet he had trouble getting his big red shoes through security.

I called a thank-you as she disappeared behind the soft blue bookcases that separated the kids' area from the rest of the store. I finally had a real lead.

CHAPTER 5

YES, I FINALLY HAD A LEAD, BUT IT WOULD HAVE to wait, at least for a few hours because I needed to clean up from the Tarzana Hookers and reset things for the evening event. I set up rows of chairs and a table with books, and made sure the signs were out front promoting *Who Are You Really, Fido?* The copy said that the author Kimball Oaks would read from his book describing individual cases in which people had used DNA tests to find out their mixed-breed dogs' heritage. According to Kimball, such information helped owners understand their dogs' behavior better. We'd already committed to this author event and one other, but Mrs. Shedd had told me to put a moratorium on arranging any others until after the bookstore's TV debut.

I expected it to be a simple evening. Kimball would read a case history, people would buy books, get them signed and leave.

Why did things never go off as expected?

Somewhere in the afternoon, I took a break, hoping to cruise by Yarnie's and get a quick answer to who owned the bag of items. Then I hoped to make a chink in the list of things my mother had to have for her visit. The initial list she'd given me on the phone had been enhanced by numerous e-mails.

My cell phone rang on the way to the car.

"Hey, babe," Barry's deep voice said when I answered.

Finally, a phone call from him. A certain tension went out of my shoulders. It always seemed to come when I didn't hear from him for a while. I mean when your job involves guns, suspects and criminal activity, it's only natural for people who care about you to worry.

"Do I have a lot to tell you," I said, cradling the phone against my shoulder as I unlocked the greenmobile. Barry said something but his voice was muffled, and then in the background I heard what sounded like someone making an announcement over a PA system.

"I just have a minute," Barry said, apparently having not heard what I said. He seemed to be talking to someone else, and I could still hear other voices in the background.

"Where are you?"

"On a plane about to take off. They're insisting I turn off my phone." In a burst of words, he told me he had to go to Philadelphia to question a witness and that he was taking his son, Jeffrey, with him and was going to drop him off at his mother's. Barry had been divorced for several years and his wife had just remarried. "I miss you," he said quickly. "I'll make it up when I get back." And then there was silence.

It took a minute for it all to sink in, and as it did, I felt the tension come back into my shoulders. Being in a relationship with a homicide detective was certainly a challenge. And again I questioned if it was what I really wanted.

My husband Charlie had worked long hours in the public relations firm and he'd traveled frequently, but when we went out to dinner we never had to take separate cars in case he got a call in the middle of our meal because somebody had just found a dead body.

I started the car and drove to the address Adele had given me for Yarnie's—a strip mall on the Tarzana-Encino border. I felt my anticipation level rise as I pulled into a parking spot. Barry was off on his case, and I was about to find out the solution to mine.

Dinah and I had always intended to check out the small yarn store but had never gotten around to it. I glanced ahead to the front window and noticed it was strangely dark. Hoping the store owner was just trying to save on electricity, I went to the door and pulled. It didn't open. Then I noticed the colorful sign on the window.

Of all the times for the owner to close for three days so she could go to a wool seminar in Pismo Beach! I couldn't hide my disappointment; I felt my mouth droop as I headed back to the car with the grocery sack stuck under my arm.

I plowed through part of the list for my mother and got the organic blackberry honey that had to come from Canterbury, New Zealand, and the organic meyer lemons, the cotton sheets and the natural detergent I had to wash the sheets in three times before putting them on the bed.

I had decided to put my parents in my room and had already begun cleaning the house and removing anything that might inspire negative comments like "You don't really use that kind of orange juice, do you?"

I dropped my purchases off at home, took care of Blondie and Cosmo and went back to the bookstore.

It was dusk when I arrived, and the bookstore looked welcoming, its warm lights shining through the windows and inviting customers in. Bob had a red eye ready for me and handed me some cookies to go with it. In a moment of humor, he had decided to make sugar cookies that looked like dog biscuits. Whatever they looked like, they tasted delicious and the strong coffee drink was a good chaser.

He set up a coffee-and-cookie stand right in the bookstore while I went to the event area. Kimball was already there taking some boxes out of a shopping bag and putting them on the table with the books.

I picked up one of the boxes and examined it.

"It's a test kit for taking a DNA sample," Kimball explained, along with the fact that he manufactured them and was offering them to the bookstore at a special rate.

I was going to object, but the crowd began to arrive. Obviously there had been some kind of misunderstanding. Who knew I needed to mention the event was for humans only? It seemed everyone in the crowd had a dog with them. And not all of the dogs were that glad to see each other. More than once I had to separate two snarling canines and send them along with their owners to opposite sides of the arrangement of chairs.

Kimball started the program, reading some sample stories from his book about how owners had found out the ancestry of their mixed-breed dogs. "And now I'll show you how to take a sample. It's the same as for people. We look for the DNA in saliva. With people you can even get a sample off a licked envelope or a paper cup. With dogs, we just take a swab." He opened up one of the boxes and asked for a volunteer. A woman with a dog that looked like a basset hound–poodle mix brought her pet up to the front.

"You just take a little swab of the inside of the cheek," Kimball said, lifting the side of the dog's mouth. The dog took it well, and then Kimball showed there was a container and a mailer in the box.

"I want to do that for my Rocky," a woman said, pointing to a brown short-haired dog that looked like he was laughing.

"Me, too," said a man, who had a tiny white fluffy dog sitting on his lap.

They made a move toward the tests and were joined by a bunch of others. I had to step in and in a nice way make sure the kits were paid for before being opened. I helped Rayaad cashier and rushed back to the event area just as Kimball was instructing the owners to open the boxes and take out the swabs. What had looked easy when Kimball did it was anything but when the owners tried. And their dogs were far less willing than the bassoodle had been.

Suffice it to say, there were suddenly dogs everywhere with owners chasing them holding swabs. Somewhere in the confusion one of the dogs got hold of the sugar cookie dog biscuits. When I looked over to the snack stand, an empty plate with some sugar sprinkles was all that remained.

Still, on the positive side, Adele wasn't there to tattle on me to Mrs. Shedd, and none of the dogs had accidents. Finally, after breaking down the chairs and vacuuming up the dog hair and cookie crumbs, I went home.

THREE DAYS LATER THE TARZANA HOOKERS MET again. The proprietor of Yarnie's was due back today, and I planned to head over there after the meeting. I had been bringing the bag back and forth to the bookstore every day, hoping the owner might show up to claim her things, but there was no such luck.

"You haven't found the owner yet?" Adele said, picking up the grocery sack. "I practically handed you the name. What happened?"

The group was sitting around the event table, and everyone looked up at Adele's comments.

"Dear, I thought you would have taken care of it by now." CeeCee seemed a little put out.

"You said I ought to wait for the owner to show up," I said.

"Yes, dear, I did, but I thought you'd use some judgement and when they didn't show up after a day or so—"

"Hey, Molly has been busy. Her parents are invading—I mean, coming to visit," Dinah said. "Have you met her mother, Liza Aronson, formerly of the She La Las?"

"Your mother was in that group?" CeeCee said. "I just loved that song of theirs—'My Man' something."

" 'My Man Dan,' " I said.

"It was their only hit, wasn't it? It must be difficult to be a one-hit wonder."

Before I could comment on being the daughter of a one-hit wonder, Adele stepped in.

"So, Pink, did you go to Yarnie's or what?"

I saw Dinah curl her lip in annoyance. Best friend that she was, she was going to say something to Adele the way she had to CeeCee, but I was a big girl and could fight my own battles.

I quickly put up my hand to stop Adele. She had her mouth open, about to say more.

"Here's the way it stands with the bag of stuff." I turned toward CeeCee. "When nobody came by the next day, I realized I should try to locate the owner." I glared at Adele. "And I went to the yarn store you said would recognize the thread, but it was closed for three days while the owner went to some yarn show. I am expecting it to reopen today."

Ali Stewart was sitting next to Adele following the conversations as if it were a tennis match. Her head was swiveling back and forth so much I was sure she must be dizzy.

"Okay, what did I miss?" Ali said. Everyone started to tell her at once, but Dinah took charge and told her the chain of events that began with us finding the bag.

Adele had her chair right next to Ali's, and I noticed they both were wearing pink tee shirts with a white thread crocheted embellishment around the neckline. Ali was a great addition to the group in many ways. She was an expert crocheter, she liked the idea of making things to give away, and she was always upbeat. The only problem was her sense of time. She always arrived late and left early. In fact, it often seemed she was just passing through the meetings.

Her hair looked as though some toddler had cut it with kid's scissors. But that hacked-off effect seemed to be in style. I guessed the shoe polish black color was in, too. Somehow on her the style and color were fun and arty.

True to form, Ali checked her watch and got up, announcing she had to leave. "I have to help my mom with something." She glanced around the group, making it clear she was speaking to all of us. "She runs a business out of the house. Don't worry. I'll have several blankets to bring in next time." As Ali started to go, Adele appeared practically heartbroken.

"Well, dear, if you have to leave . . ." CeeCee said. "But we really like having you here."

"I thought we would roll yarn together after the group." Adele held up a hank of hot pink yarn that needed someone to hold it while she made it into a ball.

Ali apologized and left, and Eduardo took the yarn out of Adele's hand and placed it over the end of the chair and started to wind the yarn into a ball.

"It's not the same," Adele said in a disappointed voice. "It's a girlfriend kind of thing."

I glanced toward Sheila to see how she'd reacted to the comment. Although she hadn't said anything, she seemed uncomfortable with Ali. But then, Ali had displaced her as the youngest member in the group. The way CeeCee fussed over her didn't help, either. Then there was the fact that Ali was always talking about her mother and father and how close they were. Sheila was alone in the world. The grandmother who'd raised her had died not too long ago and she had no other family. I sent a smile Sheila's way to reassure her, but she'd already gone into stress mode and her stitches were turning into knots. Eduardo stopped winding Adele's yarn and handed Sheila a smaller hook. He gave her a little pep talk, too, and she seemed to relax.

CeeCee glanced around the table and sighed with satisfaction. "I didn't even realize until now who isn't here. Camille didn't come back," she said.

"She hasn't come back *yet*," Adele said. CeeCee's content expression vanished.

"Did she really have you give her crochet lessons?"

Adele nodded, looking very pleased with herself. "You made it sound like she had to be a superaccomplished hooker to join us. Well, thanks to me, she's almost there. I discovered I'm a wonderful teacher. All she needs is one more lesson."

"Dear, don't say that. Didn't you hear what I said about her being a spy?"

"No," Adele said curtly. "I just heard you try to throw her to the knitters." Everyone at the table cringed, knowing any second Adele would launch into her crochet-versus-knitting rant. We all basically agreed with her, but we didn't make a federal case out of it.

Adele did about five minutes on the wonders of crochet and then sat down, and we resumed as if nothing had happened.

CeeCee took out a ball of bright yellow thread. "All this talking about filet crochet gave me an idea. Why don't we make bookmarks for the upcoming library sales? It would give those of us who haven't done filet work a chance to try it, and we could still keep up with the blankets." CeeCee stopped and swallowed. "When I tell you all what happened with the blankets we made, you'll realize how important they really are.

"I took the three blankets to the West Valley Police Station. A sergeant came out from the back to thank me and tell me about a call they'd had. There had been an awful situation where a man had killed his wife and one of the children had found her. The girl was seven and deeply traumatized. The officers who picked her up felt terrible for her and helpless to soothe her. But they had one of our blankets and wrapped it around her. Of course, it couldn't make up for what she'd been through, but they said there was something in the way she hung onto it as she rocked back and forth that made it clear it gave her some kind of comfort. It gave the officer some comfort, too, because they didn't feel so helpless."

As CeeCee relayed the touching story, we all kept our eyes fixated on our crocheting, unable to look up. I saw Sheila wipe back a tear.

At the end of the meeting, I assured CeeCee I was well on the road to finding the owner of the items. I then turned to Dinah. "I'm going to see if that Yarnie's place is open. I just want to find out who the bag belongs to and get it back to them. Want to come along?"

"I've always wanted to look in that store." Dinah sighed in regret. "But I can't go. I have a test to put together."

I promised to keep her appraised of what was going on, and we parted company. On my way out of the store, I told Rayaad I was going to lunch. I certainly hoped Adele was right about finding the owner through the unusual thread. I wanted the whole thing off my plate.

I parked in front of Yarnie's a few minutes later and went inside. It was a tiny store, three of its walls lined with yarn-filled shelves. In the middle of the store stood a small table surrounded by several chairs. Only one was filled: A woman who I figured was the owner sat taking skeins of yarn out of boxes and arranging them on the table.

"Are you the owner?" I asked.

She looked up and smiled. "My name is Dawn Yarnell, but everbody calls me Yarnie, hence the name of the store. Can I help you?"

I took out the filet piece and laid it on the table in front of her. "I'm looking for the person who made this, and a friend of mine thought you might be able to help." I mentioned the group at the bookstore.

"You're a Tarzana Hooker? Your leader comes in here a lot. Adele something. Quite an imaginative dresser, isn't she?" Yarnie said.

I nodded in agreement as the store owner picked up the piece and examined it. She seemed to focus on the panel of the odd vertical rectangle with the window in the middle.

"Adele has a good eye." She left the piece, went into a

back room and returned with an orb of thread the exact aqua of the panel. "This is the last ball of Fiji aquamarine number 10 I have. It was discontinued, and I bought out their entire supply.

"I keep records of who buys what." She paused a moment. "You can just leave it with me, and I'll check my records and give the owner a call."

I couldn't really blame her for being protective of her customers, but I wanted to meet the person face-to-face. When I said I'd really feel better if I took it back to the person myself, Yarnie didn't budge. I thought of *The Average Joe's Guide to Criminal Investigation* and what it would suggest under the circumstances. It usually advised being creative and not being afraid to stretch the truth, but I realized that in this situation, the best weapon in my arsenal *was* the truth.

"Do you know who CeeCee Collins is?" I began. Yarnie nodded and even mentioned the show. It was an easy segue into the package being left for CeeCee to deal with. And it was amazing what a celebrity name would do. "I promised CeeCee I would give it directly to the owner," I said finally.

Yarnie considered what I'd said and then opened her laptop and fired it up. She typed something in and shook her head. "I'm afraid a whole list of names comes up." She turned the computer toward me and I saw she was right.

Undaunted, I examined the piece again. "What about one of these other colors? If you look up who bought one of them it might narrow it down."

"Good thinking. I've never actually done it in reverse like this." She held the piece close and looked at the panel with the bath-powder box. "I think this is arctic blue 14." She got a sample to be sure and then typed it in the computer.

She came up with another list, and we checked back and

forth and found there were only two people who'd bought both colors.

"It's not her," she said, pointing at the first name. "She moved to Napa three months ago." She pointed to the second in the list.

Mary Beth Wells.

Yarnie seemed to hesitate then finally wrote down the pertinent information on a piece of paper shaped like a ball of yarn. "Do you know who she is?"

I shrugged and she continued. "Well, you must have heard of Lance Wells?"

Of course, who hadn't? He was before my time more or less, but Lance Wells was the premier dancing actor in all those tuxedo-and-evening-gown musicals. There was a nationwide chain of dance studios named after him. I'd just passed the one in Tarzana the other day and noticed how busy it was. Thanks to *Dancing with the Stars* and the shows it had spawned, everybody wanted to learn all the couples' dances.

"Mary Beth was married to Lance Wells Jr.," Yarnie said. "I think he died about six months ago."

"Then you know her pretty well?" I said. The shop owner gave me a noncommital shrug. "Do you have any idea what all this means?" I asked, pointing to the motifs in the panels.

"She said she likes filet crochet because it's like drawing. This is the first time I've seen anything she's made. Mostly, she just buys supplies when she comes in. She said she likes all the colors I have." Yarnie stared at the panel piece for a long time. "This is really an odd item. It's not the kind of thing I expected her to make. Filet isn't that popular. Mostly what you see are nameplates or trim on something." She reached for the phone and punched in some numbers. "First thing I'm going to ask her is what all this is." She paused and I could hear the phone ringing through the receiver. Finally, someone answered and Yarnie spoke, but it was obvious she'd reached a wrong number.

She checked her computer again and saw it was the number she'd dialed. "Oh no, I must have transposed some of the numbers." She appeared apologetic. "I'm a little dyslexic." She looked at the screen. "I think the address is right. I know I've mailed her sale notices and they haven't come back."

"I'll go there and if nobody's home, I'll leave a note in the mailbox," I said. That seemed to set okay with her, and she gave me the address and even searched out driving directions from the Internet for me.

I was glad to have the directions. Although the house was in Tarzana, it was up in the hills where the streets reminded me of spider veins. They were squiggly and branched off each other in multiple directions. After much confusion, I finally found her street, which was so steep I was afraid the car would start slipping back down the hill. Where the street ended and the signs for the Santa Monica Mountains Conservancy began, I saw the address on the curb. There was a wrought-iron mailbox in front and a solid blue-green gate across the driveway. I turned the car around and parked on the street, making sure to curb my wheels.

I climbed out of the car and stood on the sidewalk. A large house was a short distance below me, and from there a row of minimansions cascaded down the hillside. When I looked up, the whole San Fernando Valley spread before me and I suddenly felt like the queen of the world. I got caught up in the view. It was a clear day, and the San Gabriel Mountains appeared so stark, it was as if they'd been outlined in black marker. The top of Mount Wilson was dusted with snow, and farther east, I caught sight of Mount Baldy completely slathered in white. A plane at eye level was heading toward Van Nuys Airport to land. The grid of streets spread before me, and I could pick out landmarks and see how lush the Valley was, its treetops like tiny green cotton balls.

But I wasn't here for sightseeing so I began walking back toward the mailbox, noticing an intercom on a stand just before the gate. I had the bag under my arm and pressed the button next to the speaker. A moment later I heard a voice say something, and I launched into explaining my mission. But all I got out was my name before I was interrupted.

A woman's voice crackled out of the speaker, but I couldn't make out what she was saying. It sounded almost like gibberish, but I thought she repeated my name.

"Yes, yes, I'm—" There was no time to finish again as the gate made a noise and began to slide open. I walked through quickly and stood at the end of a long driveway that curved and disappeared. The laurel trees on either side were old and gnarled and made a canopy with their knife-shaped leaves. The treetops blocked out the light, making it dark and shadowy. My heart rate kicked up as I began to wonder what I was walking into.

The house didn't come into view until after I'd rounded the curve. It was an old Spanish style—two stories with creamy stucco, lots of arched windows and a red-tile roof. My breath caught as a deer darted in front of me and disappeared down into the brush on the hillside.

I reached the other end of the driveway and walked up the path toward the house. A red-tiled patio ran along the front with an overhang for shade created by the second-floor balcony. It took my breath away just imagining what the view must be like from up there. It was probably even better at night with all the lights.

The large wood door opened, and a woman in jeans and a red blouse came out. She seemed distracted and was looking past me.

"Mary Beth Wells?" I said. I took the bag out from under my arm. Her eyes focused on it, then she nodded and grabbed my arm.

She was saying something in Spanish and I couldn't understand her. She waved at the driveway and seemed to be looking for something, then dragged me inside.

The inside of the house was dark. I glanced around quickly, taking in the giant pots of mother-in-law tongues on the shiny dark wood floor. I only got a quick glance as we passed the living room. There was a light-colored sofa with a bright Native American blanket draped over the arm. By now, the woman was even more agitated; she gestured for me to hurry.

I followed her upstairs, where I was hit by a smell so bad I gasped. Just then, the woman pushed me in the doorway of what appeared to be the master bedroom. She finally seemed to remember English. "Fix her. She sick. When I got here. She like this."

I heard the sound of a doorbell coming through the intercom receiver on the wall. The housekeeper—at least I assumed she was the housekeeper—frantically rushed to press the buttons.

I stayed back but could see there was a woman in the bed who didn't appear to be moving. Pillows were propped up against the dark wood headboard, but she had fallen forward such that her face was obscured by her dark blond hair, which was spread out over the white chenille coverlet. A large stain marred the blanket.

As I took in the scene, I heard the whine of a siren and the rumble of a truck motor. Then flashing lights came through the window, and I understood why I'd been let in so quickly. The housekeeper must have called 911 and assumed I was the EMTs. No wonder she'd looked at me so oddly. She must have thought I had medical gear in the paper sack.

Even though I was across the room I had a feeling the person in the bed was beyond anybody's ability to fix. Because of my extensive reading of *The Average Joe's Guide to Criminal Investigation*, I automatically started checking out the surroundings carefully. The light next to the bed was still on, and a book appeared to have fallen on the floor. There was a carafe of water, still full, on the bedside table as well. Something next to the carafe caught my eye, and I actually took a step closer to get a better look. It was a clear plastic box of what appeared to be little apples. Several were missing.

The sounds of footsteps and voices jarred me from my observations. The housekeeper began to scream and the footsteps grew louder. Two men in dark blue uniforms rushed past me. That was when I realized what the things in the box were. Marzipan. I'd seen the almond-paste candy formed into all kinds of fruits and flowers before. As far as I was concerned, the taste never lived up to the presentation.

This seemed like a good time to leave. As I reached the top of the stairs, two firefighters came up and rushed past me. No one seemed to notice me as I headed down the staircase and toward the door. It seemed a safe guess that the woman in the bed was Mary Beth Wells. I hoped the paramedics would be able to revive her. In any case, it didn't seem likely she'd be up for discussing a crochet piece.

I got outside and walked quickly past the ambulance and small fire truck. I picked up speed, but when I went around the curve of the driveway I caught sight of the solid blue-green gate. It was closed.

I knew most of those electric gates had some kind of electric eye that made them open when you got close. As I approached it, sure enough, it began to open, but since I was walking and the gate was timed for a car, I worried it wouldn't stay open long enough. I began to run. Clutching the bag, I picked up speed. The slight downhill slope of the road only made me go faster.

The gate was still in the process of opening as I flew through it. It was only then that I saw the police cruiser pulled into the driveway waiting to come in. I had too much momentum to stop and went running past the black-and-white. Oh no. The doors flew open, and the two patrol officers jumped out and yelled at me to freeze.

I guess running out of there kind of gave the wrong impression.

CHAPTER 6

I SUPPOSE I SHOULD BE GRATEFUL FOR SMALL favors. The officers didn't handcuff me—they just gave me a lift back up the driveway. Riding in the backseat of a cruiser was not exactly my favorite mode of transportation. The seat was hard plastic and had a residue of bad odors, and there were no window openers or door handles, which made me feel more than a little trapped.

They pulled around the ambulance and fire truck and parked on the grass. I guess if you're cops you can do stuff like that. One of the uniforms opened the back door and escorted me to a bench on the lawn. Just to make sure I stayed put, he sat with me while his partner went into the house. My stomach fluttered when I saw the name on the badge.

Officer James turned toward me and studied my face. "Have I picked you up before?"

"Not exactly," I said, hoping he wouldn't pursue it. He'd been first on the scene of the very first crime I'd been involved with.

His eyes lit up with recognition, and then he appeared concerned. "You aren't going to throw up, are you?"

Ah, so he did remember. I had rambled on and on that time, telling him I was afraid if I stopped talking I might throw up.

I assured him I had changed since then, and the conversation ended except for him asking me for fingerprint and hair samples and telling me I had to wait to talk to the detective. Since Barry was somewhere on the East Coast interrogating a witness, I knew it wouldn't be him.

The one positive about waiting was I got a chance to really look at the view. It was better than thinking about why I was there, I decided, as I continued to clutch my purse and the paper sack. I knew there were houses below, but they were out of sight and I had an unobstructed panoramic view of the Valley. It was breathtaking, though I didn't need any help having my breath taken. I couldn't help it. Even though I was perfectly innocent, my heart was pounding in anticipation—and not in a good way. It was getting cold, too.

A blue Crown Victoria pulled up the driveway and stopped. By now the ambulance and fire truck had left. The fading sunlight reflected off the windshield and I couldn't see who was inside. But I had that old sinking feeling in my stomach when I saw who got out. Detective Heather Gilmore didn't look happy to see me, either.

We had a bit of history. More like a very short story. She wanted Barry Greenberg and I had him. I guessed her biological clock was getting into the red zone and she wanted to get married, so she'd zeroed in on him.

Usually, she dressed in a well-fitting suit. But this time she was wearing jeans and a white turtleneck with a safari-style jacket over it. Something looked wrong, and I realized she must have gotten the call when she was off duty. Judging by the one hand with red polish and the other hand with none, she'd been in the midst of a manicure. Then I noticed the wet white blond hair sticking out below the scarf she had tied over her head. She must have been getting her hair done, too.

I noticed a thick belt around her hips when her jacket opened, revealing her badge and gun. Did she wear it to the beauty shop?

My companion patrol officer went over to talk to her out of my earshot. Detective Heather was glaring at me the whole time he spoke. Of course, I called her Detective Heather only in my head and to my friends since it sounded a little too much like calling her Detective Barbie Doll.

"Okay, why exactly were you fleeing the scene?" she said when she finally walked over to me.

"*Fleeing* is such a strong word," I said, standing up. I tried explaining that I was concerned about the gate shutting on me, but she didn't look sold.

"Why exactly were you here to start with?" she asked, taking out her pad and pen. "How do you know the deceased?"

It was the first time I was hearing it confirmed that she was dead. Even though it seemed pretty obvious when the ambulance left without her. Still, hearing it out loud unnerved me and my legs felt rubbery. I sat back down on the bench rather hard.

I held out the paper sack and told her the story about the crochet group finding it on our table and how I had tracked down Mary Beth Wells as the owner by the color of the thread.

She slipped on a pair of rubber gloves and took the bag. She pulled out the contents and set them on the bench. I pointed to the aqua thread, but she ignored me and examined the diary entry and the note. She looked ready to roll her eyes.

"Quite the amateur detective, aren't you?" She had finished reading the note and the torn sheet from a diary and had set them aside. Her attention turned to the crochet piece. Detective Heather was an accomplished knitter, so I thought she would appreciate the filet crochet.

"I think the images in the crochet piece all mean something, like they are clues to the wrong she wanted to fix. You read the note," I said, trying to sound friendly.

"Like some kind of treasure map?" Detective Heather held the piece at a distance. I could tell by the way she was moving it around, she was focusing on the images we couldn't recognize. This time she did roll her eyes.

"Maybe somebody didn't want her to reveal something and they—"

"Killed her to keep their secret safe forever and ever." She said it in the dramatic tone I'd heard some of the romance writers at the bookstore events use when they read from their books. She turned toward me and gave her head the slightest of shakes that made it clear she thought my idea was far-fetched.

She put everything back in the bag and took it inside the house. A few minutes later she returned and handed it back to me.

"I showed it to the maid and she didn't recognize it. I'm sure you think you were very clever, but there doesn't seem to be anything to connect it to Mary Beth Wells."

"But . . . but," I sputtered.

Detective Heather impatiently rocked her head from side to side. "There is nothing on the note with her name. I looked around; there isn't a crochet hook or even a stash of yarn. The maid doesn't know anything about any secret. She also corroborated your story about just getting here. It looks like natural causes. The maid's been off for two days, but she said the woman was feeling sick the last time she saw her." Then Detective Heather stopped herself. "Why am I even telling you this?"

"You should check for poison."

Detective Heather glared at me. Clearly, she didn't like anyone telling her her business. She started to dismiss me, but then her expression changed to one of smug satisfaction. "Haven't seen much of Barry lately, have you?" She didn't wait for me to answer, because she knew what the answer was. "Not much fun being left behind all the time, is it? It's hard for civilians to understand. That's what I told Barry over dinner the other night."

I knew the "dinner" was probably a couple of burgers in a paper sack from the local drive-thru during a break from interviewing a witness, but she had hit a sensitive spot. I could tell by the way her eyes lit up that I had been unsuccessful at hiding my flicker of upset.

"Is that really what you want?" she said as I got up to go.

She stood watching me as I began walking down the driveway. The sky was almost dark, and the canopy of laurel trees made it even darker and more sinister. I was sure the things in the bag belonged to Mary Beth, and I was sure the cause of death wasn't natural. But most of all I felt terribly guilty. If only I'd gotten here sooner, maybe she wouldn't have died. On top of the guilt there was something else. Detective Heather's words echoed in my mind. *Is that really what you want?*

Was it? I had been asking myself the same thing.

This time I walked through the gate. Several news vans were setting up on the steep street, and before I could get to my car Kimberely Wang Diaz of Channel 3 News rushed over to me.

"You again," she said in an excited voice as she shoved a microphone in front of me. Oh no, not this time. I was not going to end up on the news leaving the scene where someone died. My son Peter would be embarrassed and my son Samuel worried, and everybody else would think I'd earned the title "crime scene groupie."

The reporter was dressed to be on camera and had on a thick layer of makeup to keep her from looking washed out. I had neither going for me. "So was it murder?" Diaz asked with all too much excitement in her voice.

For once I wised up. "No comment," I said, stepping away and going toward my car.

I drove directly to Walter Beasley Community College and found Dinah's classroom. I waited ten minutes before the bell rang marking the end of class. Before it had even stopped sounding, freshmen exploded through the door. I had a momentary distraction watching the fashion show. It made me glad not to be young anymore. What was with the boys in skinny jeans pulled so low they waddled and their underpants hung out? And the girls—I still didn't get the gaudy tattoos and too many earrings in all the wrong places and hair that looked as if it had been dipped in melted Popsicles.

Dinah came out last with a good-looking young man whose face was twisted in upset.

"I just don't understand why I can't take the test now since I missed it," he said, almost running to keep up with her.

Dinah appeared about to pop her cork. "Because, Vincent, we just went over the test answers in class after I asked three times if there was anyone who hadn't taken the test."

"I didn't hear you," Vincent said. "I guess I fell asleep," he muttered.

That didn't seem to go over well with Dinah, and she threw up her hands. Then she saw me. I must have looked a little done in because her brows knit in concern. She told Vincent they were finished and no was her final answer. "If you have a problem with that, take it up with the dean. And be sure and mention the part about falling asleep in class," she said before coming toward me.

"Omigod, what happened?" she said when she got close. I started to open my mouth, but she ordered me to hold my thought. "I have to pick up the twins from preschool, and if I'm late, they start charging five dollars a minute."

I didn't get a chance to talk until we'd picked up the kids with thirty seconds to spare and had gone to a Mexican fast-food place. Dinah was strictly ixnay on the kiddie meals and had gotten each of them a cheese quesadilla and half juice–half sparking water—her version of soda.

"I feel like it's my fault. If I could have found Mary Beth sooner, maybe I could have done something."

"But Yarnie's was closed," Dinah said, trying to make me feel better. But I persisted.

"If only I'd been able to talk to Mary Beth at least I could have found out who she was worried about and what all this means."

"Did you consider that maybe Detective Heather was right? There really isn't anything on here that says 'Mary Beth Wells.'" Dinah had taken the grocery bag I was still clutching and was examining the contents again. She read over the papers and picked up what I'd started calling the "crocheted clue." "It would be nice to know what all these things are supposed to be." Dinah pointed to the panel next to the one with the rectangles. "It looks like a bunch of shapes that make no sense."

My cell phone interrupted us as Ashley-Angela took the crochet piece from Dinah and turned it around. She tried to show us something, but Dinah just told her to finish her food.

Barry was on the phone. Apparently, he'd crossed paths with Detective Heather.

"Molly?" He sounded concerned and exhausted. "Are you okay?"

"Am I ever going to see you again?" I said.

"Babe," he said with a sigh of apology, "as soon as I'm done with this case, I'm yours." Then someone called him and he signed off.

The kids took their cups and food wrappers to the trash and went off to play in the indoor playground. Dinah watched them go and then turned to me. "They're going home. For real this time. Jeremy called this afternoon," she said, referring to her ex-husband. "I'm almost afraid to believe it. I'm going to get my life back." Then her normally perky expression drooped. "But I'm going to miss them. Suddenly I'll have all that time—"

"Don't worry. I know just what to do with it," I said. The crochet piece was just where Ashley-Angela had left it. Leave it to a four-year-old to figure it out. All the motifs were upside down now except one. I traced the shape with my finger. Instead of looking like a bunch of odd shapes stuck together, it was clear what it was supposed to represent. Dinah saw me staring and followed my gaze.

"No connection to Mary Beth Wells—yeah right," I said. Viewed at this angle it was clearly a wishing well with an *MB* embedded in the texture of the roof.

"Wow, there's even an *s* to make it *Wells*," Dinah said, pointing to the shape holding the bucket.

"I can't just do nothing," I said, not taking my eyes off the crochet work. "I'll feel better if I at least find out what Mary Beth was trying to fix and take care of it for her."

Dinah touched me to get my attention. "You know the secret and her death are probably connected." I nodded and Dinah perked up. "Count me in. An investigation will keep me from slipping into the empty-nest blues."

I turned the piece back around right-side up, and we both went over the motifs to see if the new information made a difference in understanding the whole. It didn't.

"Didn't you say Detective Heather said the death was from natural causes?"

"No. She said it *looked* like natural causes. I bet anything that when they do an autopsy they'll find out it wasn't." I caught a glimpse of the clock on the wall and jumped up. "I have to go."

CHAPTER 7

I GOT HOME WITH BARELY ENOUGH TIME TO TURN on the lights and take care of the dogs before the grand arrival. I was fluffing the pillows on the couch when the SUV pulled up to the curb in front of the house. Who would have thought my parents would get a sport-utility vehicle?

I opened the door and waited for them. My mother floated in on the scent of Chanel No. 5 and hugged me. Then she stepped back and looked me over. They were hardly in the house and I was already girding for the onslaught.

"Molly, the last time I saw you, you were wearing the same thing. Is your whole wardrobe khaki pants and white shirts and a black something? You need some color, some pizzaz."

Nobody would accuse my mother of lacking pizzaz. In fact, my mother, Liza Aronson, had pizzaz to spare. I wasn't as obvious as she was, but I checked out her outfit, too. Unfortunately, there was nothing negative to say. It was depressing to realize my mother had more style than I did. She had on black jeans with a black turtleneck and a woven scarf of blues and purples wound loosely around her neck. An armful of silver and turquoise bracelets and long dangle earrings complemented the look, which she finished off with silver-toed black cowboy boots. I looked like queen of the frumps next to her. Even her hair was better. When I went for a cut, I just sat in the chair and let Gerardo decide how to snip. Not her. She always went to the salon with an exact plan of how she wanted her hair. It was a golden brown with mink highlights, cut to shape her face perfectly. But then, as she had always reminded me, she was a performer and I wasn't.

Next my father came in carrying some bags. I offered to help, but he insisted he had it under control. He wore slacks and a blazer, and though his hair was almost white he still had a nice head full. He dropped a bag of samples on the table. "I brought some of this great new sunblock," he said, narrowing his eyes as he studied my face. I knew the look. He was checking my skin. It was second nature to him. He was always on the lookout for skin cancer. He seemed satisfied with what he saw and asked where to take their luggage.

"I suppose you're going to put us in one of the boys' rooms," my mother chimed in. Before I could stop her, she headed for Peter's old room. When she turned on the light, she yelped in surprise. The last time she'd seen it, there was a pullout couch, a dresser and a bookcase full of sports trophies. Now it was a riot of color and plastic grocery bags. When I'd first turned it into my crochet room, I'd kept it orderly. All the yarn was in the bookcase, arranged by color. But then I'd gotten more yarn than there was shelf space for, and even though I had tried to squeeze it in, it had popped out and sort of landed everywhere. Then there were the projects. I'd start something and work on it for a while, then something else would excite me and I'd set the first one aside thinking it would just be for a moment until I got the next one started. And on and on. I'd discovered the best way to keep track of my works in progress was by putting each in a plastic grocery bag along with the instructions, notes on what I'd completed, a yarn wrapper and a hook. The grocery bags seemed to have multiplied like rabbits.

"See, I do have some color in my life," I said as I prepared to turn off the light.

"What's all this?" my mother said with concern in her voice as she stepped farther into the room and poked into the grocery bags. "You know, disorder is a sign of mental illness."

What? My mother was barely in the door and already she was calling me crazy.

"It's my crochet room." I left the light on and proceeded to show her how sane I was. Would a crazy person be able to follow the pattern for an afghan that was finished except for half the fringe? I didn't think so.

"You made this?" My mother actually sounded impressed, and I figured she was now clear that I wasn't nuts.

"What about this?" She didn't sound so impressed anymore, and when I looked to see what was diminishing her opinion of me, I saw that she had picked up Mary Beth's piece. "Is this some kind of art piece? Were you trying to mix representational art with abstract?"

"I didn't make it, so I don't know." I debated whether I should tell her about Mary Beth being dead and my thinking it was some kind of clue map. But considering that she already seemed to have some doubts about my mental health—well, even I knew it sounded kind of crazy.

"What is all this supposed to be?" my mother said, turning the piece around as if a different view would change things. "I recognize this—it's the Casino Building on Catalina Island."

"Huh?" I said, looking over her shoulder. Then I saw she was right. I'd seen the round-shaped building countless times during the weather segment on the news. Here she didn't even know anything about the mystery and she'd already turned over a clue. A bath-powder box, indeed. I almost wanted to hug her.

My mother lost interest in it after that. "Then I suppose we get Samuel's old room," she said, heading down the hall.

"No. I'm putting you and Daddy in my room," I said. "Just stay here for a moment." I dashed across the house to make sure I hadn't left anything embarrassing around. Sure enough, there was the bottle of ylang-ylang pleasure oil next to my bed that Barry had brought over. I slipped it in my pocket just as I heard footsteps in the hall.

"Irv put the bags in the hall," my mother called to my father before coming in. She looked around with interest. She'd never spent much time in here before. When my parents had come to visit while Charlie was alive, our room had been our domain.

It was really a wonderful large room with vaulted wood ceilings and a fireplace. There were large windows on two of the walls and a glass door leading to a little private patio. The bathroom was roomy with a window looking out on the same patio, and there was a hall with two closets and a door at the end. With the door shut, the bedroom suite became like a separate world from the rest of the house.

I had gotten a new bedspread with pink flowers on a green background; an abundance of pillows complemented the decor. They also made the bed seem like a wonderful sleep nest; I was going to miss nestling in there. I closed the shutters on the windows and pulled Blondie's chair with me. The two dogs followed me out. As I was going, my mother wanted to make sure the bed had the all-cotton sheets she'd asked for. "Yes, and I washed them three times in the organic soap," I called out.

As soon as I got across the house to my office—the tiny bedroom off the laundry area where I kept my computer—I turned it on and typed in *Catalina*.

CHAPTER 8

"SO YOUR MOTHER HAS NO IDEA THAT SHE UN-covered a clue?" Dinah said. It was a few days later and Dinah and I had met for a pregroup breakfast. Truthfully, we both needed a diversion. Her ex had picked up the twins the day before and her house felt too empty. My mother was in diva mode and my house felt too full.

"And it's going to stay that way. My mother already thinks I'm mentally unstable because of the mess in my crochet room. She'd probably try to call in some television shrink if she knew I got involved in solving murders. Anyway, it's not the most important clue, so far. That was the wishing well, which was like Mary Beth's signature, and Ashley-Angela is the one who turned the piece around."

Dinah's perkiness fell. "I wonder how they're doing? I hope Jeremy doesn't just forget them somewhere. He's so irresponsible." Dinah poured some coffee and steamed milk in her mug and nibbled on her roll. "Let's talk about Mary Beth. Thinking about the twins is upsetting."

"What is there to say? All we know is that she liked filet

crochet, had a secret and was married to the son of a famous dancer-actor."

"And there's a Lance Wells Dance Studio down the
street," Dinah said, sounding like her usual self again.

"Let's go there now," I said, downing the last of my coffee. We finished up quickly and headed down the street.

The Lance Wells Dance Studio was on the second floor
of a building facing Ventura. A stairway between the clothing store and real estate office on the ground floor led the
way up. A plaque near the bottom of the steps announced
that both the dance studio and the corporate office were
upstairs.

When we got to the second floor, a paper sign on the
inside of the glass door said the studio and offices were
closed due to a death in the family.

"So much for trying to find out about her here," I said
as we came back out down the stairs and headed up the
street to Shedd & Royal.

When we got to the bookstore, a painting crew was just
finishing up.

"It's about the TV shot, isn't it?" Dinah said, watching a
guy in white coveralls carry out a ladder.

"Mrs. Shedd might have gone a little overboard. She
figures this is the bookstore's chance to become a star, and
she doesn't want to leave it to the production people to fix
it up."

"Still no idea who the subject is?" Dinah asked on our
way back into the event area.

"Nobody's talking, so your guess is as good as mine."

Dinah helped me set up for the crochet group. Once we
had the table and chairs in place, we put out our things. The
paper grocery bag had gotten a little worse for wear given
all the dragging around and now seemed ill-suited to carry
something as important as the filet crochet panels and the
notes that came with it. I had put each of the notes in its
own plastic bag, and I'd wrapped the filet piece around a

piece of cardboard and put it in another, larger plastic bag. Then I'd put all of it in a Gelson's plastic grocery bag and tucked it in my tote. I had saved the original paper one just in case it turned out to be some kind of evidence.

"Nice presentation," Dinah said as I laid all the clear plastic bags on the table.

"I thought since all this was left on the group's table at the park sale, I ought to tell them what's happened."

CeeCee and Sheila arrived next. CeeCee had brought some balls of bedspread-weight thread and an array of small steel hooks for the bookmarks. She regarded Sheila with concern.

"Dear, I don't know how you're going to do this. If your stitches get too tight . . ." CeeCee shook her head rather than complete the sentence. Sheila had been known to turn her stitches into little fists. So far she'd always gotten them undone by changing to a smaller hook, but the steel one was so tiny to begin with, her only alternative would be to try to loosen any too-tight stitches with a pinhead.

I was actually a little concerned for myself, too. When I'd played around with crochet thread at home, I'd spent most of the time picking up the silvery hook after it slipped out of my hand.

Adele came over from the children's department. She was wearing some kind of long, loose yellow tunic over black leggings. She'd pinned crocheted flowers in pinks and oranges and yellows all over the top and had finished the look with a crocheted headband pulled over her head like a crown. As she sat down she looked at my attire. "Pink, you're such a dull dresser. Do you own anything besides khaki pants and white shirts and black somethings. You look like an ad for bland."

I was used to Adele's barbs, and they usually rolled off my back. This time, though, she got to me because her comment echoed my mother's exactly. I wondered if there was some truth in their remarks.

Eduardo made a stir when he joined us, beaming a

bright smile as he greeted everyone. He knew he was fabulously good-looking, but he never let it get in the way of being a really nice guy.

"More blankets, ladies," he said, pulling out two blankets of cream and beige stripes from his leather bag. "There was so much waiting on my last photo shoot, I had plenty of time to crochet." He started to hand his creations to CeeCee, but she pushed the blankets to me.

"She's the one with police contact." CeeCee took in my surprised expression and then continued. "I know I set it up originally, but I was thinking your boyfriend is a homicide detective and you know that Detective Gilmore. You can just give the finished ones to them."

"Speaking of homicide detectives," I began. I pushed Mary Beth's things toward the center of the table where everyone could see them. I had planned out the order in which to tell them everything, but I blew it by pointing out to CeeCee that it wasn't really a bath-powder box after all.

"You're right, dear. Of course that's the building on Catalina," CeeCee said. She had taken the panel piece out and unwound it from around the cardboard. She held it up in both hands and stretched out her arms to get more of an overview. "But you have to admit the Casino Building is shaped like a bath-powder box."

"Casino?" Sheila said. "Is it one of those Indian casinos with bingo and slot machines?"

"No, it's not that kind of casino. It turns out the actual meaning of *casino* is something like 'meeting place.' The one on Catalina has the only movie theater, a ballroom, a small museum and nothing related to gambling. It's the landmark building on the island."

"Oh, I wouldn't know. I've never been," Sheila said. Against CeeCee's orders, she was trying the thread and steel hook and was working very slowly.

"You'd like it, dear," CeeCee said. "It's very relaxing and charming. Even though it's just a short boat ride off the coast, it's like another world."

"Avalon is my kind of town," Adele announced. Then suddenly something registered with her. "Pink, why do you still have the stuff? Haven't you gone to Yarnie yet?" Adele turned toward the others and repeated her cleverness at sending me to Yarnie's. "I ask you, who is the real Sherlock Holmes here?"

I held up my hand to stop her. "There's something I need to tell you." I shot Adele an annoyed glare and said I had gone to Yarnie's. Then I told them who the things belonged to—emphasis on the past tense.

"Mary Beth Wells?" CeeCee said, putting a hand to her heart. "Didn't I hear on the news that she died? It belonged to her?"

As I was explaining what happened when I'd tried taking the bag to Mary Beth, Adele interrupted. "Geez, Pink, you're really attracted to dead bodies. You really are a—"

"Don't even say it." I stopped Adele cold. "I am *not* a crime scene groupie." Adele snickered because I'd just said what I'd tried to keep her from saying.

"Of course you're not," CeeCee said, patting my hand. She turned to the others. "Molly isn't some kind of thrill seeker. She was trying to get the woman's handiwork back to her." Then CeeCee gave the floor back to me, and everyone wanted to hear all the details. They were on the edge of their seats as I described walking into the house and seeing the body, and when I got to the part about running out of the gate and nearly slamming into the cop car, they all squealed. All except Adele, who just kept rolling her eyes.

"I showed the bag of things to Detective Heather, but she acted like I was ridiculous for suggesting they belonged to Mary Beth. She said nothing on either of the pieces of paper gave an indication they were from her, and she wouldn't even listen to me when I tried to explain about the unusual thread. She said the death looked like it was from natural causes."

I noticed Sheila shrank back at the mention of Detective

Heather's name. She reached out and touched my hand in support.

"Did she take you to the station and lock you in one of those interview rooms?" Sheila had been caught in Detective Heather's sights when a local shopkeeper was killed. She was still getting over the shock.

"No interview room or even a trip to the station. I think she was closer to laughing at me. Too bad I hadn't noticed this." I took the panel piece from CeeCee and laid it on the table the other way.

"Oh," Sheila said with a tremble in her voice. She touched the *MB* embedded in the roof of the wishing well. Suddenly Sheila sat back and looked pale. "There's a member of the gym who has a relative who works at the West Valley Police Station. She came in this morning just before I left. I heard her talking to some friend." Sheila's eyes were big and round. "She was talking about someone named Wells and saying something about her being poisoned."

"I knew it," I nearly shouted. "They must have done an autopsy. Did you hear what kind?"

"What's the difference?" CeeCee asked. "It obviously did the job. I played a murderess once in an episode of *Keeley Crumpfort, ME*. It was so against character, the director thought no one would be able to figure out it was me until the denouement. My character used poison to kill her husband. She, I mean, *I* fed him small amounts of it so he had a record of being sick, and then whammo, I gave him a double dose and he died."

"I bet that's what happened with Mary Beth. Detective Heather said the maid mentioned Mary Beth had been sick," I explained. A picture of Mary Beth's bedroom flashed in my mind. "And I bet I know how they could have done it. There was a half-eaten package of marzipan apples on the bedside table."

CeeCee and Dinah both made faces, not about the poisoning, but rather about the marzipan. CeeCee said it tasted like gritty paste.

"It was probably a woman who did it," Eduardo said. "Poison is considered a woman's weapon." We all looked surprised at his comment. "I read a lot of true crime," he said with a shrug.

I laid my hand on the display of items. "Since these were left on our table, I feel it is my responsibility to finish what Mary Beth wanted to do, and since the first panel has an image of the Casino Building, I think the place to start is Catalina Island."

For a moment there was silence at the table. Then Cee-Cee spoke. "I could use an outing, and since I'm sure the package was left for me, I should go along. Count me in."

Sheila looked up. "I've always wanted to go there, but I don't know . . ." I knew she was worried about the cost. She was chronically short of money. I told her I'd pay her boat fare and she could do something for me in return. I would have just paid it, but I knew Sheila had her pride.

Dinah's face lit up suddenly. "I forgot the kids have gone home. I'm free. Count me in."

Eduardo had to beg off because he was booked to do a talk show back east. "The idea is to turn me into more than just a face. I'm going to show my funny side."

"Good idea, Eduardo," CeeCee said. "It's always good to be multidimensional. Did I tell you I used to sing, too?"

"We're getting off topic," I said. "So, all of you except Eduardo are coming to Catalina with me?" After some back-and-forth over when to go—everyone had something to rearrange—we finally agreed on a day later in the week.

"I'm here to join the group." At those words, we all looked up from our conversation to see Camille Rhead Katz holding a swatch of off-white yarn. CeeCee's face fell so low I thought it would hit the floor, and I heard her groan under her breath. Camille's swatch had rows of single and double crochet and then a pattern with double crochets and shell stitches. She dangled it in front of CeeCee. "See, now I can crochet."

CeeCee sputtered, but there was no legitimate objection

she could make and she finally muttered a welcome to the group while sending an annoyed flash of her eyes in Adele's direction.

"Did I hear you talking about a trip to Catalina? Is the group meeting there?" she said in a friendly voice.

CeeCee stepped in before anyone else could speak. "It's a separate thing some of us are working on."

Camille looked a little miffed, though not enough to leave. She set her bag on the table. It was made of black fabric covered with a pattern of small red hearts, each of which bore the initials *VT*. I had seen a lot of similar bags lately and initially thought they were one of those cosmetic-counter giveaways. Adele had been the one to set me straight. They were the latest bag from the Vladimir Tucci collection, and they cost a fortune.

Her crochet supplies were equally elegant. She pulled out a full set of hand-carved wood hooks in a padded roll and a set made out of plastic that featured little lights on the curved part. Next came a clear plastic case that held scissors shaped like a crane, stitch holders, a measuring tape, a space pen and a tiny notebook. She glanced Adele's way. "Did I get the right stuff?" Adele nodded.

Camille noticed Mary Beth's filet panels on the table. "Why do I keep seeing this?" She surveyed the group for an answer.

I opened my mouth to explain but caught sight of Cee-Cee giving me one of her cease-and-desist stares, and I closed it without saying a word. I got CeeCee's drift. She couldn't keep Camille out of the crochet group, but that didn't mean she was really one of us.

Just then Ali rushed up to the table and skidded to a stop. She was out of breath, and between heavy gasps she apologized numerous times. CeeCee's face softened. She liked Ali. She and her late husband had never had children, but I think she regretted it now. Ali was the kind of girl she would have loved as a daughter, except maybe for her problem with time management.

"That bag is wonderful," CeeCee said as Ali set down her purse.

"You like it?" the young woman said with a grin. "Some people think it looks a little odd. It's improvisational crochet. I put on music, take out a bunch of hooks and bits of yarn, beads and charms and go crazy." I ran my hand over the texture. It went from smooth to bumpy and had beads and charms crocheted right into it. "The best thing is you can't make a mistake; it's whatever you feel like."

Ali looked at the panel piece, too. She didn't ask any questions; she simply stared at it for a long time, almost as if she were trying to remember something.

"Ladies—and gentleman," a male voice said. We all looked up, and there was Bob holding a plate of cookie bars. "I'd like to get your opinion on whether these have enough chocolate in them." He went to CeeCee first. He knew all about her sweet tooth and valued her opinion. CeeCee glanced toward Camille while she was looking away. I could almost see CeeCee's mouth watering, but I knew she didn't want any stories of her gorging herself on sweets getting back to Camille's husband, particularly now when they were negotiating her contract.

"Not today," CeeCee said. Bob quickly recovered from his surprise and moved on to Camille. She practically laughed at the offer and took out a pack of diet cookies— little meringues with a tiny dot of chocolate.

"Maybe Bob's the one CeeCee's show is doing," Dinah said, nudging me.

I supposed anything was possible.

CHAPTER 9

NOT KNOWING VERY MUCH ABOUT MARY BETH Wells was a definite disadvantage in figuring out her secret and who killed her. I wanted to know more about her before we went to Catalina. There was one person I thought of immediately. He knew everybody and as long as there was no attorney-client privilege involved, would probably share his information.

Mason Fields was a big-bucks attorney with a reputation for keeping naughty celebrities out of jail. We had what I'd call a flirty friendship going. Before I left the bookstore, I called his office and left a detailed message. Then I headed home.

The curb in front of my house was parked up when I got home, so I walked through the backyard savoring the last few minutes of peace as I prepared myself for the onslaught.

Cosmo and Blondie were waiting by the kitchen door and took off into the yard when I opened it. The lights were on in the kitchen, and the deli delivery guy was just bringing in some trays. My mother didn't cook, but she knew how to order. By the time the delivery guy was finished, there was a tray of meats and cheeses, along with a selection of salads, fresh bread, condiments and cheesecake.

It wasn't his first trip here. Apparently my parents hadn't found a Santa Fe deli to measure up to their favorite west Valley haunt. They were like shipwrecked sailors when it came to deli food and had been ordering every night since they arrived. This was a bigger order, which implied more people.

"Help yourself, honey," my mother said. "There's plenty of everything."

She sailed out of the room, and I waited for the dogs to return. When they came in, I fed them their dog food, though the way they were sniffing, they clearly hoped the deli trays were for them.

I followed the sound of voices to the living room. Lana and Bunny, the two other She La Las, were sitting on the couch next to my mother. Their husbands and my father came in from my former bedroom.

When all of them saw me, there was a lot of hugging and telling me how sorry they still were about Charlie and apologizing for not keeping in touch. Finally, we all headed into the kitchen. The three men got their food first and started to file out of the room.

"I hope you don't mind, Molly, but I set up a table for us guys in the bedroom. There's a basketball play-off game on." My father squeezed my shoulder as he passed.

I glanced down the hall just as my son Samuel came out of the room that was my current bedroom. He was dragging a keyboard and a bunch of wires. "Hey, Mom," he said when he saw me. "Grandma asked me to be the musical director."

Samuel was a barista at a coffee shop by day and a musician by night. He sang and played all kinds of instruments, though it was either guitar or piano for most of his bar gigs. He went into the living room and started setting up his equipment.

I followed him back into the living room. The She La Las had put down their plates of food and were in the empty area in front of the fireplace. One of them started singing "My Man Dan" and the others joined in. It wasn't like in the movies where suddenly it was like no time had passed and they were great. Actually, they were terrible. They weren't even singing together. At least one of them forgot the words, and when they tried to do their signature dance steps they almost tripped over each other.

Even though I had just gotten home, I knew I had to get out of there. I grabbed the dog leashes and my cell phone, threw on a warm jacket and went out into the night. The dogs and I wandered around the block, but all too soon we were back at my house again. I looked through the big front window and saw the She La Las jumping around. I sat down on the stone porch. It was a little cold on the butt, but a lot quieter than inside.

When my cell phone rang I jumped in surprise. As I tried to open it, it slipped out of my hands and landed in the bushes. I frantically tried to retrieve it before it stopped ringing. Finally, I flipped it open.

"Hey, sunshine," Mason said. "I got your message. Why do you want to know about Mary Beth Wells—" He paused a beat. "You're not a suspect are you?"

"Not this time." I started to tell him the whole story starting with the park, but he stopped me.

"You sound funny. Where are you?"

I told him about the She La Las taking over my house, and he chuckled when he heard I was on the porch.

"Have you eaten?" he said.

"There's a ton of deli food, but no."

"I'll be there in a few minutes. Information is always better over dinner."

"But I have dogs with me," I said.

He didn't miss a beat. "No problem. I know just where to go. I'll even bring mine."

"You have a dog?" I asked, surprised.

"Yes. I'm a lawyer. I need to get unconditional love from someone."

I considered whether I should tell my parents I was leaving, but there was so much going on inside, I doubted I'd be missed.

A few minutes later, Mason pulled his black Mercedes into my driveway and walked across the lawn.

"Don't you look cute," he said when he got closer. The black mutt and the strawberry blond terrier mix got up as they considered whether to bark at him. He ruffled both of their heads before they had a chance, and both dogs went into tail-wagging mode.

They looked even happier as we headed toward the car.

"Where's your dog?" I said, checking the backseat before Cosmo and Blondie got in. Mason pointed to the front seat.

"I hope you don't mind sharing."

I didn't see what he meant until I tried to sit in the passenger seat. A tiny short-haired white dog with black markings eyed me suspiciously.

"Meet Spike," Mason said, introducing his toy fox terrier.

Cosmo and Blondie were sticking their noses through the space between the front seats trying to do what Mason said. Spike took one look at them and gave them a commanding bark. Both my dogs jumped back and sat down.

I lifted Spike up and got in. He started to bark at me, but I stared him in the eye and shook my head. "Not after the evening I've had."

Leave it to Mason to know a restaurant where dogs were not only welcomed, they were catered to—as long as you sat on the patio. There were heat lamps and plastic siding that made it warm despite the chilly night. In no time, the dogs had bowls of water and dog snacks and we had menus.

As soon as we ordered, I tried to get down to the business of pumping Mason for information, but he stalled.

"So, where's the detective?" he asked.

"On a case," I said, trying to sound like it was no big deal. One of the reasons Mason was a good attorney was he saw through things—like my answer.

"Tough being left behind, isn't it?" His dark eyes caught mine. He was still wearing his suit pants, but not the jacket. The opened collar of his cream dress shirt showed above the neck of his pullover sweater. The patio was warm enough that we'd both taken off our coats. "Look, I deal with homicide cops. I know the life."

Mason was easy to talk to, and I eventually admitted I was having my doubts. He looked all too happy. Mason was divorced and had made it clear he wasn't looking to get married again—something I could completely understand. I was really more interested in casual companionship, too. It was Barry who kept pushing for more.

"But that's not what I'm here to talk about. I need to know who Mary Beth Wells was," I said just as the waiter arrived with dinner. Mason had ordered a platter of barbecued everything for us to share, and there was plenty to pass down to the dogs.

"Ah, playing detective again, are you? This is fun," he said as we began eating. "I got your message just as I was leaving the office, so there was no time to check anything. All I can tell you is what I know offhand."

Mason was on the board of directors of practically every charity there was. In his usual self-deprecating way, he always joked that he had to do something to make up for his profession. Since he was on all those boards, he was a regular on the circuit of dinners and events the charities put on. So, it turned out, were Mary Beth and Lance Wells Jr.

"They made a good-looking couple. She had honey blond hair and refined features. He had his father's dark coloring and athletic build, but none of the dancing talent. Couple that with a little too much alcohol. Well, there were a few events when Mary Beth had to gracefully get him off the dance floor before he totally embarrassed himself."

"What about the dance studios?"

"I don't know much about them except that I think Matt Wells took over as the front guy when Lance Sr. died," Mason said.

"Who's he?" I asked.

"Sorry, I should have explained. Matt is Lance Sr.'s nephew. He's on the charity-dinner circuit, too. Matt doesn't have the star quality his uncle had, but he's certainly competent to be the spokesperson for the dance studios."

I told Mason again about the note and diary entry along with what I described as the crochet code map. "I'd like to find out what the secret was that she was about to reveal." Mason was sympathetic when I told him I felt guilty somehow because I hadn't figured out who the things belonged to sooner.

"Molly, I'm sure you couldn't have done anything to change things." He reached across and laid a hand on my arm. By now, the dogs were full of barbecue, and Spike, apparently used to being an only dog, was getting tired of having friends around. He jumped up on the bench, crawled under Mason's arm and started to squirm, making it clear he wanted to go.

Mason had given me more information than I'd had, but not as much as I wanted. On the way home, I told him about the Casino Building being on the crochet piece but that I had no idea what it was supposed to mean.

"It sounds like she must have been very successful at keeping the secret a secret. Didn't you say the diary entry was more than twenty years old?"

"You're right." I mentioned my coming trip to Catalina and said I hoped it would turn up something. He wished me luck and mentioned what a romantic spot it was.

"I'm going with the crochet group," I said, rolling my eyes. "At least most of the crochet group." I told him how CeeCee didn't want our newest member to come. When I mentioned Camille's name, Mason blinked in surprise.

"I wouldn't have figured she'd join a handicraft group." he said.

"Then you know her?" I asked.

"She's Alexander Rhead's daughter. Who doesn't?"

When we got to my house, Mason, ever the gentleman, insisted on escorting me and the dogs to the door. Maybe it wasn't all gentlemanliness. When we got to the porch and I started to say good-bye, he put his arms around me and kissed me. He'd kissed me before, but always more in the just-friends vein. This was a full-throttle, deep kiss. And much as I hated to admit it, it sent a shock wave down to my toes.

In the middle of it, the front door opened and my mother looked out saying something about having heard some noise.

"You must be Barry Greenberg," she said, making no attempt to mask the fact she was checking him out. She invited him in and I started to make excuses, but he was all charm and introduced himself as he followed her inside. The She La Las were just packing up, and my mother told him all about their big audition.

I couldn't believe what Mason said then or that my mother fell for it. He said it was hard to believe she was my mother. That she looked so young she could be my sister. I mean, isn't that the oldest line there is? But she lapped it up anyway.

CHAPTER 10

"WHAT KIND OF BOAT IS IT AGAIN?" SHEILA asked from the backseat. I had borrowed my parents' Explorer, and CeeCee, Dinah, Adele, Sheila and I were on our way to catch our ride to Catalina. The boats left from a small harbor in Long Beach. We'd found the one window in time just after rush hour and before midday when traffic was light, and we were practically zooming down the San Diego Freeway.

Just like Sheila, I, too, had never been to Catalina. And also like her I was very nervous about the boat. It was the whole boat thing that had kept me away all these years. I had a terrible feeling I would get horrendously seasick on the way over and not want to take the boat back and have to spend the rest of my life on Catalina Island. Okay, maybe my fear was a little over the top. But who says fears are rational?

My son Peter had been to the island a couple of times and had mentioned to me that helicopters flew there, too, but that sounded even worse.

Adele started talking about the steamship that used to

go to Catalina and how that trip took two hours. "But that was back in the seventies. The boats they have now don't seem to pitch so much, and it only takes an hour anyway," she said, patting Sheila's hand in reassurance.

Who was reassuring me? But then I hadn't even disclosed my fears to Dinah. I hoped the fact that I was on a mission of good would somehow help. Maybe the fairies of the sea would make the ride smooth or just knock me out for the trip.

"You know, ladies," CeeCee said, "this isn't really the season. I hope the sea isn't too rough."

My stomach did a flip-flop at that. Then she went on talking about how all her trips there had been on her friends' boats.

"Private boats go there?" Sheila asked with a little nervous squeak in her voice.

"My, yes. The harbor at Avalon is practically on the beach. But you'll see when we get there," CeeCee said. Then her cell phone rang and she made a big fuss about having to take the call and asking if we could all keep it down because she was sure it was her agent. "We're in final negotiations about my new contract." She held up crossed fingers and finally pressed the button to answer the call.

Arranging the day had taken some doing. Mrs. Shedd had been okay about me taking the day off. I had hoped she would object to Adele being out, too, but somehow Adele had pulled it off. Then I had realized the greenmobile was too small for all of us, so I had to convince my parents to trade cars for the day.

I'd asked my parents—well, my father—to take care of the dogs. When I'd mentioned it to my mother, she had looked as if I'd asked her to move the moon or rearrange the tides, instead of opening the door to the yard a few times and pouring some food in a couple of bowls.

When I pulled into the parking structure at the boat terminal, CeeCee lost her cell reception and got cut off midcall. She held the phone in her hand as if waiting for it to ring as we got out of the SUV and walked into the terminal building. The *Catalina Express* waiting room was beyond plain. Just a counter, some hard plastic seats, a small snack bar and a counter to arrange island tours, which was closed.

We picked up our tickets. Dinah looked over at me with concern.

"Are you all right? You look pale."

I nodded. I didn't want to say it was because suddenly the boat trip had become all too real. I decided the best way to deal was by looking out for Sheila, so I wrapped my arm in hers as we headed outside to the dock.

Since it was a weekday and February, only a trickle of people were waiting to board. The boat was kind of odd looking, but before I could comment, Adele stepped forward.

"Good. We got one of the catamarans," she said, then continuing with one of her in-the-know speeches she went on to explain that only four of the Catalina Express fleet were catamarans and she personally thought they had the best ride. Whatever it was called, I thought it resembled a sled.

I didn't say anything to Sheila about it and hoped she didn't notice the boat looked as though it were on stilts. CeeCee seemed impatient with the whole procedure.

"I'm afraid I'm not used to all this business with tickets and bomb-sniffing dogs." She adjusted her wide-brim straw hat as two hunky Coast Guard guys walked a German shepherd past us as we prepared to board. "There was none of this on my friends' boats. We just sat on deck chairs and sipped margaritas."

No more stalling. I took a deep breath and led the way. Since the temperature was a bit cold, CeeCee suggested we sit inside. We had our choice of seats and took one of the booths along the window.

The engine started and the boat backed out of the slip

and then turned around. We slid under a bridge and past the huge, permanently docked *Queen Mary*. All the while it felt pretty much like riding in a car.

"This isn't bad," I said to no one in particular, but Adele answered anyway.

"Pink, we haven't even left the harbor yet."

I tensed all over again, and Sheila hid her face in my shoulder. The motor made a louder sound, and the boat began to move faster. We passed the giant clawlike things used for unloading the cargo ships from all over the world, and then suddenly there was nothing ahead but open water. Sheila held tighter. I readied myself for the first wave of queasiness. The boat at last began to rock as it picked up speed. I waited for that sick feeling to come . . . but to my surprise, it didn't.

I realized I'd been holding my breath, and in a gush I let it out and began to breathe again. "It feels like we're sailing over small hills," I said, relief spreading over my body. I wasn't going to have to stay in Catalina forever.

"They're called swells," Adele corrected

Whatever they were called, they were just fine. The color returned to Sheila's face, and she finally let go of my arm.

I had brought the crochet piece with me, and I laid it out between us on the table. CeeCee pointed to what we now all acknowledged was the landmark Casino Building.

"You have to admit it really does look like a bath-powder box," the actress said still trying to cover her error.

Adele rolled her eyes. As usual, she had dressed over-the-top for the occasion, wearing white cutoff pants, a middy blouse with a heavy blue sweater and a white sailor's cap. Even the crew on the boat snickered when they passed us.

CeeCee held up her cell phone as an excuse and then pushed out of her seat, moved to the middle section of the boat and took a seat with no one around.

Looking a little peaked, Sheila was pressed against the

window and holding the chair handles with a white-knuckled grasp. The rocking of the boat was soft but unrelenting and seemed to have renewed her worry.

I thought it might help her get her mind off of the fact we were on a boat if we talked about Mary Beth.

"I had dinner with a friend who knew Mary Beth Wells," I began. Dinah peered at me with a question in her eyes, and I mouthed, "Mason." Her eyes opened wide, and it was clear she wanted more information, but that would have to wait until it was just the two of us. "Nothing he said about her seems to go with any of these motifs. She was married to the son of Lance Wells, the famous dancer-actor. She was connected to his dance studio, but her husband didn't inherit any of his father's talent. She and her husband went to all the entertainment-industry charity dinners." I shrugged as I looked over the panels. "There's nothing here that goes with any of that. We have the Casino Building, Sagittarius guy, a house, a sitting cat, a standing cat, the Arc de Triomphe, the weird circles, the vase of flowers, the wishing well—which we know is Mary Beth's signature—and then the double-size panel with the rectangle. Since the very first panel is the Casino Building, does that mean that everything else refers to something on Catalina?"

"The diary entry referred to time she spent on an island, so that makes sense," Dinah said. "But whatever happened, it happened over twenty years ago." She was holding the sheet of paper and turned it over as she put it down. "Hey, look at this," she said pointing. There were words on the back: *Catalina, I'm going to miss you.*

"How could I have missed that?" I said, surprised.

"Well, Pink, it's not such a mystery," Adele began as she stood and picked up the page. "Sometimes I think I should be the detective around here." Adele held up the diary entry and pointed out it only covered a little over half the sheet. "It's a complete thought, so why would you look for more on the other side? And even if you did," she said demonstrating turning over the paper, "the line is written in such light pencil and just where your finger is likely to cover it up, you could easily just not notice it." Adele took a bow as she finished and laid the sheet down before returning to her seat.

I glanced over to see if I had succeeded in distracting Sheila, but she still looked upset.

I pointed to the image of the house. It was certainly not a generic house. The overall shape had a Victorian feel, but it was the roof that stood out. It was shaped like an inverted ice cream cone. "I bet this house is on the island. Maybe if we find it we'll get a way into the puzzle."

Dinah looked skeptical. "But how are you going to manage that?"

"We could ask somebody. Maybe it's Mary Beth's house."

Adele snorted. "Not really, Pink. People married to famous dancer's sons have unlisted phone numbers and people don't give directions to their houses." Adele adjusted her sailor cap, which had fallen forward. "But there might be another way." Adele knew she had our attention and held onto it for all it was worth. She innocently looked out the window and back toward the snack bar and finally at all of us. "Oh, you want to know what that way is, huh?"

She dragged the suspense out another beat or two and then continued. "Obviously you've never been to Avalon." She addressed the three of us. "It's basically the only town on Catalina, and it's where our boat will be landing. There are only around thirty-five hundred residents, and it's only a mile square. Most of the town is spread up the side of the hills."

Adele stopped. Dinah and I looked at her, waiting for the punch line. Adele looked confused and then apparently realized we hadn't gotten her meaning.

"Okay, Pink and everybody else, the point is, it's not that big, so finding a house shouldn't be that hard."

I was glad Adele didn't ask me what I was going to do when I found the house. I hadn't figured that out yet. There didn't seem to be anything else to discuss, so I put the piece back in my tote bag.

"Let's explore the boat," Dinah said. She nodded toward Sheila. "C'mon, walking around will make you feel better." Now that I knew I wasn't going to be seasick, I was up for it and got up quickly. Sheila, still looking at me as though I were her lifeline, followed.

CeeCee had fallen asleep with her mouth open, her cell phone still in her hand. She was snoring softly and her straw hat was cockeyed. I looked around for anyone pointing a camera at her. It was just the kind of picture she worried about showing up on some tabloid website. It wouldn't be hard to come up with a good caption: *CeeCee Collins passed out in public and even her hat looks drunk.*

We went upstairs and outside. The air was brisk and I was glad for my jacket. Our boat zipped past cargo ships hanging around waiting for their turn to come into the harbor to get unloaded.

Further on we caught up with and passed a barge with a big Vons grocery store truck on it. Adele had stuck with us like glue and continuing with her in-the-know news about Catalina explained the barge was the only way for things to get to the island. Weather permitting, it made the trip five times a week. Weather not permitting, nothing got to the island, which was why all the residents had a stash of frozen bread, dried milk and canned goods.

We had the outside deck to ourselves, for a bit, but when the boat's captain announced over the intercom that we were going to pass through a pod of dolphins, a few people came from inside and joined us to look over the side.

I saw a dolphin just below the water swimming alongside. It was pretty neat but turned out to just be a hint of what was to come. The one was joined by many, and they began to jump out of the water in an arc as they swam next to the boat. More and more dolphins showed up. We looked at them and they looked back at us.

Sheila finally had some color in her face and let go of

the death hold on my arm as she became lost in dolphin magic. Even Adele was speechless. Only CeeCee missed it all. She was still inside, dreaming about her deck chairs and margaritas.

"The dolphins are a good omen," Dinah said as we leaned against the railing and savored the moment.

"I hope you're right."

Dinah glanced around. Sheila and Adele had moved to the back of the boat to watch the dolphins as they swam around in the wake.

"So, you had dinner with Mason?" she said.

"It was nothing," I responded. "I'd called him thinking he would have some information about Mary Beth." But it was useless. I couldn't just gloss over the details with my best friend, so I told her the whole story about being stuck on my own front porch because the She La Las had taken over. And, yes, I mentioned that Mason had kissed me.

"When's Barry coming back?" she asked.

I shrugged. "When his case is over. Whenever that is."

Dinah rocked her head from side to side. "If he doesn't hurry, he may not have a girlfriend—" She stopped herself. "I know you think *girlfriend* and *boyfriend* sound stupid past a certain age. So then, how's this: He may not have a friend of the female persuasion anymore?"

I rolled my eyes in response.

When I looked ahead I saw the island. We seemed to be traveling parallel to it but getting closer at the same time. From here it appeared mountainous and empty, and I wondered about everything I'd read online about it. Other than the occasional boat near the shore, it looked uninhabited. Adele had mentioned that most of the island was wild. Besides Avalon, there was only one other village, Two Harbors.

The engines began to slow just as Avalon finally came into view. Boats bobbed in the harbor and beyond that was the town. Adele had been right: The town seemed to be draped on a slope and looked almost too adorable to be true.

Glancing over to the side of the harbor opposite from where our boat moored, I got my first view of the Casino Building. With its round shape and red roof, the landmark definitely stood out. Even in person it looked like a bath-powder box or maybe a giant casserole dish.

CeeCee was just waking up when we walked through the cabin to collect her. Then we joined the crowd waiting to get off. Once we'd disembarked, I realized just how small Avalon was. After walking maybe a block, we had curved around the harbor and were on the town's main drag.

Since it was February and a weekday, the small crescent-shaped beach was deserted. Most of the people getting off the boat seemed to be locals. The few tourists followed the same path we did down the street of restaurants, shops and hotels that faced the water. A green pier sticking out in the water offered boat rides and fishing trips. Everything was small and cute.

"I feel like I'm inside a snow globe," I joked to Dinah, who nodded in agreement. When we got to the center of the business district, we stopped beside a fountain.

"Meet you guys later," Adele said, heading back toward the pier. "I'm going on the submarine and then on a trip to the Airport in the Sky."

Sheila seemed to have recovered from the boat trip and went after Adele, saying she wanted to go, too.

CeeCee was still a little dazed from sleeping on the boat and was clutching her cell phone. "I have to make a call," she said, starting to walk away.

"I guess that leaves us," I said to Dinah. "Unless you're planning to bolt, too."

"I'm all yours," she said. She glanced at the small sandy beach with the water softly lapping against it. "The kids would have loved this." She shrugged it off. "Okay, you can tell me to shut up now."

Since I hadn't come up with a more specific plan than to try to find the house in the crochet piece, I suggested we get food before we began our search. The sun was out and the air was warm enough that I took off my jacket as we walked toward the eateries. It was a nice change from the chilly gray days we'd had lately.

We agreed on a restaurant right on the water that featured a patio with umbrella tables. It turned out to be a wait-on-yourself kind of place, and a few minutes later we carried our order out onto the patio. All the tables were empty except one. CeeCee had her back to us and was just putting her cell phone on the table. She was getting up as we walked over.

Seeing us apparently changed her plans and while we put our food down, she went back in to get a refill on her coffee and as she put it "a little something sweet to go with it."

I had gotten a strawberry-banana smoothie and Dinah a mango-pineapple, and we'd ordered French toast to share.

I took a sip of my drink and set it on the round bistro table. Dinah sat across from me and slid the plate of French toast to the middle of the table. We hung our tote bags on the chairs and walked to the railing. The harbor was literally right next to us, and we had a nice view of the boats, though there were quite a few empty slips.

"If I had to pick one, I'd want that one," Dinah said, pointing at a boat that was twice as large as any of the others. Its back deck was facing us, and a table and some deck chairs were set up there. A woman came out from below. She took off her hat and I got a view of her face.

"Is that Camille?" I said, leaning over the railing for a better look. By now CeeCee had rejoined us.

"I tell you that woman is following me," CeeCee said. Camille glanced our way and saw us. She began to wave and we waved back. CeeCee had put on a smile but was talking through gritted teeth. "I was hoping my contract would be settled, but the production company is being difficult. My agent said I had an offer of another show. I'm sure Camille is here to find out if it's true. Oh dear," CeeCee said. "Her husband is here, too."

Camille held up something, and I realized it was her

crochet work. I could only make out the raspberry pink color. Her husband was on his cell phone with his back to us, running his hand over his hair. Camille flagged down a water taxi and rode the short distance to the pier.

Dinah shook her head in disbelief. "There's a dinghy attached to their boat. She couldn't row herself to the pier?"

CeeCee let out a little of her trademark tinkly laugh. "Dear, we're talking about Camille Rhead Katz here. I bet she has somebody to brush her teeth. You do realize how ridiculously wealthy they are. All those years of successful shows—I think Alexander Rhead pays her a salary just for being his daughter."

Money was a sensitive spot with CeeCee. She had done well over the years and should have been set up, but though her late husband had been a world-class dentist, he'd been an idiot when it came to money. When he died, she found out about all the bad investments. She had lost everything and had to start all over. I knew that was why she was so tense about the contract for *Making Amends*. She needed the job.

The water taxi left Camille off on a small floating pier that had dinghys tied to it. We had a perfect view of her taking the few steps to the stairway to the pier. We watched her progress as she came closer and closer to us.

"Oh no," CeeCee said, looking at the chocolate-covered donut in her hand. Suddenly something flew past me and I heard a splash in the water. Personally, I thought CeeCee was going a little overboard with her concern about Camille tattling on her eating of sweets, but I guessed she didn't want to take any chances. CeeCee put on her theatrical smile as Camille walked across the patio and joined us at the railing.

"Small world, isn't it?" Camille said.

"Yes, it is," CeeCee said. "How did you happen to come here today?"

"It was Hunnie's idea."

"Whose idea?" I interrupted.

Camille laughed. "My husband's. That's my nickname for him. It's kind of a play on sounds. You know, the endearing term and his nickname sound the same."

"Oh," I said, getting it.

"Hunnie's going to be taking over my father's position next week. He's going to be so busy after that. It was such a beautiful day—and we thought it would be nice to have an outing together."

"You knew we were coming to Catalina, didn't you?" CeeCee said. Her voice had gotten a little shrill, but she quickly reverted back to her usual sweet tone.

"I might have mentioned it to Hunnie," Camille said, pouting ever so slightly. "You said it wasn't a group trip, but I saw Adele and Sheila on the pier in line for a boat ride and you three are here. The only one missing is that girl with the chopped-up haircut.

"You mean Ali? Exactly," CeeCee said. "If it had been a group trip she would be here."

Camille turned toward me. "If it isn't a crochet group trip, then why are you all here?"

CeeCee, Dinah and I looked at each other, and it was clear I was the intended spokesperson. It was also clear by CeeCee's pointed look, she didn't want me to tell Camille the truth.

"I've always wanted to come to Catalina and we got a deal on the tickets," I said finally.

Camille's eyes narrowed then went back to normal. "Now I get it. You came because the tickets were cheaper. My life coach wouldn't be happy with me for not getting that right away." She sighed. "I must sound like an idiot. Living the way I have has its own shortcomings. I've never had to be concerned with how much anything costs, and so it's hard for me to understand how the price of something could keep you from doing it. This is why I need this group so much."

She hugged each of us and gave us air kisses. It was probably her version of sincere.

"Hunnie suggested I invite you on the boat."

Dinah and I both started to nod, but CeeCee answered a firm "No, thank you" for all of us, saying we'd already made plans for the day.

Camille took out her crochet work. It was clearly the work of someone new at it. The stitches were uneven and she seemed confused about what loop of the stitch to go in, but she was so proud of it, even CeeCee didn't say anything. She was off to the local craft shop to pick up some special yarn.

When she finally left, CeeCee sighed. "I know she's spying, but I actually believe she's serious about wanting to be part of the group. And her life actually has had its share of difficulties." She went on to tell us that Camille had had a hard time with dating. "I heard she always had to be concerned about whether someone was really interested in her or just getting close to her father and all his money and power."

"What about Hunnie?" I said, trying not to choke on the homophone.

"He was already working for her father—a line producer or something. I think Alexander is the one who introduced them. And now, they're referred to as one of Hollywood's enduring couples." CeeCee finished and then shuddered. "This was a day to get away from them. Thank heavens I stopped you before you accepted the invitation to go on their boat."

"I thought it was a good idea," Dinah said. "It's not every day I get asked aboard a luxury boat like that. I wonder if they would have let us look around."

"Shouldn't you two be spending your time thinking about Mary Beth Wells's secret?" CeeCee said. "And I can't believe that was the best you could do about why we came here. *Because we got a deal on the tickets*."

I shrugged off the criticism. "What's the difference? She went for it."

CeeCee glanced in the direction Camille had gone and

sighed with relief. "I'd love to help work on the mystery of the filet panels, but between waiting to hear what's going on with my contract and Camille's showing up, I need a little pampering. I'm off to the country club. I want to check out their spa services."

CHAPTER 11

"IT LOOKS LIKE IT'S JUST YOU AND ME AGAIN," I said. Dinah and I finally went back to our table, rolling our eyes about CeeCee's plans and Camille's quest to get in touch with her inner regular. "Do you think we should tell her if she wants to be like us, she ought to leave the yacht at home?" Dinah joked.

I reached for my drink, then I made a face. "I think this is yours," I said, trading cups with Dinah.

"How'd that happen?" She looked at the table perplexed and then, seeing which tote bag was hanging on the back of which chair, realized we'd gone back to opposite sides of the table.

"Now what?" Dinah asked after we'd finished our drinks and the now-tepid French toast.

"Now we go house hunting," I said with a smile. Thanks to Miss Information Adele, I already knew the only mode of transportation available was a rental golf cart. Golf carts were what most everybody used to get around. The number of cars allowed on the island was very limited. And likely to become even more so since no one could bring one car over unless two people got rid of theirs. Adele said there was a ten-year waiting list.

We found the stand that rented the small vehicles and got one for two hours, which we were assured was plenty of time to cover all of Avalon with time for stops. I considered showing the crocheted house to the rental guy, but I was afraid it would make us seem a little weird.

Dinah offered to drive so I could keep my eyes on the houses. After a few false starts, she got the hang of it and soon we were motoring down the street. The area just behind the business street was called the Flats. We drove through it checking out the houses. They were so close together, you could lend your neighbor a roll of paper towels without going outside. But none of them had the odd shape of the house in the panel.

Beyond the Flats, a few streets were closed to rental golf carts, so we walked those but again came up empty. We got back into our open-air vehicle and followed the route on the map the rental guy had given us. When we reached the top of the town, we stopped by the roadside and checked out the view. From here we could look down on rooftops and out into the water. But we saw nothing close to the house we were seeking.

I slumped against the golf cart. "Maybe I was wrong. Maybe Mary Beth meant the word *casino* instead of the building here," I said. I pulled the multicolored panel piece out and laid it on the backseat.

"But she mentioned the island in the diary entry, remember?" Dinah said, smoothing out the piece. "And missing Catalina."

"I guess that eliminates Las Vegas," I said.

"I think if that's what Mary Beth had been trying to depict, she would have done a motif of Elvis Presley," Dinah said with a chuckle. "Let's not give up on here yet. We have the golf cart for another half hour. We might as well finish exploring." We got back in and followed the map as the road wound around the top of the town. Dinah continued driving while I did the looking. We were clearly in the super-high-rent district. The houses were built into the hill, and some of them were huge.

As we began our descent, we followed the scenic route signs.

"You might as well enjoy the ride, as long as we're here," Dinah urged. She pointed toward the Zane Grey-Pueblo Hotel, which stood out from the design of the other buildings. "It's supposed to look like a Hopi Indian pueblo," Dinah explained, going on to say it had originally been the famous writer's home. She threw out other tidbits about the island as we drove back into the heart of town. At one time the Wrigley's Gum family had owned the island, but now almost everything outside Avalon was part of the Catalina Island Conservancy and was maintained as a natural preserve.

"Oh, and the other town, Two Harbors, is located on an isthmus, hence the name," Dinah said. "Two Harbors sounds pretty small—one lodge and campgrounds." I guess my face must have registered surprise because Dinah laughed. "What can I say? When I knew we were coming I did a little reading." She steered the golf cart back toward the drive along the water.

"Did I tell you about the buffalos?" she said. "They brought some over for some Zane Grey western filmed here in the thirties, and they've just kept having little buffalos ever since. Too bad we don't have more time. We could take one of the tours that goes into the interior and see them."

The road ran toward the Casino Building. As we passed it, Dinah suggested we stop and check it out on the way back. We zoomed past a diver's beach after which the road seemed to disappear around a curve and go inland. Dinah pulled over so we could check the map to see what was up ahead.

"I guess this is it," Dinah said, pointing at the map. "The road goes only a short distance past the curve before it's marked Hamilton Cove Condominium Residents Only."

"Maybe the house is part of the condos," I suggested, but Dinah shook her head. During her pretrip research she'd seen a picture of the condos, and she assured me they didn't resemble anything on the crochet piece.

"It makes me glad Adele didn't come with us. I can hear her saying, 'Well, Nancy Jessica Drew Fletcher Marple, you're some detective.'"

I was about to tell Dinah to turn around when I saw a cat run across the road just where it curved. And then another cat, and another.

"Let's see what's around the bend," I said as Dinah turned the golf cart back on. We drove ahead to the spot where the road curved, and Dinah slowed down as we went around the base of the hill.

At first I saw only a grassy spot with a stand of trees. But when I studied it a little more, I saw the cats. Dinah pulled up a little farther. Now I saw there were cats everywhere, along with a bunch of food bowls. That's when I saw the house.

"Dinah, look," I said, my voice shaking. She followed my finger and gasped. I took out the crochet piece, and we looked from it to the house and back again. There was no mistaking it: This was the house. I pointed at the two panels with cat images. "They're a clue, too."

Unlike most of the houses we'd seen in Avalon, this one was off by itself. It was well shaded and had a clear view down to the water. I moved closer and got a good look at the structure. The crochet image had broken it down to its geometric basics, but the real house was intriguing. I realized we were looking at the back of it, and we walked through the grass to the front. The cats ignored us and went about their business.

A small porch led up to the door of the white wood-frame house. The front featured a bay window, probably perfect for admiring the great view. But it was the top portion that stood out. I had thought the roof resembled an inverted ice cream cone, but now I saw it was wider—more like a snow-cone holder. Just below it was a round porch.

Bravely, I walked up the steps to the door and knocked, though I had no idea what I was going to say if someone answered. It turned out not to be a problem because no one did. The fact that no one was home meant I was free to look in the windows. Or try to. The view was blocked by window coverings that I realized, on closer examination, were made out of filet crochet. Someone had had a lot of time on their hands.

"We have to find out about this place," I said, walking quickly back to the golf cart.

"But first we have to return the golf cart," Dinah said, holding her arm up to show me her watch. "Our two hours are up."

A few minutes later, we pulled into the rental lot and left the golf cart. Before I could work out a plan to find out about the house, I was distracted by throngs of people coming from various directions and all going into a large doorway.

"What's going on?" I asked a woman wearing a ruby red poncho.

"Mail call. This time of year it's the event of the day." She explained that there was no mail delivery on Catalina. The mail came by plane to the Airport in the Sky and was driven down to town and then put into the mailboxes that lined the wall of the Atwater Arcade.

Curious, Dinah and I followed her into a dark walkway on the ground floor of an old hotel. Along one wall people were eagerly opening their mailboxes. On the opposite side a window looked in on a hardware store and down the way a door was open with a sign proclaiming, "Vacation Rentals."

"That's just what we need," I said as a plan began to form.

"We do?" Dinah said, following me in.

"I have an idea. Just go along with anything I say."

"Okay, captain," Dinah said with a nod.

Inside a woman sat behind a desk reading a book. We set off some kind of bell when we walked in and she looked up. It took a moment for her to focus, and then she took off her glasses and let them hang from the chain around her neck.

"Renata Baker at your service," she said. "Can I help you with something?"

"My friend and I just came for the day, but we've fallen in love with the island and we're interested in renting a place."

Renata pointed to a couple of chairs and invited us to sit. "You ladies came at just the right time. You can have your choice of rentals and such a bargain price—luxury accommodations at the bare basic rate. How long are we looking for?" She was already pulling out an album and thumbing through the plastic-coated pictures.

"Actually, I saw the house I want to rent," I said and described the place, but before I could get to the cats, she was already shaking her head.

"That's the Wells place. They don't rent it. Well, actually I don't know what's going to happen to it now." Her expression dimmed. "There's been a death in the family."

Undaunted, I didn't give up. "I'd really like to see the inside. If you think it's going to be for sale soon." I let it hang, implying I'd be interested in buying it, hoping she'd have visions of a giant commission and find a way to show it to me.

"It belongs to the Lance Wells estate, and I don't expect it to be for sale," she said, obviously trying to dismiss it as a possibility. She pointed to a photo of one of the houses we'd passed in the Flats. "This place is just darling. I can show it to you now."

Feeling dejected, I glanced at the floor. I wanted to get inside the Wells house, sure that some huge clue to Mary

Beth's secret was waiting there. Maybe all it would take was one look around and I would have the whole mystery solved.

I glanced out at the street and saw that CeeCee was window-shopping nearby, eating an ice cream cone. I had a sudden flash of inspiration. A cousin of mine had been in the TV and film location business and he always told the same story: people who wouldn't open the door for anybody threw it open and invited him in as soon as he said he was looking for a location for a TV show.

"You watch television, don't you?" I said to the woman. Her eyes narrowed at the strange question and she nodded. "Not much goes on here in the winter. I watch a lot of television."

"How about *Making Amends*? Do you watch that?"

"Sure," the woman snorted. "I can't believe the things people confess to. What about that guy who admitted he'd been having an affair with his wife's sister? I thought his wife was going to kill him during the program." Renata leaned toward me. "I wonder what really happened on that trip to Honolulu they gave the couple. Are they still together or did he mysteriously drown?"

Dinah stepped in to help. "Some things you just can't make amends for," she said in a serious tone.

"That's what I thought," Renata said.

I pointed toward the street. "There's CeeCee Collins—the host of the show."

The woman looked closer. "You're right. It is her. We don't get many celebrities this time of year. In the summer they arrive on their own boats and come in to shop or eat. Wow." She moved toward the door and I heard her start to tell the mail gatherers who were out front, but I stopped her just in time.

"My associate and I are actually looking for locations for the show," I said. "And that house seemed perfect. Are you sure there isn't some way we can have a peek inside to see if it's what we're really looking for?"

The woman knit her brows and seemed to have an inner conversation. "We're supposed to aid in any filming done here—it's a boon to our economy. But the Wells house is kind of a tough one since it isn't a rental and I don't have a key."

"There must be a caretaker," Dinah said. "Someone puts out all those bowls of cat food."

"Of course, you're right. Where was my head?" the woman said and went out in the hall. A moment later she came back with a tan man who had a head of thick white hair, introducing him as Purdue Silvers. She excitedly pointed out CeeCee, who was savoring the last of her cone, and in an animated voice explained we were looking for a location to shoot the program on the island.

"Do that show here? What a great idea. I could tell them about some wrongs that need righting," Purdue said. Then Renata pointed out the house we were interested in. He seemed hesitant until she reminded him that productions brought business to the island.

"I suppose there's no harm in letting you have a look-see. Though I'm not the one who can give you the permission to use it. I can give you the name of the law firm that's handling it now." He cast his eyes downward. "There was a recent death in the family."

Dinah and I made somber nods. He left to pick up the keys, returning a few minutes later, and led us out to his golf cart. He had individualized it to look like a woody station wagon, complete with a miniature surfboard attached to the roof.

Purdue turned out to be a talker and during the short drive back to the house, we learned he was named for his father's alma mater and that he was one of the few natives who still lived on the island. He said he felt blessed to be able to live in such a paradise. When he stopped to take a breath, I asked him how long he'd been a caretaker.

"It's my profession of choice. So many people have houses here they don't live in and don't rent, it's been a nice living. I drive the submarine once a week to add some money to the pot, and I bartend at a couple of beachfront places," he said. "And I do the late afternoon city tour."

He pulled the small vehicle onto the grass and turned off the motor. The cats surrounded him when he got out; it was obvious he was the source of their food.

Dinah and I followed him up the few steps and he unlocked the door. Purdue certainly liked the sound of his own voice. He was still talking. By now we knew that he had stayed in most of the houses he took care of, though not the Wells house.

"Some of the owners have regular times they come to Catalina, but not Mary Beth Wells. She was all over the place. Summer, winter or fall, I'd just get a call that she was arriving on such and such a day and to please stock the refrigerator for her." His voice dropped when he said her name. "You know, she died. I heard they thought it was natural causes, but it turned out to be poison." He sighed and lowered his gaze. "I can't imagine who'd want to kill her." When he looked up his eyes were sad and watery. "She was a nice woman—a very nice woman."

As we walked inside, I noticed a stuffy smell with that touch of mildew places near the ocean seemed to get. He walked into the living room, saying he thought it was the best spot for the show to film.

While he pointed out the view, which was outstanding, and the various spots he thought would be perfect to set up cameras, I tried to look around. I nudged Dinah and she attempted to distract his attention but had only limited success. I was able to admire the filet crochet window coverings, but when I tried to move into the other rooms, Purdue pulled me back, wanting to show me the handmade molding on the fireplace.

Mary Beth might not have had even a crochet hook hanging around in the Tarzana house, but she'd made up for it here. There were examples of her handiwork everywhere. She seemed stuck on filet crochet; I noticed only one yarn piece—an afghan with stripes of varying shades of green draped over the upholstered forest green couch. There were framed examples of her filet work on the walls. Most were done in white or ecru, but some were done in colors.

"She was quite the crochet artist," Purdue said, noticing I was admiring one of the long panels hanging over the windows. "Maybe we should go back and pick up Ms. Collins. She probably wants to see the place." He took a breath and then launched into questions about how the show was done and how he could get on with his story. He stood in front of me, expectant for answers.

I did exactly what the *Average Joe's Guide to Criminal Investigation* suggested for dealing with questions you didn't want to answer. The book advised you to completely ignore the questions and ask one of your own, preferably on a different subject. I asked him about the history of the house, noting how unusual it was.

"Lance Wells Sr. had it built. The round porch up top was his idea. He used it to practice all those ballroom dance moves. And he used it for parties, lots of parties," the caretaker said with a knowing nod.

"It was a little different with his son. Lance Jr. came here exactly once. He was so seasick I heard they had to practically knock him out to get him back on the boat to go home."

"But I thought you said his wife came here all the time," I said, talking to him but moving around the room and dramatically using my hands to "measure" what a camera would see. Dinah had taken out a piece of paper and a pen and was pretending to make note of things about the house for the show.

"She did. She came without him," Purdue said, standing in the middle of the room. "Yep, once was enough for Lance Jr. But then from what I hear he was nothing like his father." He mentioned that Lance Jr. had died about six months ago. He'd driven his car into a pole. The caretaker didn't give any more details, but from what Mason had said about Lance Jr., I guessed the accident was alcohol related.

"Now, Matt Wells is a different story than his cousin," Purdue said. "You ladies probably know who he is. He does all the commercials for the Lance Wells Dance Studio. He has no trouble with boats. He only comes once in a while, but he always slips me a hundred when he does. Mary Beth was the one who used the place the most," he added.

As I did my fake measuring, I commented on how it must have been lonely for her. Purdue shrugged. I thought he wasn't going to comment further, but when Dinah and I didn't say anything, he kept on talking.

"I think it was her getaway place. She said something once about him being very controlling, like he wouldn't even let her do this crochet stuff in their mainland house." He stopped for a moment and seemed to be thinking. I looked longingly at the row of photos on the mantel and the filet pieces on the wall. I wanted to get closer and examine them. Maybe they were a key to why Mary Beth had included the house in the crochet panel. But every time I made a move away from the center of the room, the caretaker corralled me back.

I noticed how Purdue's voice softened when he talked about Mary Beth. He obviously felt something toward her.

"I'd forgotten," he went on. "When she first started coming, she used to bring a woman with her. I barely knew her then. They kind of looked alike, but then maybe it was just that they both had long hair and wore baggy sweats all the time. Now that I think about it, they spent a lot of time here that year. First it was mostly just a few days, but then when it was really dead around here, they came for a month."

By now Dinah had stopped writing her phoney notes and was pretending to be looking them over. I moved my camera hands so they framed Purdue.

"About how long ago was that?" I asked, hoping he

would continue with his rambling and not realize the question had nothing to do with our purported purpose.

His eyes gazed at the ceiling, and he knit his brow in thought. Then he let out kind of a snort. "Time sure flies. It must have been around Christmas twenty some years ago."

I felt a buzz of excitement; it sounded like he had just described the time mentioned in the diary entry.

I opened my mouth to ask him for more details, but he suddenly consulted his watch.

"Ladies, I have to get to my other job." He rounded us up and directed us toward the door.

Not giving up, I asked him as we walked outside whether anything strange had happened during that month-long stay all those years ago.

He gave me an odd look, and I expected him to ask me what that had to do with the televison-show taping there, but instead, he shrugged and said, "I never exactly had the details, but I remember Delia—she works at the grocery store down yonder—saying there was something they wanted to hide."

He pulled the door shut and locked it tight before herding us back into the fancy golf cart. Five minutes later, he stopped the golf cart in the business district. "Ladies, I have to get back to the plaza. I'm doing the city tour. You're welcome to come. I give lots of background on the island," he said, trying to sound tempting.

I thanked him for the offer but declined, and we got out.

As soon as he drove off, Dinah and I walked out to a bench and sat down. I opened my bag and pulled out the crochet piece. I moved right past the image of the casino and the house. Dinah and I both studied the other motifs and then had the same realization at the same time.

"It's not the Arc de Triomphe," I said, pointing at the panel done in tan thread.

"It's the fireplace," Dinah said with exasperation. "If

only we'd looked at this while we were in there, we would have realized that's what it was."

"The Casino Building brought us here and led us to the house. And the house was supposed to lead us to the fireplace," I said, sharing Dinah's exasperation. "*If only* is right. Damn." I pulled out the diary entry and read it over again. "It sounds like Mary Beth was saying good-bye to someone. Maybe the woman. Maybe she wasn't her sister. Maybe their relationship was something altogether different," I said in a hushed voice.

Dinah glanced down at her watch. "What time are we supposed to meet everyone?"

I shrugged off the question. "I have to go back in that house."

CHAPTER 12

DINAH WINCED. "I SEE YOUR POINT ABOUT wanting to look inside the house again, but I don't see how you're going to do it. You heard the caretaker. He's off to his next job, and if we catch up with him, I doubt even you could charm him into giving you the keys."

"Don't have to," I said with a satisfied smile. "I can let us in myself." I proceeded to explain that while I'd been admiring the window covering, I'd unlocked the window and opened it just a touch.

"You're good. If the bookstore thing doesn't work out, you could always try a life of crime," Dinah said with a teasing smile.

Since we didn't have the golf cart anymore we walked back to the house. We were all alone except for the occasional golf cart heading to Hamilton Cove. We quickly hatched a plan. Dinah would keep watch while I went inside. I promised to be quick so we could get back and meet the others in time for our boat trip back to the mainland.

I checked the area, and the only eyes watching me were those of a sleek gray tabby. The window opened with ease, and I slipped inside quickly. I made a beeline for the mantelpiece in the living room. I had never noticed before how much the Arc de Triomphe resembled a fireplace—well, if it were in the house of some giants.

My eyes swept the top. I stopped at each photo and knickknack, wondering if it was a clue. I was sure the first photo was of Mary Beth. I hadn't seen her face in the Tarzana house, but I immediately recognized the long golden blond hair as what I'd seen spread over the bed. So this was Mary Beth. Her features were refined, and a touch of patrician arrogance showed in her expression. The familiar hair hung loose around her shoulders, and she was dressed in a scoop-neck top that accentuated her long neck. When I looked again, I noted that despite the coolness of her expression, there was a seductiveness to her smile.

I felt a rush of emotion—seeing what she looked like alive after having seen her dead. I thought of the crochet piece and how connected to her it was. And now I had it. Would it have made any difference if I had figured out where it belonged sooner? Whatever her secret was, Mary Beth had wanted to make right by it. I mouthed a promise that I would try to do it for her.

But first I had to find out what the secret was. I moved down the photos and doodads. Most of the pictures were of Mary Beth at different ages and in different locations. There was one taken in the living room of the Tarzana house. She was dressed in sparkly evening wear standing between two men in tuxes. They made a good-looking group, but who were the men? Lance Jr. and Matt?

I looked at every photo on the mantel twice and even slid the photos out of the frames in case there was something behind them, but I found nothing. Maybe the fireplace meant the area. I gazed up at the wall above and studied the filet pieces hanging there. Some were of people but because of the geometric quality of the designs, they weren't recognizable.

Could there be another fireplace? I rushed into the hall to check the other rooms and came up empty. I took the stairs up and at the top, opened a door and found I was on the round porch. It did seem perfect for dancing, but it was empty of everything but a view. I saw the *Catalina Express* pulling into its dock and realized it was probably our boat.

Sure I must have missed something on the mantelpiece, I rushed downstairs. The fireplace had to be important, otherwise why spend the time to make a motif of it? My eyes rushed over the row of photos, a collection of seashells and a display of old postcards with views of the island, but I saw nothing new. I stepped back and looked at the fireplace as a whole. I hadn't focused on the tiles around the opening until now. They appeared to have been custom-made and together created a scene of some trees and beyond them, the ocean. When I glanced toward the window I realized the scene was a re-creation of the view. Did that mean something?

I was so intent on staring at the fireplace and everything on it, I didn't notice the noise at first. When it finally registered and I looked up, Dinah was at the window waving madly. I leaned toward it to make out what she was trying to say. But before I could, I heard the door snap open and the rush of footsteps.

I felt a surge of adrenaline as a deep voice ordered me to turn around slowly with my hands on my head.

I did as I was told and found myself face-to-face with a tall man in the green pants and khaki shirt of the sheriff's uniform. He had his gun drawn, but when he saw me, must have realized I wasn't that much of a threat because he quickly holstered it. He ordered me to put my hands behind my back. He stepped around me, and I felt the metal rings of handcuffs on my wrists and heard an unpleasant click as they locked shut. I knew it was useless, but I tried pulling my hands anyway. They didn't move.

He patted me down checking for weapons as I tried to explain I had to get to the dock because my boat was leaving.

"I don't think so," he said as he marched me outside. The area had been nearly deserted before but not anymore. A couple of men in black wet suits had come up from the beach, and several golf carts had stopped by the side of the road, their riders watching. Three people in warm-up suits stood beneath a tree, walking in place no doubt to keep their aerobic heart rates from dropping while they watched me being led to the sheriff's SUV. The commotion must have scared the cats, because there wasn't even one hanging around. Dinah had tried to blend in with the golf-cart people. She mouthed, "I'm sorry."

I was glad she hadn't been caught. But I really wished I hadn't been, either. The black SUV looked big and out of place next to the golf carts. As the deputy opened the back door, I noticed the tour trolley stopped up the road. There were only three people on it, and they were all staring at me as though I were a point of interest. Purdue saluted to the man in uniform.

Only later did I find out the caretaker had seen CeeCee on his way to the tour plaza and tried to pitch her on his services, during which time she made it clear no one from the show was on the island.

Oops. I should have filled her in on the plan.

The SUV drove slowly down the road back toward the main part of town. The roadway was lined with people. Apparently, seeing a suspect being taken in was a big event here on Catalina. I had the sudden urge to wave, like a beauty queen on a parade float. I resisted.

"You don't understand," I said from the backseat. At least there was no cage and no icky plastic covering on the seat like in the usual patrol cars. "I dropped my keys when I was in the house. I didn't want to trouble Purdue to let me in since I knew he had to get to work."

The deputy seemed unmoved and turned up toward the

sheriff's sub station. He pulled into a parking space, then helped me out and led me in the back door. A fluffy white dog stretched out on the floor got up, sniffed my ankle and then jumped up like it wanted to be petted.

I started to go for it, but the handcuffs made it impossible and I apologized to the dog. I was in some kind of office, but I saw three doors with tiny windows off to the side; a sign warned officers to stay safe by keeping prisoners locked in.

I felt light-headed. Was I going to get thrown is one of those cells? Would they give me one phone call? Who would bail me out? Would I ever get off the island?

Instead of putting me in the cell, however, the deputy sat me in a chair and scratched his head. "Okay, so you say you dropped your keys, but Purdue said you falsely said you were looking for locations for some TV show."

I had to think fast and talk faster if I was going to get out of there. I explained that it was true that I didn't exactly work for the show. I was just going to pass on the information to CeeCee Collins, my friend, and to the executive producer of the show, who happened to be a customer of the bookstore where I worked.

By now the dog was sitting in his lap and the deputy— Deputy A. Daniels, according to his name tag—looked confused.

"I didn't take anything. You can search me if you want." I stood up and turned model fashion. The young officer's face suddenly turned very red.

"Ma'am, sit down."

Oh no. He had misunderstood my offer. I slipped back into the chair feeling sleazy. It was probably useless to explain that I wasn't suggesting what he thought I was suggesting. I went back to trying to talk my way out of there.

"It was just a misunderstanding. If you want, you can go get CeeCee Collins. She knows me. She'll vouch for me."

He sighed a few times and ran his fingers through his hair. "Okay, I'm going to do what I do when I catch the local kids making trouble. I'll give you a warning. But if it happens again—" He pointed toward the three doors.

I assured him he had nothing to worry about. I'd only come for the day and he'd never see me again. He unlocked the cuffs and showed me to the front door. I didn't need any help getting through it.

The lobby was so tiny there wasn't even room for a chair, not that I cared because I was out the door in two seconds into the tiny government plaza.

Dinah was pacing out front and ran up and hugged me. "I was so worried." She held up her phone. "I called Mason. He was ready to hire a helicopter."

I flopped on the bench in front of the closed one-room library. My legs still felt rubbery and I needed to recover.

Officer Daniels peered out through a window and his expression dimmed. He opened the door. "I thought you were leaving."

I thought I was, too. Until Dinah told me we'd missed our boat, which was the last one of the night. Luckily, Officer Daniels hadn't taken me up on my offer to have Cee-Cee vouch for me, because she and the others had already left.

Dinah and I had no choice but to spend the night. I felt obligated to explain to Officer Daniels, who by now clearly wished I would just disappear. I promised I'd be no trouble and follow all the rules. Shaking his head, he shut the door.

Getting a hotel room was no problem, and the local drugstore provided us with toothbrushes and some extra-large tee shirts to sleep in. We shared a pizza and some ice cream and went to our room.

I called my father and asked him to continue his dog care until the next morning. We'd be on the first boat out.

I fell into the bed exhausted. The sound of the waves lulled me into a deep sleep—for a little while, anyway. Was I dreaming or was there screaming coming from the bathroom? I stumbled out of bed trying to figure out where I was and what to do about the screaming. The door was ajar so I went in. Dinah was in the dark, pointing at the toilet. There were tiny lights swimming in the water.

Dinah was rarely that jumpy, and I attributed it to the long day we'd had and set her mind to rest, thanks to more information from Adele. Although Catalina was surrounded by water, it had very little on the island, so they had dual water systems: fresh water for sinks and drinking, salt water for toilets. There were some kind of iridescent creatures that lived in the salt water and glowed in the dark.

Dinah climbed back in bed, and we both fell back asleep. Sometime later my cell phone began to vibrate and then play the royal flourish that was its ring tone. I caught a glimpse of my watch. It was 3 a.m. I sat bolt upright and grabbed for the phone. Nobody called at this hour with anything but trouble.

CHAPTER 13

DINAH TURNED ON THE LIGHT AS I SWUNG MY legs over the side of the bed. I needed to be sitting up to deal with bad news. Dinah had her eyes glued to my face, reading my expression and mirroring it. Judging by how she looked, I must have appeared pretty worried.

"What?" I said into the phone. Through the earpiece I could hear multiple people talking at once, and I couldn't make out who they were or what they were saying.

"Molly?" Barry's voice broke through the din. "Where are you?" he demanded in an upset tone.

Before I could answer my mother was on the phone saying something about almost having a heart attack, which was neither here nor there. She said stuff like that when the bag broke on some take-out Chinese and her egg foo young flipped out of the container.

Finally, there came the even voice of my father. "Don't worry, honey, there was just a little incident."

As I listened to the story of "the incident," I could feel my expression change from one of concerned confusion to one of suppressed laugher. Dinah was trying to figure it out from my end of the conversation, but there was no way that my uh-huhs gave away what I was hearing.

As soon as I snapped the phone shut, she was on me like cream cheese on a bagel wanting to know what was going on.

I was smiling, picturing what I'd just heard. "Okay, Barry finally got back from his out-of-state trip. And he decided to surprise me . . ."

Dinah covered her mouth and started to laugh. "Oh no."

"Oh yes. Apparently he used his key to come in the house, then he stripped and started to climb into bed with—well, he thought it was me, but it was my parents. My mother started freaking and called 911. My father has been taking some kind of martial arts classes and elbowed Barry in the face. You know how people always complain it takes the cops too long to get there? Not this time. They were there before Barry could get his pants on. And I guess he has a black eye."

"Omigod," Dinah said, laughing so hard she fell back on the bed.

My cell rang again. This time it was Barry only. He was sitting in his Tahoe, apparently with his clothes back on. The patrol officers—friends of his—had left after laughing their pants off.

"Don't worry about the front door. I'll fix it," he said.

"Front door? What's wrong with my front door?"

Barry sighed. "I'll fix the doorbell, too, so that next time somebody rings it, you'll hear it and they won't have to kick in the door."

"They kicked in the door?" I was incredulous.

"Yeah, when they get a call from a screaming woman who doesn't answer the door, that's what they do."

"The dogs?"

Barry groaned. "They're fine. They hid in the closet. I think your dog is turning my dog into a wimp. He didn't even bark." He stopped for a minute. Dinah was behind me

trying to cover her face with a pillow to muffle the laugher.
"I hear someone laughing. This isn't funny."

When he said that, I had to bite my lip to keep from
laughing, too. I couldn't stop picturing Barry coming into
the bedroom with big plans on his mind and pulling back
the covers to discover my parents.

"Where are you?" Barry said with an edge to his voice.
He didn't sound happy when he heard the answer.

"Catalina?" he sputtered. "Why didn't you tell me your
parents were sleeping in your bed? Why didn't you tell me
you were going to Catalina? And what are you doing there?
Who are you with?"

"Hey there, Mr. Detective, I don't know why you're getting so testy with me. You were gone, remember, off on a
case somewhere. When you called, you always had to get
off the phone."

A deep tiredness seeped in his voice. "I was working.
What can I say?"

"What about Jeffrey?" I said, asking about his son.

"He's spending some more time with his mother and her
new husband."

I could tell Barry missed having Jeffrey with him. He
and Jeffrey argued over the boy's acting ambitions, but
Barry loved the kid.

"Don't try to change the subject and get the spotlight
off of you. Just cut to the chase. I hear somebody else in
the room," he said.

I told him it was Dinah, and then he started to ask why
we were there but stopped himself.

"This wouldn't have anything to do with Mary Beth
Wells's death?" he asked suspiciously. There was just some
dead air on my end and he continued. "Heather told me all
about it, but she made it sound like you were involved. Something about you playing detective and thinking some dishcloth had a secret code and belonged to the victim."

"Is that what she said?" I felt my anger rising. I slowly
explained that it wasn't a dishcloth but it did seem to have

a code. "And no matter what Detective Heather said to you, I am sure the piece belonged to Mary Beth Wells. Not only did I see an *MB* embedded in the image of a wishing well, but when I saw the inside of her Catalina house—well, there were pieces similar to it everywhere."

"What were you doing in her house? Let me rephrase that. How did you get in her house?"

"The usual way, through the door."

"Molly," he said, dragging my name in that warning tone of his. "Let's save time. You know how good I am at getting confessions, and you know how much better you'll feel when you lay out the whole story."

He *was* good at getting confessions, but I doubted I'd feel better telling him about my skirmish with the sheriff. I decided to skip over that part and only explain why I went to the house. I started at the beginning and told him about how we'd found the package at the sale and CeeCee had thought it had been left for her to take care of, but she had dropped it in my lap. I told him what was in the note and the diary entry.

"You know how you said you feel like you're speaking for the victim when you investigate a homicide? Well, I feel like I'm speaking for Mary Beth Wells. I want to finish what she started."

"I understand your motivation, babe. Your heart is in the right place." His voice was soft, and I suddenly wished he was there with his arms around me. "But assuming the cloth really did belong to her and has some kind of code and there is some kind of secret—it's probably why she got killed."

"I suppose that crossed my mind," I said.

"Did it also cross your mind that if somebody killed her to keep the secret a secret they won't take kindly to you mucking around?"

The hairs on the back of my neck stood up. I hadn't really thought of that. But I knew he was right. "Nobody really knows I'm looking around."

"Molly," he said in a voice full of frustration. "Just let it be. When are you coming home? We can talk about it then." His voice became husky. "Babe, I've missed you and I can't wait to show you how much."

The tone of his voice was a pretty good indication of what he had in mind. Even though I was sitting down, my knees suddenly felt wobbly.

I told him we were taking the early morning boat back. After telling me a few more times how much he was looking forward to seeing me, he finally hung up.

Dinah had fallen back asleep while I was talking. I curled up under the covers, looked out the window at the view of the harbor and thought about the day. I was too wide awake to sleep, so I leaned over the side of the bed and grabbed the bag of things I'd gotten at the drugstore. I pulled out the reporter-style notebook that was just like what I'd seen Barry and Detective Heather carry. I thought it would be so much more efficient than trying to keep everything in my head. I began to write down everything I knew so far. I fell asleep with the pen in my hand.

DINAH WAS DRINKING COFFEE WHEN I AWOKE. Through the open curtains I saw the boats bobbing in the small harbor.

"I brought one for you, too," she said, giving me a paper cup with a lid. "It's a red eye and there's some pastry." She indicated a bag on the night table.

The strong coffee sent a nice jolt to my fuzzy brain. I took a few bites of the pastry and headed for the shower. At least I'd be clean and fresh even if I had to wear my clothes from the day before.

"Our boat doesn't leave for an hour," Dinah said as we checked out. "We could get some real breakfast."

I shook my head. I had other plans. Dinah was a little concerned when she heard what they were.

"But didn't you guarantee that deputy you were going

straight to the boat and back to the mainland?" she said as we stood in front of the hotel. The business walkway that ran along the water was empty. The air felt fresh and the sky was a cloudless blue.

I started to walk the other way. "I'm not leaving without talking to Delia. You heard what the caretaker said she said: There was something Mary Beth and that woman wanted to hide."

I kept walking, but Dinah stood her ground. I heard her make an exasperated snort and mumble something about it not being her fault if I ended up in the Catalina pokey. A moment later she caught up with me.

We walked into the small grocery store. There were a few shoppers and one cashier. She had curly black hair and a friendly smile. Her name tag was clearly visible on the red smock. I'd found Delia. Or more correctly, she found me.

"You're the one the sheriff took in," she said pointing at me. She had heard the whole story already, including my explanation that I'd dropped my keys. "The deputies don't have a lot to do around here so they get real excited when they have an actual perp." She punctuated her comment with a laugh and roll of her eyes. "I know what you're really up to."

I swallowed hard. "You do?"

"I may live on this tiny island, but I get around. It's obvious you're a PI investigating Mary Beth Wells's death."

I nodded and said nothing. She was right—almost. I was investigating and I was private, but I didn't have a license nor had I been hired by anybody.

When I glanced toward the door, I saw the deputy from the day before stop outside the store. He clearly saw me—and his expression was grim.

He walked inside. "Aren't you supposed to be gone?" he said, stopping next to me.

Delia made a gesture to wave him off. "Relax, Allen. She just stopped in to buy some snacks for the trip before she goes over town."

At first I wondered at the comment but then remembered more of Adele's travelogue. The islanders used the expression *over town* when they referred to going to the mainland.

"I'll just be waiting outside to make sure you get to the dock okay," he said.

As soon as he'd stepped back outside, Delia leaned over the counter.

"I don't want you to get in trouble, so I'll just tell you what I know. Mary Beth came in here to shop and she was always nice, though maybe a little distant. It was a different story with her cousin-in-law Matt Wells. What a doll—all personality and pretty good to look at, too."

"There was something a long time ago. Mary Beth made a lot of trips with another woman—" I said, afraid she was going to get lost in talking about the cousin-in-law's dreamy eyes or something.

"Oh, that's what you want to know about? It was when Mary Beth first started coming to the island. I guess for the first year, she didn't come because that husband of hers had the seasick problem, but then she started coming on her own. Mostly, she came with another woman. I don't remember her name, just that it reminded me of a flower. They kept to themselves. I'm the only one who knew anything about them because they came in here to shop. And believe me, even I didn't know much, except the woman with the flowery name had a baby here. Just popped it out at home with old Doc Bender assisting, or so his wife told me.

"That doesn't happen much anymore," Delia said with a dismissive wave. "Everybody goes to Long Beach. I'm guessing they were pretty quiet about it because the father wasn't around, if you know what I mean. Back then people still felt some shame at having a baby and not having a husband." Delia laughed and waved the air. "Not anymore. What with women going to sperm banks or having affairs just so they can get pregnant and then dumping the guy once he's done his job."

I noticed the deputy looking in at us. He was shifting his weight and obviously getting impatient. Delia launched into a rant about maternity clothes, rambling on about how women used to try to hide their condition. "Not like now where they're all wearing tiny tee shirts that don't even cover their baby bump. You should see them on the beach here in their bikinis," Delia said in a disapproving tone.

I was beginning to get uneasy. How long would Officer Daniels continue to believe we were paying for some snacks? I rushed to speak. "So after that, did the three of them come back to the island a lot?"

"Who? The women in the bikinis?" Delia said, perplexed.

"No, no," I said quickly, looking toward the door. The deputy was holding the handle. "I was talking about Mary Beth and the other woman."

Delia shrugged and shook her head. "I never saw the woman or the baby again. And like I said, Mary Beth was always kind of aloof, so I couldn't ask her."

The deputy opened the door and pointed at his watch and then the water. It was time for our boat to leave, and I was pretty sure if we missed it, I'd see what the inside of the Catalina jail looked like.

I thanked Delia before Dinah and I left. The deputy followed us all the way to the boat and stood there until it pulled away from the dock.

"Hmm, you realize that gives the Sagittarius figure a new meaning," Dinah said as we sat around one of the window tables on the boat. "It's the baby's sign."

CHAPTER 14

"PINK?" ADELE SQUEALED WHEN I WALKED INTO the bookstore office. "They let you out, huh? I was just telling Mrs. Shedd about what happened and offering my services to take over for you until you got out of jail."

Mrs. Shedd looked at both of us. "Molly, you certainly lead an interesting life. Adele said you're in the middle of another murder. Well, actually she said you were in a muddle over a murder and you got caught breaking into a house."

I gave Adele a frozen smile, and Mrs. Shedd continued. "You don't have a felony on your record now or anything?"

"I wasn't even arrested, just detained," I said.

"I'm sure it was just a misunderstanding," Mrs. Shedd said. "Catalina's so small, they probably don't even have a jail."

"Believe me, they do."

I was relieved when Mrs. Shedd dropped the subject and went back to bookstore business. She wanted to know if either of us had any idea who the subject of the *Making*

Amends episode was going to be. "I heard a rumor that it's Bob," Mrs. Shedd said, glancing out the door of the office in the direction of the café. "Something about his father walking out on the family when Bob was three and now wants to come back into his life. What about you, Adele? Do you have some secret wrong that needs to be righted?"

"I sure do," Adele said, glaring at me. I knew what she was thinking: Her big wrong was me getting the job she wanted.

Mrs. Shedd didn't ask for any details and again urged us to cooperate with any of the TV people who came in. "This could be a major move for the bookstore. We could become a tourist stop," she said, putting some things in her tote bag. "Well, I'm off. You two enjoy the day."

Adele wanted to know how I had avoided getting arrested. I couldn't tell whether she was disappointed or just interested. "Luckily, William came and picked the rest of us up since you weren't around to drive us," she continued. "He was waiting when we got off the boat." I wondered if he would use the experience for his next book, *Koo Koo Hangs Out at the Harbor*.

Dinah and I had gotten off the boat and I'd dropped her home and come right to work. The caffeine jolt of the red eye she'd gotten me had worn off. I went into the café and ordered a black eye.

"Tough morning, huh?" Bob said, pushing the coffee with a double shot of espresso across the counter. I nodded as I picked it up.

Back in the bookstore, I took my drink to our television-and-theater section. There was a coffee table book about Lance Wells Sr., and I dragged it to one of our reading stations.

The black eye definitely cleared my mind, and my eyes were now fully opened. As I thumbed through the pictures, I recognized the inside of the house in Catalina. The windows had real curtains instead of the filet panels, and there were blank spaces on the walls where I'd seen the crocheted pictures. Lance Sr. was standing by the fireplace. There was a grace in the way he held himself. The copy below it mentioned the house in Catalina, which turned out to have a name: Paradise Found. It also mentioned that the dancer-actor often brought groups of people over for parties, and he entertained them with his magic tricks. It went on to explain he was fascinated with illusion and that the house had secret panels. I stared at the fireplace and suddenly knew why Mary Beth included it: There must be a secret hiding place in it.

I rushed back to the office and took out the crochet work. When I examined the fireplace motif, there in the midst of all those double crochet stitches that formed the picture was an open spot with no stitches. I had vaguely noticed it before but had thought it was a mistake. Now I saw it in a new light. Was it meant to mark the spot where the secret panel was?

"Why couldn't you have put that in the note Mary Beth."

What could I do with the information now? I couldn't turn around and go back to the island without getting in trouble. I surveyed the crochet piece. I was going to have to rely on it for the rest of the puzzle.

Then I went back to the book on Lance Sr. and thumbed through the rest of it. I stopped when I got to a photo of Lance Sr. cutting a ribbon on his first Lance Wells Dance Studio. He was standing in a doorway, and I caught a glimpse of the address written in gold lettering. I realized it was the studio down the street. There was nothing on the crochet piece to indicate the dance studio, but I wanted to try again to check it out anyway.

I took a short break and went down the block. But when I went up the stairs, the sign stating they were closed due to a death in the family was still on the glass door. Defeated, I returned to the bookstore.

The rest of the day went by in a tired blur. By the time I drove my parents' SUV home, all I could think about was barricading myself in my son's room and crashing. After putting on clean clothes, I would put up my feet and crochet. Did I really think any of that was going to happen? Not likely.

I walked in through the kitchen and was greeted by the sound of banging coming from the front door. My mother swirled in with the deli delivery guy close behind carrying a bag of food. Samuel came out of his old bedroom, muttering something about all of my stuff in there. The dogs were barking and scratching from somewhere.

"I had to put them somewhere," my mother said when I asked about the dogs' noises. "We were practicing our dance steps and they kept getting in the way." The deli guy went back for the rest of the food. I followed him to check out the damage to my front door.

Barry was on his knees and had a hammer in his hand. When he looked up at me, I was shocked to see one of his eyes was ringed in a sickly blackish green.

"Where did that come from?" I asked, stepping closer for a better look.

"Your father, remember? He said he'd been learning some kind of martial arts," Barry said, setting down the tool. I did a double take. Who knew my peaceful father could do so much damage? Barry pointed at the spot where he'd been hammering a piece of plywood to the lower portion of my front door. "I just patched it until the new one I ordered arrives."

He stood up and came over to me. His eyes flared with heat and he held his arms wide open, but the deli guy came through the doorway and interrupted the moment.

Barry let out a disappointed groan as the delivery guy passed between us and headed for the kitchen with a bag of bread and rolls. That's when I noticed the living room.

"Mother," I yelled, throwing my hands up. It looked as though I'd been robbed. All the furniture was gone. The only seating was a few folding chairs where the couch had been. Some kind of electronic music equipment had been set up in front of the fireplace. And some lights had been added to give the illusion of spotlights.

"The furniture is all in the den," Barry said. "I checked."

I rushed through the living room and on to the den. I could barely walk in as all the living room furniture had been pushed in there.

"We had to move everything out," my mother said, coming up behind me. "There was no room to practice the She La Las trademark dance steps. Lana almost went over the couch. And our musical director needed someplace to set up his equipment."

"You mean Samuel?" I said to my mother.

"Yes, but it sounds better to say *our musical director* than *my grandson*," my mother said, finding her purse and handing a generous tip to the deli guy.

Barry stepped closer to me and dropped his voice. "Why don't you come with me? We'll get some dinner. My place is empty," he said with a heavy touch of suggestion.

Being somewhere else sounded appealing, and I was about to accept and tell my mother I was leaving, but she beat me to the punch.

"You're not thinking of going anywhere, are you, Molly? I thought it would be nice if we had a family dinner. Samuel's here already and Peter's coming by later."

My mother had me and she knew it. Even with all the chaos, I was a sucker for a family gathering.

"Join us?" I said to Barry. I thought for sure he'd refuse. If I had been him, I sure would have. Either he didn't know what he was in for or he liked awkward confrontations, because he accepted.

And he got it in spades.

The dining room was still intact, and once my father and I had put all the food on the table, we all sat down.

"I guess we all know each other," I said, trying to ease the awkward moment. Barry and my parents exchanged uncomfortable glances. Samuel just took the platter of meat and put some corned beef on his plate. For a few moments we passed the food in silence, exchanging bowls of coleslaw and platters of cheeses and meats, along with a basket of rye bread and rolls.

As my father passed the mustard and pickles to Barry, his gaze stopped on Barry's shiner. He apologized, but I detected a dash of pride in his voice that he could inflict so much damage.

And then the inquisition began.

"So, I understand you have a son," my mother said. "What does he do?"

I wondered how the questioner felt about being the questioned. I was just waiting for her to use his line and say, "Do you want to tell me the whole story? I'm sure it will make you feel better."

"He goes to school."

"College?" my mother asked.

"No, middle school," Barry answered. I had to admire how he looked her right in the eye when he answered.

"So you must have waited a long time to have children," my mother the questioner continued.

"Actually, no."

"Then you waited a long time to get married. You must have been what, about thirty-six or thirty-seven? Being a bachelor all those years must have made it hard to get used to a family."

For the first time ever, Barry appeared uncomfortable. He was looking down at the table.

"My job made it . . ." Barry began. Then he cleared his throat and looked directly at my mother. "Okay, I wasn't single all that time."

My mother leaned closer to the table, her eyes locked on him. "What exactly does that mean?"

Barry turned toward me. "This isn't how I planned to tell you, but I was married twice before."

The news hit me like a boulder in the chest. I could feel everyone staring at me. At that moment Peter walked in. My older son looked around the table and quickly assessed that something was going on. As he pulled out a chair and sat down, I pushed mine back and went outside.

Barry followed.

I walked far out into the yard and flopped on a bench in the corner.

He stopped in front of the bench and stood over me. "I always planned to tell you. But when I didn't mention it at first, it became awkward."

"Kids?" I said in a low voice.

I heard him blow his breath out. "A daughter, but she stayed with her mother and I've had virtually no contact."

My head swirled with all this new information. "Do you think that makes it okay not to mention her?"

"No," Barry said with regret. "I didn't mention it at first because being divorced twice makes me sound like a relationship washout."

"Is that why you're so intent on getting married again? Do you think three times is the charm?"

He pulled me up to face him. "No, I think *you're* the charm."

My stomach was doing flip-flops. I had been wondering about a relationship with someone who always had one foot out the door and who disappeared for days. I wanted something casual, but with someone who was there. And now this news. How could he have just left out a wife and daughter?

I heard the back door open and turned away from Barry. My father walked across the yard.

"There was someone on the phone just now. They asked for you and when I said I'd get you, they said just to give you this message." He held out a piece of paper. "I wrote it down to make sure I got it right. The person wouldn't leave a name. They said to stop meddling or else. Molly, are you in some kind of trouble?"

I could feel Barry's eyes boring in my back.

"What did I tell you?" he said in a low voice.

I ignored him and laughed, saying I was sure it was just my friend Dinah's idea of a joke.

My father appeared relieved and patted my arm reassuringly. Then after a quick glance at Barry, he walked back to the house.

I'd had a moment to think, and I turned back to Barry.

"I can't do this anymore. You're gone all the time, and now I find out you left out a big hunk of your life. A whole wife and daughter."

"Molly, we can work it out. I promise that's the only wife and daughter I didn't mention," he said in a vain attempt to lighten the moment.

The back door opened again and the dogs came flying out. Cosmo ran up and sat between Barry and me.

"I'm sorry. The reason—" His cell phone interrupted him. His eyes held mine with a pleading look while the phone continued to go off. For a moment I thought he was going to ignore it—that this moment between us trumped everything, even his job. But then his features evened out and the emotion disappeared in his expression as he flipped open the phone.

"Greenberg," he said, all business again. He pulled out his notebook and wrote something down before hanging up. "I have to go, but we're not done. Okay?" He didn't wait for an answer, probably because he was afraid of what it would be.

Cosmo followed behind him and then sat at the gate watching as Barry walked down the driveway. I called the dogs and went back inside to the table, trying to act as if nothing had happened. As my mother focused on my face, she began a speech about how sometimes bad things happened for good reasons. It was some spiritual mumbo jumbo and my back started to go up, but then I realized she meant it. She got up from the table and hugged me. "I'm sorry, honey. I was just trying to make conversation. It's for the best," she said finally. "Anyway, I liked the other one better."

That's when I heard a rustle behind me. When I looked, Barry had come back and was picking up his toolbox. All the emotion was back in his eyes and his jaw was clenched.

"Other guy?" he said in a voice so low only I heard it.

WHEN I FINALLY WENT TO BED, I HAD A HARD time sleeping. The combination of Samuel's small bed, Cosmo taking up too much space and the events of the evening made it impossible for me to get comfortable and turn off my mind. Instead, I got up and tried crocheting. I took out the chart for the bookmark and a ball of number 10 thread. But instead of calming me, working with the steel hooks and fine thread only made me more tense. The work was too intricate, and I had trouble getting the hook into the tiny loops.

I wondered how Mary Beth had managed to make all those filet pieces. I gave up and reached for some comfort crochet. Working on the purple worsted scarf with its repetitive rows of single and double crochet stitches was easy and soothing. I would have relaxed completely, but a dark thought kept wandering around the back of my mind. What if the warning call was real?

CHAPTER 15

"WHAT?" I SAID, TRYING TO KEEP THE SQUEAL out of my voice. It was the next morning, and Dinah had just returned my call and told me she hadn't left me any message, joking or otherwise.

"Is there something you're leaving out?" Dinah said, reacting to my anxious tone.

I glanced over my shoulder. My mother had just come in the kitchen and was making a breakfast drink for herself and my father. This was the closest she got to cooking. The mixture in the blender resembled pond scum. She'd been making it every day, and each time she offered to make enough for me, too. Even though both my parents looked great and seemed to have lots of energy, I always politely passed.

She seemed intent on pulsing the blender on and off, but I knew my mother well enough to know it might be a cover for eavesdropping. She didn't know anything about my sleuthing activities, and I thought it best to keep it that way. If she was concerned about my mental health from the state of the crochet room, I could just imagine what she'd say if she found out I was in the middle of a murder investigation and might have gotten a threatening phone call.

"Let's get coffee," I suggested. I didn't want to discuss the Barry situation in front of my mother, either. The hug and sympathy had been the extent of her understanding. Later she'd said she couldn't understand what I'd want with somebody in such a dangerous line of work. She did think he was sexy, and when I blushed, she put her hand on her hip and gave me one of her famous Liza looks.

"I know an attractive man when I see one," she had said, laughing at my embarrassment.

A few minutes later I was at Dinah's door. She grabbed her coat and we took the short walk to Ventura Boulevard and the heart of Tarzana. Although the sun was out, the air still had a cold sting.

"Okay, tell me everything," Dinah said, winding a deep rose–colored scarf around her neck and pulling her gray sweater coat tighter.

I started with the threatening phone call, and her jaw dropped in response. "What made you think it was me?"

"Maybe wishful thinking," I said as the impact of the call began to sink in.

"Did you ask your father about the caller's voice?"

I nodded and said I'd tried to be nonchalant about it. He'd said the voice was whispery and he hadn't been able to tell if it was a man or a woman. I swallowed hard. "If it was for real, you know who it had to be?" It was more or less a rhetorical question, but I answered it anyway. "Whoever didn't want Mary Beth's secret to come out." I hesitated before I said the rest. "And probably the person who killed her."

"Have you considered dropping the whole thing?" Dinah said.

I shook my head. "I haven't had a chance to think about it."

Dinah's sixth sense kicked in. "There's something else, isn't there?"

My shoulders sagged, and I told her the Barry story as we walked down the main street. At this time of day the foot traffic was limited to people in sweats or stretchy pants out for an exercise walk while clutching the necessary accessories: a coffee drink in one hand and a cell phone in the other.

"He left out a wife and kid. Wow," Dinah said. She'd never really understood my hesitation for not taking our relationship to a more permanent level, but she certainly understood why I was upset this time.

"Well, there is always Mason," she said. "You always said he seems to want the kind of relationship you do. He's nice looking, has a job, et cetera."

"There's just one problem," I said when we'd reached Le Grande Fromage. I threw in a nice pause before I finished the thought. "My mother likes Mason."

Dinah and I both laughed. It felt good after all the grim news.

Dinah opened the door and was about to go in when I looked up the street. A man walked out from the stairwell leading to the Lance Wells Dance Studio. Excited, I detoured and headed down the street. I heard the Le Grande Fromage door *woosh* shut and Dinah's footsteps as she followed me.

"What's going on?" Dinah asked. "It must be important if you chose it over French-press coffee."

"I think the dance studio is open again," I said, walking faster. "Maybe we can get some answers about Mary Beth there."

"What are you going to say?" Dinah said, keeping up with me. Then she shrugged it off. "You think well on your feet."

After walking through the arched entryway, we went up the exterior stairs. I pulled open the studio's glass door, and we walked into a large room. A small reception area was formed by a counter with a screen behind it. The front wall was one big window with a view of the north mountains peeking above the low building across the street. The reception desk was empty, and Dinah and I walked to the side of it and looked into the lesson area.

Considering the early hour, I was surprised to see two couples on the floor dancing to tango music. It was easy to tell teachers from students. Both male teachers wore black bowling-style shirts with "Lance Wells Dance Instructor" embroidered in white across the back.

When I looked over at Dinah, I saw that her eyes were practically bulging out of their sockets. She pointed at the back of one of the instructors. "It's Vincent, my student. The one who had the problem with his test." I watched him for a moment. Whatever problems he had with English, he had the tango down.

Dinah wanted to leave, but just as I stopped her, a door opened on the side wall and a man and woman came in. As soon as they saw us, they became very animated and moved quickly toward us. She started her pitch as soon as she was within earshot. The man was barely a step behind her. "Welcome, welcome ladies. Here about lessons?" She didn't wait for an answer before continuing. "Everybody wants to dance like the stars now. The first lesson is complimentary. We can do that right now if you'll just wait until our fabulous instructors finish with their current clients." The couple went behind the reception counter and before I could blink, they were handing us clipboards with questionnaires attached.

Now that I was closer to the counter, I saw the row of photographs of Lance Wells Sr. on the temporary wall. Below them a banner read, "Dancing is the Footwork of the Gods."

When I didn't take the clipboard, the woman explained the questionnaire had to be filled out before we could take our complimentary lesson.

"It's for insurance purposes," the man said, stepping out from behind her.

Since I was more interested in talking than dancing, I took the clipboard but didn't do any writing. Dinah didn't even pick hers up.

"I work down the street at the bookstore." I introduced myself and Dinah. "And you are?"

"Roseanne and Hal Klinger," the woman said, speaking for both of them.

"I saw the sign on your door. . . ." I let it trail off, hoping they'd explain their connection to Mary Beth Wells. My words hung in the air for a moment, and I saw the woman's eyes tear up. Hal stepped in and explained Roseanne's sister had died recently.

"Maybe you heard about it. Her name was Mary Beth Wells," he said in a somber tone.

I did my best to appear surprised. This was a golden opportunity and I didn't want to blow it. When I glanced at Roseanne again, I saw her resemblance to Mary Beth, although the overall look was totally different. Mary Beth had appeared glamorous, with her golden hair and fine features. On Roseanne, those same features were sharp and foxlike, and her hair was short and red. Mary Beth seemed to have done better in the husband department as well. Lance Wells Jr. might not have been much of a dancer, but he'd inherited his father's good looks. Hal Klinger had bland features and a fringe of hair around a bald spot that gave him an insipid aura, which his demeanor matched. He seemed to stay one step behind his wife.

Both Dinah and I expressed our condolences. Roseanne nodded in recognition of our sympathy but then shut the door on her emotions and went back to business. She motioned toward the questionnaires, which were still not filled out. Meanwhile, the tangoing continued on the dance floor. I picked up the pen attached to the clipboard. If I wanted her to talk, I was going to have to act like a customer. I nudged Dinah and with a grunt of protest, she began to fill out her sheet as well.

"Is that Lance Wells?" I said, glancing up from my writing and gesturing toward the row of photos on the wall. I noticed he was in a different outfit in each picture. The first showed him in a tuxedo, the next in a theatrical version of a cowboy outfit, then in a pirate getup and the final picture was when he was older. He was dressed in normal clothes and flanked by two younger men, both of whom resembled him. It wasn't much of a stretch to figure they were Lance Jr. and Matt.

"Yes, that's Lance Sr."

"Then he owns this place?" I said innocently.

"He started the dance studios, but he died a number of years ago," Roseanne said.

"Are you the owners now?" I asked.

"We manage—" Hal started to speak, but his wife gave him a sharp flash of her eyes and he stopped.

There was an edge of impatience in her voice. "What possible difference could that make?"

Dinah stepped in and said we wanted to know who we were dealing with before we committed to lessons. "You know how it is—you pay for a bunch of lessons and the place suddenly goes out of business."

Roseanne seemed offended at the comment. "I assure you we have been in business for a long time." She launched into the studio's history. "Lance Wells started the dance studios to get Americans on their feet. The tradition is being carried on by Lance's nephew, our artistic director, Matt Wells.

"We've been managing the studio for years. If anything, it's doing better with all the television dancing shows."

As Roseanne finished, I noticed another man had come in the side door and joined us.

"New students?" he said, beaming a charismatic smile in Dinah's and my direction.

Hal introduced him, though I had already guessed who

he was. Matt Wells looked better in person. The photo didn't do justice to his thick dark hair and sparkling gray eyes. Hal went on to explain to him our concern about the ownership of the place.

Roseanne gave her husband a sharp stare—for what, because he dared to speak?

"I have it covered," she said to Matt. I tried to calculate how Matt and Roseanne were related. He was Lance Wells Jr.'s cousin and she was Mary Beth Wells's sister, did that even make them family? How ever they were related, I sensed hostility in the way Roseanne and Matt looked at each other. Roseanne had positioned herself so she was standing between Matt and me. But I wanted to talk to *him*. So, I grabbed the dancer by the shoes, figuratively speaking, and stepped around Roseanne.

"If you're an actual Wells, does that mean you're the owner?" I'm not generally a flirty kind of person, but something about Matt brought it out in me, and it seemed like a good way to get some information. I started twirling my hair and batting my eyes, and I heard Dinah choking back a laugh. But it worked. Matt's expression softened and his smile broadened.

"I'll take care of them," he said. Roseanne's eyes grew stern and she didn't move. Nor did Hal. I explained our concern to Matt.

"I'd just like to know who owns the dance studio," I said, eyes batting all the while.

His face lit with understanding. "There's nothing to be concerned about. This is our flagship studio, and I can assure you, it's not going anywhere."

"I understand that. I'd just like to know who owns the place." I had to stop batting my eyes—it was giving me a headache, as was their reluctance to answer what seemed to be a simple question.

The charm abruptly drained from Matt's face and he appeared almost annoyed. "Why don't you stop worrying about who owns what and just take your complimentary lesson."

The *Average Joe's Guide to Criminal Investigation* emphasized the utility of saying nothing. Silence—particularly in response to someone's leading comment—made people uncomfortable and encouraged them to divulge all kinds of useful information. So I simply did not respond. I looked around at the two couples winding down their lesson. I looked out the picture window at the view of the street. I looked at Matt Wells and then Roseanne and then Hal. Dinah knew what I was doing and leaned against the counter. I could see the tension mounting in all their faces.

"What's wrong with you people?" Hal said at last. "It's not secret information." He turned his gaze to me. "The dance studio belongs to the Lance Wells estate."

Roseanne shot her husband another angry look, and he seemed to slink into the background. The tango music stopped and the two students headed toward the door. I had the feeling Roseanne had decided we were more trouble than we were worth. She gave up on trying to get us to fill out the forms on the clipboards and instead, with a sigh of resignation, just took them from us and told the instructors we were here for a complimentary lesson. When Vincent saw Dinah, his face lit up.

"I'm taking her," he said to his coworker. Dinah was making choking noises. "We'll see who's the teacher now," he said with a smirk. I was about to say we'd changed our minds about the lessons, but both instructors were already pulling us out onto the dance floor.

Mine must have been a bodybuilder in his other life, because he had an iron grip on me. Someone turned on the music, a waltz began and my teacher told me to watch his eyes and follow his lead. I did okay for the first few steps, but then I stumbled on the instructor's feet and I saw annoyance flare in his eyes. When I made a move to pull away, he simply held on tighter.

"We always start with the basic waltz," my teacher said before taking off around the room. Things went from bad to worse when I looked away for just a moment and saw Detective Heather come in the door. I tried to steer my partner over to the front, but he kept pulling us toward the back of the room.

Detective Heather was talking to Roseanne and Hal, neither of whom looked very comfortable, though Hal at least seemed to be enjoying ogling the blond detective. Matt Wells had disappeared into the side room when Dinah and I started our lesson, but now he came back out. As he approached the group, I could see him turn on the charm. But Detective Heather stayed all business. That is until she noticed me dancing by. Her eyes narrowed and she shot me a dirty look.

The music changed and went into a polka, and my partner began to pick up speed. I swear my feet left the floor as we began whirling around the room. Vincent was smiling as he swung Dinah to-and-fro. It was hard to keep my eyes on Detective Heather without getting dizzy, so I turned toward my partner, and when I looked back Detective Heather was gone. I was ready to cut the lesson short, but before I could suggest it, the music changed to a jitterbug and my partner held me by one hand and did some maneuver where he reeled me in and then spun me out. I was breathless—and so thankful when the music finally stopped.

"Wasn't that fun?" Hal said, coming up to Dinah and me. "Just like the TV show, huh?"

We insisted we had to think about it as we headed toward the door. We ran down the stairs and out of the building, where we practically smacked into Detective Heather. She ignored Dinah and zeroed in on me. "I'm not even going to ask you what you were doing there. I'm just going to tell you straight out: Stay out of this investigation."

I couldn't help myself; I just had to ask her one

question. "Did you know that Barry was married more than once?"

She looked at me directly with a little self-satisfied smile. "Of course."

CHAPTER 16

ALL THAT DANCING LEFT US PARCHED AND NEI-
ther of us had had breakfast, so we went back to Le Grande
Fromage for café au laits and croissants.

"Maybe we should sign up for some lessons," Dinah
said, sinking into a chair after we had placed our order.
"We shouldn't be so pooped after a partial lesson. But if we
do, I'm insisting that somebody other than Vincent be my
instructor."

I agreed with our need for exercise and took out my little notebook and pen. Dinah watched as I flipped it open.

"What's that?"

"You know how Barry and Detective Heather always
take notes when they talk to people. I thought it was about
time I started doing it, too. But if I'd taken out my notebook
at the dance studio, I think it would have seemed kind of
weird."

Dinah nodded with comprehension. "They already
thought we were kind of strange—that would have pushed
it over the top."

I showed her the first few pages where I'd drawn a diagram of the crochet piece and written in the meaning of the motifs we'd figured out.

I held the pen over the paper. "Let's see. Now we know Mary Beth had a bossy sister with a wimpy husband. I don't think she and Matt Wells get along," I said, beginning to write. "And the studio is owned by the Lance Wells estate." I blew out some air. "I wonder what that means." I started to slump, then straightened. "Ah, but I know how to find out."

Mason took my call right away. "Hi, sunshine," he said cheerfully. "The other night was nice. Calling for a repeat?"

"It was nice," I said, smiling at the memory. "But I'm really after some information. I found out the Lance Wells estate owns the Lance Wells Dance Studio, but what does that mean? Also, what else do you know about Matt Wells besides what you told me about his dancing ability?"

"I don't know off the top of my head, but I can find out. However, I'm sorry I can't give out any of that information on the phone. It has to be in person, preferably someplace dark with good food," he said, a tease in his voice.

Telling myself this was in pursuit of finishing Mary Beth's mission, I accepted.

Dinah listened to my end of the conversation and was grinning when I clicked off. "Good move. No downtime. Get right back on the horse."

She was trying to make me feel good, but it had the opposite effect. I got a queasy feeling in my stomach.

"Doesn't that make me seem pretty shallow and man hungry? It's just dinner, and it's really about information," I said. "Though I do like him."

"Molly, you're not twenty anymore. Time is moving on and you need to, too. When the issue with Barry was that he wanted to get serious, I didn't understand your problem. But this is different. You're objecting to Barry's lifestyle, which isn't going to change, and the fact that he didn't mention a whole other wife and daughter. Just because he has no contact with them doesn't mean they don't exist." She gave me a solidarity arm squeeze.

"I LIKE PLAYING DETECTIVE," MASON SAID THAT night as we were led to our table. "Particularly since I have a staff to actually get the information." He had found a place nestled in Laurel Canyon I'd never been to. The walls were a brick red, and the candles flickering on each table softly illuminated the dining room.

"Roseanne and Hal have been married for twenty years and have two daughters in college. One is nineteen and one seventeen. I'm sure Mary Beth worked it out so they would get the job managing the dance studio," Mason explained once we were seated.

He stopped for a moment, caught the waiter's eye and ordered a bottle of merlot, then continued. "All I've been able to find out so far is what the Lance Wells estate owns. The house in Catalina, the one in Tarzana, all of the dance studios and a portfolio of investments all belong to it. It's just a guess, but I would imagine with Lance Jr. and Mary Beth both gone, the estate will go to Mary Beth's sister and Matt Wells."

He tasted the wine when it was delivered, nodded with approval, and the waiter poured us each a glass.

"So Lance and Mary Beth had no children?" I said before taking a sip of mine.

"No, and Lance was an only child so he had no siblings. Lance Sr. had a whole slew of wives. When he died he was married to his nurse," Mason said. The waiter had returned and Mason ordered for us. The restaurant featured a tasting menu, which meant you ordered a lot of different items and got small plates of each.

"What about the nurse? Would she be an heir to the estate?" I asked once the waiter left.

Mason didn't think so. He imagined she'd been awarded a lump sum when the elder Lance died; she would have gotten her share long ago. Then he went back to talking about Lance Jr. and how surly he'd been when he was sober.

"If he was so unpleasant, why did Mary Beth stay with him?" I asked.

Mason raised his eyebrows in surprise. "You really don't know?"

I shrugged, and he tilted his head and blinked. "I didn't realize you were such a romantic. She stayed with him because she liked the money and position. I don't know for a fact, but I bet she signed a prenuptial agreement, and with no kids as a chip, she wouldn't have gotten much. Her sister and husband would have lost their gig. Mary Beth would have had to give up the big Tarzana house, the one in Catalina and all that went with being Mrs. Lance Wells Jr. And she would have gone back to being a nobody. My people checked. She grew up in Van Nuys and was working for a caterer before she married Lance Jr. I think her goal was to get on the other side of the tray."

"Oh, yuck," I said. "I can't imagine marrying someone for a reason like that."

Mason's face and voice softened. "That's what is so wonderful about you—and rare around here." Then his tone changed back to business. "Mary Beth was young and beautiful and ambitious. I've seen lots of women like her. They're bold and go after what they want, planting themselves and ignoring rejection while treating the guy like he's a god."

"You sound like you know about it from personal experience," I said.

"Let's say, I saw through it," Mason said as our dinner began to arrive. It took two waiters to handle all the tiny plates.

Hearing all these details was changing my perception of Mary Beth and Lance Jr.; I could see them now as three-dimensional people instead of just names. I picked up my fork and prepared to eat the tiny mound of Caesar salad. I almost laughed at the artful presentation: baby romaine lettuce mixed with dressing and neatly arranged between two large croutons, a shaving of Parmesan cheese set like a tent over the top.

"The house on Catalina was probably a refuge for her. And maybe a rendevous spot," Mason suggested.

I put down my wineglass. "I don't know about that. The caretaker seemed to know everything, but he didn't mention anything about that."

Mason seemed unconcerned. "Maybe he was being discreet, or maybe she was, or maybe she just went to be alone."

I told him about the fireplace motif and the book about Lance Sr. and his fascination with magic. "I'm thinking there is some kind of secret panel in the fireplace and that Mary Beth hid some important clue there."

Mason turned serious. "Don't even think about it, Molly. As your lawyer, I am advising you to stay away from Catalina. You saw how small it is. Do you think there's any way you can avoid being seen by that deputy?"

What could I say? He was right. I changed the subject as the main course arrived. We each got four plates, each one with a tablespoon of food and a lot of fancy garnish.

"Did you find out anything about Matt Wells?"

Mason's expression darkened. "Is this about the murder or are you interested in the guy?" It was my turn to look surprised.

"It's about the murder—only."

Mason ran down the information quickly. Apparently, Mason had gotten a staff member to call the dance studio claiming to be writing an article for *Dance Journal*. She found out Matt was divorced and had had a few small parts in some musical movies and plays but had never really broken through. When Lance Sr. died, he stepped in as the artistic director of the studios. In the old days they sent around movies of the dance methods. Later they sent videos and now it's DVDs. It was the artistic director's job to make up the DVDs and travel around to the studios. To ensure the quality of the instruction he was also the spokesman for the commercials.

"Pretty good job of getting you information, huh?" Mason said as he poured the last of the wine in my glass. I nodded and he appeared pleased with himself. "I shouldn't jinx my good luck, but what happened? How long have I been trying to get you to go out with me, and now two dinners in a couple of nights. Did you finally have enough of being abandoned all of the time?"

"How'd you know?" I said, looking at the wineglass stem.

Mason had his usual easy smile. "I told you, I've dealt with a few homicide detectives. I know how they work."

I broke down and told him the rest. "How can you trust somebody who would do that?"

Mason gave my shoulder a comforting squeeze. "For perfectly selfish reasons I'm glad it happened. I can't believe he didn't tell you."

Mason's cell phone went off just as dessert arrived. The waiter was very serious as he set down a small plate of fingernail-size chocolates, and a big plate with a shot glass in the middle. The glass held a tiny hot fudge sundae next to which were two doll-size sugar cookies. I automatically stiffened at the sound of the phone and prepared for Mason to have to leave. Instead, without what appeared to be a second thought, he shut it off. As we tried not to laugh at our dessert, Mason asked if Camille was still in the crochet group. He seemed surprised when I said yes.

"She and my ex are friends of a sort. They always work on the Crystal Ball committee," he said, referring to one of the top yearly charity events.

I explained Camille seemed committed to doing a down-to-earth kind of activity.

Mason found that amusing. "She's spent her whole life with wealth, privilege and every advantage that money could buy. People always think the grass is greener on the other side."

After dinner Mason drove me home and walked me to the door. He had suggested a detour to his place, but I said no and he didn't argue. There was a comfortable feeling about being with him—maybe because he wasn't always pushing the envelope, trying to talk me into more of a relationship than I wanted.

Through the window we could see the She La Las. They were doing their dance moves, which were showing improvement. I invited Mason in, but he took another look at the dancing trio and passed.

Who could blame him?

I went in quietly through the front door, but the dogs heard me and followed me to the kitchen door. Then they charged off into the dark while I checked the phone for messages. There were three from Barry. He wanted to tell me he was coming to feed Cosmo. The next message was after he'd left, saying since I wasn't home he'd fed Blondie, too. The third call was just to say hello and tell me the new door was being delivered tomorrow.

"Barry was here while you were gone," my mother said, coming into the kitchen to get some drinks for the group. "He's pretty handy. We were having trouble with our microphones," she said, showing me her headset. He knew just how to fix them. Then he stayed and listened and said we sounded great."

Omigod, Barry was trying to soften up my mother.

And me.

When I went out into the yard to round up the dogs, I saw a vase of flowers on the umbrella table. The note said, "I know I'm sorry doesn't cover it, but believe me I am." And he signed it, "Love, B." I came back inside just as my father was walking into the kitchen. "The doorbell just

rang and I found this on the front porch," he said, holding
out a package to me.

I unwrapped the paper and saw it was a box of marzipan apples, with a note that said simply, "Enjoy!"

CHAPTER 17

"WHAT DID YOU DO WITH THE CANDY APPLES?" Dinah asked. We were sitting around the event table waiting for the rest of the crochet group to arrive.

"I brought them with me," I said, pulling the plastic box out of my bag to show her. "I couldn't leave them home. Suppose my mother or father decided to try one. No matter where I hide stuff, she always finds it. Can you believe she found the bottle of love oil I hid in the back of the linen closet?"

"Love oil?" Dinah said with a chuckle.

"Never mind. Back to the apples. Obviously, I'm not going to eat them, but beyond that I'm not sure what I'm going to do with them. Even if I didn't think they might be poisoned—marzipan, yuck," I said with a shudder.

"You can leave them at my house," Dinah offered. "Now that the kids are gone, I don't have to worry." She examined the box of almond paste candies. "Maybe you should get them tested."

"I think someone gave them to me for the shock value. Besides who would I take the candy to?" I said. "I'm not contacting Detective Heather. If I showed her the candy apples, it would be like waving a red flag that I'm investigating. And I'm not calling Barry about anything."

"I see your point. Nobody will bother the candy at my place," Dinah said, tucking the package in her tote. She put her hand on my arm. "First the phone call, now the candy. Maybe you should think about dropping the investigation. You never even met the woman, so why should you feel so obligated to take care of her business?"

"I know, but I keep thinking if I had been quicker on the uptake and found her faster, she might not have died."

Dinah didn't buy that as enough of a reason, nor did she think that either the She La Las practicing practically twenty-four hours a day at my house or my father's martial arts skills were much protection. But best friend that she was, she was staying in it if I was. "It's much harder to kill two people than one," she said.

"So you made it back." CeeCee pulled her wheeled craft carrier up to the table and then took the bag off her arm and laid it down. "You really left us in the lurch. It wasn't until we got on the boat that we remembered you drove. I offered to call a car service, but Adele insisted her boyfriend would pick us up." CeeCee appeared perturbed. "I don't know what he does, but he has some weird stuff in his car. I had to ride next to a pair of giant red shoes."

Adele arrived as CeeCee made her comment. She glared at Dinah and me and then her look changed to pleading. Adele always described William as being a serious author of important nonfiction topics when she mentioned him to the group. The way I looked at it, just because Adele was always trying to give me a hard time was no reason to do the same to her, so I said nothing.

Adele appeared relieved when she realized I wasn't going to out her boyfriend. "William was wondering if the subject of *Making Amends* had to be a bookstore employee. He thought it might be an author—perhaps him." Adele continued on about how William's spirit had almost been crushed by his third-grade teacher and he was sure that now that he was a well-known author, she'd like to apologize and give him the grades he truly deserved on his workbook.

Once Sheila got close to the table, she rushed over and hugged me. "I'm so glad you're all right. When I heard you got arrested—"

"Arrested? Who got arrested?" Camille stood at the head of the table, looking over all of us.

"Pink did," Adele said.

CeeCee addressed Camille. "Maybe you want to rethink being in this group. I'm sure you don't want to associate with jailbirds."

"Wait a second," I said, interrupting. "First of all, I wasn't arrested, just detained. It was a misunderstanding."

"What kind of misunderstanding?" Adele said with her hands on her hips.

I was going to try to talk around what had happened, but Dinah's words about it being harder to kill two people suddenly rang in my ears. It would be even harder to go after a group. I decided my best defense was to keep them all in the loop.

There was a collective "ooh."

I stepped next to Camille. "Did you know Mary Beth Wells?" I asked.

Camille swallowed hard. "I heard about her murder. I was shocked."

"But did you know her?" I asked while Adele rolled her eyes.

"Here goes Nancy Jessica Drew Fletcher Marple."

Camille ignored Adele and looked at me. "I'm not sure if this counts as knowing her. I contacted her a few years ago for donations for the silent auction for my children's school—Welton Preparatory. They're off on their own now. And not following in the family business, I might add," she said. Her daughter was in med school with plans to work in a third-world country, and her son was a park ranger on the big island in Hawaii. "They won't even come back for the party I'm throwing for Hunnie next week. My life coach said my children should be an inspiration to me. Like them I should branch out and try new things with new kinds of people. She particularly mentioned ordinary people, like you." Camille gestured toward the whole group.

CeeCee blanched. I'm sure she didn't like being referred to as ordinary. She hardly seemed ordinary to me. She'd had her own sitcom for years and was hosting *Making Amends*. It was CeeCee's choice to act like a regular person and do things like run the crochet group. I watched CeeCee swallow her annoyance. As long as her future on the show was undecided, she wasn't about to ruffle Camille's rich feathers.

"Hi, everybody," Ali said as she sprinted up to the table and pulled out a chair. She might as well have made a recording of her apology for being late; then she could just hit the play button whenever she arrived anywhere. She could have included the part about having to leave early, too. The funny part was for once she was on time.

I didn't care if she had time-management issues; she always made me smile. Something about Ali's bright eyes, impish smile and interesting assortment of clothes made me think of a tall pixie. It was funny how styles had changed. In the days when I was her age, if I'd mixed all those patterns and worn all those layers, someone would have stamped me as weird with no taste. She came across as cute and original.

"You were saying how you knew Mary Beth Wells," I said to Camille, trying to pick up the thread of conversation.

Camille took a moment to collect herself, then continued. "I got a donation of a dance lesson with Matt Wells himself." She looked sheepish. "I remember it so well because my husband bought them for me at the auction. The school was starting a tango club and I wanted to join. Mary Beth is the one I contacted for the donation."

"So she worked in the dance studio business?"

Camille shrugged. "I guess so because I called their corporate office and she was there. I never saw the office or the actual dance studio. Matt came to my home gym and did the lessons there." She paused and appeared to be making some mental calculations. A flicker of realization suddenly crossed her face. "Does Mary Beth Wells have a house on Catalina? Is that the house you broke into?"

"*Break in* is such a strong term. I climbed in through an open window."

Camille seemed fascinated. I guessed her elite friends didn't do stuff like that.

"Yeah, Pink. And how far along are you with unraveling the code?" Adele said with a snort.

"Molly's doing great," Dinah interjected, glancing sharply at Adele. "She's already figured out what several more of the panels mean."

"Well, Pink, and what great clues did you find in the house?" Adele asked snidely.

"For one thing," I said, trying to be evasive, "Mary Beth Wells was certainly very fond of filet crochet."

"What kind of crochet?" Camille asked. Eduardo had just joined us, and CeeCee told him to do the honors of answering her question since he was such an expert at it. While Eduardo talked to Camille, Ali showed us her latest creation. She'd made a crocheted cactus and stuck it in a terracotta pot filled with a hunk of green florist's foam. Then of course, she had to leave.

AN HOUR LATER, THE GROUP WAS GONE AND I was putting away the table and setting up for the night's program—a book called *Unbreak My House*. It was a guide to home repairs, and I wondered if it would attract much of an audience. Author Felix Lyndstrom was planning to demonstrate how to repair the inside of a toilet. He hadn't exactly explained how he was going to do the demonstration. I certainly hoped water wasn't involved, but I rolled out plastic under the demonstration table just in case.

"Mrs. Pink," a voice said from somewhere in the vicinity of the chairs. I peeked out from under the table and saw Detective Heather. Today she was wearing another one of her suits, black with white pinstripes. She had on heels that made my feet hurt just looking at them and her makeup job was so perfect she seemed not to be wearing any at all. Her white blond hair almost touched her shoulders.

"I think you can call me Molly," I said, getting up. "Is this about the dance lesson? It's a public place, and I had every right to be there getting my complimentary lesson."

Detective Heather put up her hand to stop me. "It's not about the dance lesson." I waited to see if what she was going to say would make it obvious Barry had told her about our breakup. But her attitude and tone were still just short of hostile, so apparently he hadn't.

"I'm here to pick up the blankets your group made. Tell your group thank you," she said in a gruff voice. She stopped a moment and her face softened. "They really help." She went on to tell me that a man had been brought in for questioning about the death of his wife and he'd had his eleven-year-old son with him. She knew the man was going to end up being arrested and the boy would have to go to social services. They tried to give him some game to play with while the father was in the interview room, but the boy had withdrawn completely, no doubt over what had happened. "On a chance, I handed him one of the blankets. At first, he pushed it away. But I left it on the bench next to him. When I looked back, he'd picked it up and was holding it next to his face."

I was stunned. This was the closest thing Detective Heather and I had ever had to a real conversation. I'd never seen her let down the hard exterior before, and I almost wanted to hug her. Almost.

Instead, I walked her up to the front counter and got the

large plastic bag that held the next batch of blankets. As she turned to go, she paused and said, "I heard you were a visitor at the Catalina sheriff's station because you were found inside the Wells house." Detective Heather gave me an exasperated groan. "If I hear you do anything like that here, there's going to be trouble. And I won't let you off with a warning."

I held my breath, waiting to see if she was going to ask for the filet crochet piece, the diary entry and the note, but either she'd forgotten about them or completely discounted their importance.

"You don't know what you're missing," I said under my breath as she left. I was glad I hadn't followed through with the hug.

CHAPTER 18

I HAD SOME TIME BEFORE THE EVENING PRO-
gram, and I didn't want to go home to watch the She La
Las do their number again. Though they had gotten the
lyrics down and were singing together, the dance steps
were still an issue. My mother kept insisting it was like riding a bicycle and the synchronization would come back to
them if they kept practicing. But they were getting panicky
since the day of the audition was fast approaching.

Instead of heading home, I called Dinah. She loved
having her house back to herself, but she still missed the
kids, particularly in the late afternoon. We decided to go to
Los Encinos State Park. It was a dual mission. Neither of
us had to deal with what we were avoiding, and we got to
look over the place where we'd first found Mary Beth's
package.

We met inside the gate near a low building by the natural warm spring that fed the guitar-shaped lake. The late
afternoon sun glistened off the water as the ducks swam
toward the fence where two women and three kids stood
with bags of feed.

"Maybe she stopped writing so abruptly because she saw someone," Dinah said, referring to the note accompanying the filet crochet in Mary Beth's bag.

"If that was the reason, I bet that someone knew what the crochet piece meant." I stopped for a moment as the full impact of what I'd just said sunk in. "And that someone didn't want her to disclose the secret." I choked on my breath. "And was probably right in front of us at the sale."

A goose came chasing behind us, thinking we had food, as we walked down the long porch of the adobe house where the sale tables had been set up. I noticed a bench nearby. "I bet that is where she was sitting when she wrote the note," I said, picturing her scribbling quickly while she looked around. "Whoever it was must have been nearby."

Dinah looked wistfully over at the kids feeding the ducks. "Isn't it amazing how they can have a good time doing the simplest of things?"

"Focus," I said to her. "We're trying to figure out a mystery here."

"Well, it's no mystery that I'm cold," Dinah said, pulling her jacket around her. By now the sun was almost down and the sky was orange near the horizon. She suggested we continue our discussion at her house. I guessed it didn't seem as lonely with me there. It was a good stop for me anyway since I had to go back to the bookstore, which was just down the street from Dinah's place.

Dinah went to put on the kettle as soon as we walked in. I noticed the house was back to normal with all the knick-knacks returned to their rightful place. I sat on the chartreuse couch, which no longer had a protective sheet over it.

"Maybe we should go over what we know," I called out to Dinah. I took out the notebook and flipped back almost to the beginning. The fact that I'd found Mary Beth through the color of the thread didn't seem to matter anymore.

I'd written down *poison is women's weapon*, and I had some notes about what Mary Beth's maid had said at the house. She'd been off for the two days prior to the death. Given the way she'd acted, I didn't think she was involved.

I flipped past the section of notes about the filet piece. And as I'd realized my mistakes, I'd written in the correction over the images with some notes. I'd crossed out *Arc de Triomphe* and written in *fireplace that must have a secret panel*. In frustration I'd scribbled *If only I'd known!* I also regretted not paying more attention to all the filet crochet pieces hanging in the house. I had a feeling that kind of crochet was Mary Beth's means of expression.

Next I read over the notes I'd written when we were in the hotel room in Catalina. There were a lot of *whews* and *that was a close call* and *boy, am I glad to be out of the sheriff's station*. Then, below Purdue Silvers' name there was a list:

woman who looked like Mary Beth
name like a flower
baby

"Dinah," I called as I got up and went looking for her in the kitchen. Her kitchen was really more like a hallway, probably designed by some man. No woman would ever make a kitchen so small. I waved the notebook, and Dinah looked up as she poured hot water in a teapot.

I read her the list under the caretaker's name. "Who does that sound like?" I asked.

Dinah put down the kettle. "Who would look like her more than her sister, and *Roseanne* sounds like a flower to me."

I started figuring. "The diary entry was written the same year Samuel was born. The baby would be twenty-three now." I flipped ahead in the book and found the notes from my dinner with Mason. Besides mentioning what a good time I'd had and how different he was from Barry and a few sentences about feeling strange and maybe a little like I was cheating on someone, I'd written down the facts he'd shared. Mason had said Mary Beth's sister had two daughters, but they were only teenagers.

Dinah and I carried the steaming cups of Earl Grey back into the living room. "What if Roseanne had a baby before she married Hal and gave it up and Mary Beth decided to tell him?"

Dinah had zoned out. She was looking toward the bedroom where the kids had stayed. All this talk of babies and children had made her think about them. Suddenly she zoomed back in. "I have pictures."

"Pictures of what?" I asked, feeling a tinge of annoyance that she had missed my big aha about Roseanne.

"I have pictures of the park, the day of the sale. I was taking pictures of Ashley-Angela and E. Conner before the babysitter took them home. Remember how serious they were about feeding the ducks and geese?" Dinah said before disappearing into the other room. She returned holding her digital camera. She flipped through the photos and then held out the camera so I could see the image display.

I looked at the kids holding out their hands with food for the animals and was about to hand the camera back to Dinah. I was seriously going to try to find a love interest for Dinah. She was way too fixated on two kids that by all means she should resent.

"Did you look at them?" Dinah asked.

"Yeah, yeah, the kids are very cute."

Dinah rolled her eyes. "That wasn't the point. You must really think I've lost it if I'm trying to show you photos of the kids when we're talking about Mary Beth. This is too small anyway. Let me print a copy."

A few moments later, she handed me a piece of paper. This time I looked at everything except the kids. The angle wasn't the best, and since Dinah had been focusing on the kids, she hadn't paid attention to getting in the background. I saw the adobe house with the sale tables set up. CeeCee and I were behind our table, and Ali was handing someone a package. I moved my gaze to the adjacent benches. My heart skipped a beat when I saw the figure with long golden hair bent over something. The paper bag was on the bench next to her. It had to be Mary Beth. I felt a sudden wave of sadness. If only . . . Dinah noticed me hesitating and pointed beyond a giant cactus. I followed her finger. There were some other figures I couldn't make out, but there was no mistaking Camille.

"*Camille* sounds almost like *Camellia*," Dinah said, looking at me with wide eyes.

I scribbled some notes before drinking my tea in one gulp. There was no time to deal with it now. I had to get back to the bookstore for the evening program.

BOB WAS BAKING MAN-SIZE COOKIES SINCE THAT was who we expected the audience to be. I was just hoping there would be any audience as it was mostly women who came to our events. I wondered if men would be open enough to admit they needed a fix-it book.

I was relieved to see a crowd had already started to gather. My relief ended when the author arrived toiletless and explained there was nothing quite like demonstrating on the real thing, at which point he grabbed his bag of tools and took the group into the men's room.

I pushed to the front of the group standing around the stall and tried to stop him, but he insisted it was win-win. He'd do the demonstration, and the toilet he worked on would be like new. The audience turned to me expectantly.

"C'mon, let him do it," a man said. "I came all the way from Calabasas."

What was I to do? I gave him the go ahead, then left him to his work and went to get the signing table ready.

I walked out of the men's room, and when I glanced up, Barry was standing in front of me.

"The men's room?" he said, giving me an odd look.

"What are you doing here?" I asked, flashing an odd

look back at him. He pointed to the sign for *Unbreak My House*. I knew Barry could fix anything. Like I was really going to buy that story.

"Am I too late?" he asked, nodding toward the empty event area. I started to shake my head and was going to direct him to the men's room, but I'd had something on my mind and wanted to discuss that first.

"It's about the other night. I realized we can't exactly make a clean break. There's Cosmo, and we're going to run into each other like this."

There was just a hint of smile on Barry's lips, which I did my best to ignore.

"I think I've figured out a solution," I said.

Barry stepped closer, apparently assuming it was something about not breaking up after all. "I knew you'd reconsider once you thought about it. One of the things I like best about you is how understanding and forgiving you are." He went to touch my chin, but I stopped his hand.

"Not exactly. I was thinking we could be friends."

Barry froze, then dropped his hand to his side. The smile faded to his blank cop face and his jaw clenched a few times. He didn't seem happy with my suggestion.

"Friends?" he said in a low voice between gritted teeth.

"Yes. It's the perfect solution. Cosmo can continue living at my house, and you can come over and take care of him. And if we run into each other like this, we can be cordial. No problems, no expectations, no commitment."

"And no sex," Barry said, looking disgruntled to say the least.

"Well, yeah, that is sort of the line drawn between friends and something more."

"It's because of the other guy your mother mentioned, isn't it?" Barry said. His eyes had gotten that piercing look.

I felt a *woosh* of air as Dinah rushed up, holding some papers. "There you are. I found some more pictures." As an afterthought she noticed Barry and the fact that we were standing adjacent to the men's room.

She looked at Barry and at me. "Is this a bad time?"

He said yes, and I said no. I noticed he didn't make a move to leave as I examined the prints she'd brought.

"See, there's Camille. Doesn't it look like she's staring at Mary Beth?" Dinah said, pointing at the trajectory of Camille's gaze.

Barry's head shot up at Mary Beth's name. "Molly, what are you doing? Heather told me you were in custody on Catalina, but she seemed to think you had learned your lesson and dropped your detective game."

"It's not a game. I'm telling you this crochet piece is definitely . . ." Then I stopped. I didn't want him to take it from me.

"There's a problem in there," a man said, coming out of the men's room. Just then, I noticed water seeping out from under the door and the rest of the group made a hasty exit. The author came out last and with his head down in embarrassment mumbled something about how I should have told him we had faulty toilets and he'd changed his mind about the signing.

I looked at Barry. "There's another thing about friends. They fix things."

CHAPTER 19

I DIDN'T KNOW WHAT TO DO ABOUT CAMILLE. She had admitted to knowing Mary Beth only in relation to the dance lessons. Yet there she was not ten feet away as Mary Beth wrote her note. Maybe Mary Beth had sensed she was being watched—that whole thing about feeling eyes looking at you. Maybe Mary Beth had looked up and seen her and panicked and stopped writing. In any case, there was definitely more to the relationship than Camille had said.

Still grumbling about his new designation as friend, Barry had stopped the flood in the men's room and fixed the author's error. Dinah had helped me mop up and had reminded me that the caretaker of the Catalina house had said the woman with Mary Beth had resembled her.

"Camille doesn't look like the picture of Mary Beth I saw in the newspaper," Dinah said as we put away the cleaning supplies.

"True, but Purdue was talking about over twenty years ago, and he said something about long dark hair and loose sweats. And he's a man. If we both had long hair and sweats on now he'd probably think we looked alike," I said, standing almost a head taller than my friend.

"What are you going to do?" Dinah asked.

"I can't lock Camille in an interview room and interrogate her like the detectives do. I'm going to have to find another way to get information. In the meantime, I'd like to find out what all the discord at the dance studio was about. I have an idea, but I need your okay."

"YOU HAVE MY BLESSING, BUT I DON'T KNOW IF it will help," Dinah said the next morning as we walked through the Beasley campus to the bungalow where Dinah's class was held. Vincent stood out from the clump of people waiting outside the prefabricated building.

Unlike his fellow students, who looked as though they picked their clothes from the dirty laundry, he had a sense of style. He was all in black with a red bandana tied over his wavy dark hair. Men sure had a lot of head options these days. When I was Vincent's age, everyone just had long, often straggly hair. Now men's heads ran the gamut from dreadlocks or tiny little braids to the intentionally bald look. Then they covered it all up with all kinds of caps, hats and scarves. I wondered if their goal was the same as that of male birds with bright plumage.

Vincent straightened when he saw Dinah and made a little dance move. He snickered when she dismissed it with a wave. I stayed behind as Dinah unlocked the door and went into the classroom. This was one time she was glad to be left out. I was still hearing about how much her teacher advantage had been ruined by taking the dance lesson with Vincent.

I snagged him as he was starting toward the stairs to the bungalow. He gave me a puzzled look as I pulled him off to the side.

"What? You want a dance lesson now?" He had an amused smile.

"No. I'm more interested in information. It looked like there was some disagreement between the managers of the studio and Matt Wells. Do you know what it was about?"

"Is this because of the dead chick?" He regarded me with new interest. "Are you some kind of cop?"

"No, just an interested party. So, what were they arguing about?"

Vincent shrugged. "I'm just a hired hand. I try to stay out of stuff. Just like I never really listened when the dead chick came to the studio and started arguing with Roseanne. Hard to believe those two are sisters. Mary Beth Wells was sure hot, for an older babe."

"Arguing? About what?" I tried not to sound too eager.

He shrugged. "Look, Mary Beth Wells was an owner, but Roseanne Klinger was my boss. I didn't want to get in the middle, if you know what I mean." He glanced toward the door to the classroom. "I gotta go. Ms. Lyons won't cut me any slack, even for talking to you. If you want information, talk to Matt Wells. He knows more than I do anyway. He always has breakfast at Le Grande Fromage. Just don't tell him I told you."

It was already too late for this morning. Besides, I had to get to the bookstore. Someone was coming from the production company to figure if they were going to need to bring in plants and extra power, and since Mrs. Shedd considered the TV shoot an event, it had become my baby.

When I walked into the bookstore, the people from the production company were already moving around, checking light levels and angles. I introduced myself and offered my services, but they seemed almost annoyed by my presence. Finally, I excused myself and said I'd be in the event area if they needed me. Between Barry's surprise arrival and the disaster in the bathroom, I hadn't had time to clean up things from the aborted signing.

As I walked by the children's area, I saw Adele. Story time had ended and the kids were gone. She was sitting at one of the tables working on a filet bookmark. Even if I hadn't known the morning's book was *Being with the Bee Family*, I could have guessed by her outfit. Yellow had become her color of choice lately. She looked like a beehive with the golden yellow cropped pants and long tunic, topped with an oddly shaped hat. I watched the rhythmic motion of her hook for a moment, recalling how I'd tried working on a bookmark at home.

I had finally gotten the hang of working with the tiny hook and fine thread and actually done a couple of rows of filet. It had taken me some time to adjust to working on so small a scale, but once I had gotten going I really liked it. And when I saw what I had done, I was impressed. The fact that the work went so slowly made me appreciate how much time Mary Beth had put into making the panel piece.

I had taken to carrying Mary Beth's panel piece with me all the time. When I'd put away all the unsold books, I pulled it out of my tote bag and laid it on the table. I skipped over the panels I'd already deciphered and went over the rest. The vase of flowers was at least a recognizable motif, though I didn't know what it was supposed to mean. But some of the other pictures just seemed like odd shapes. I tried stepping back as sometimes the images in this kind of crochet work were hard to make out. But even halfway across the event area, they still made no sense. The panel piece reminded me of one of those puzzles where you have to unscramble the letters and figure out a phrase. When I succeeded at those puzzles, the answer always seemed to come in a flash of inspiration. It just wasn't happening here.

I wondered if I would ever be able to figure it out without knowing what was hidden in the fireplace.

Eventually the people from *Making Amends* finished and gave me a schedule of setup and shooting time. We'd actually have to close the bookstore for two days, but having our name in front of millions of viewers was priceless.

I knew the subject of the show was supposed to be a

surprise, but I thought that maybe asking straight out, as if of course I was supposed to know, would make them tell. I pulled over the person who seemed in charge. "I wonder if you'd tell me who the subject of the show is?"

He regarded me with a self-satisfied smile. "Sorry. Nobody but a few insiders know who it is. Who knows, it could even be you."

Me? It had never occurred to me that I was even a possibility.

BARRY WAS AT MY HOUSE WHEN I WENT HOME. He was working with a contractor for the police department installing my new door. The dogs had been fed, and Barry had fixed the light that wouldn't turn off. He'd been missing in action for days, but now that we were just friends, he seemed to be crossing my path constantly. Things must be slow homicidewise in the west Valley.

The She La Las had just finished dinner and were looking over their costumes. I felt as though I were invisible since nobody seemed to notice me. It was pointless to try to cook. My mother had ordered in again, so I just helped myself to the Caesar salad and pasta and took it in my crochet room.

Barry stuck his head in the door and then stepped into the room. He did a double take at all the balls and bags of yarn and half-done projects.

"You're really serious about this hook stuff." He picked up a partially finished rust-colored afghan and then looked at me with a question in his eyes. "Weren't you making that for me?"

"It's almost finished. Just because we're friends now doesn't mean I won't finish it. Friends make afghans for their friends all the time even if they leave out important elements of their lives." That last part just slipped out.

"Your door is back in place," he said, ignoring my remark. I noticed his black eye had begun to fade. I held up my plate and showed him the food and told him there was plenty in the kitchen. He didn't move. "Molly, I can't do the friends thing. Maybe you should just keep Cosmo for now, until I make some arrangements." He put the key down on the arm of the chair. "You know where to find me," he said as he left. A moment later I heard my new front door open and close.

I was still sitting there feeling a little stunned when Dinah called for an update.

"I think we broke up even as friends," I said.

"You had a problem with Vincent?" she said, surprised.

"No. Barry." I re-created the whole scenario for her, and she said she wasn't surprised.

"Men don't like to be friends, particularly when it's a step down from what they've been. I was really calling about your confab with my student, who by the way tried to use his being helpful as a way to get to take the midterm test he missed."

"Obviously, he doesn't know who he's dealing with." I repeated what he'd said about Mary Beth fighting with her sister and how I wished I knew what they fought about. "Vincent was no help. He said to talk to Matt Wells, which is exactly what I intend to do tomorrow."

"Not a bad assignment. And who knows what else may come of it. Now that you're single again," Dinah said, "the world is your man buffet."

"Single again. You make it sound like Barry and I were married. We were just seeing each other."

"If you're not seeing someone, you're considered single in the current lingo," Dinah said.

"What about Mason?" I said.

"I thought you wanted to keep it to a casual dinner now and then," Dinah said.

"Well, yeah . . . It is, well, it was. It's just that . . ."

"What did you leave out?" Dinah repeated, her voice lighting up with interest.

"Nothing. It's about his good night kiss . . ."

"Cheek or lips? You never said," she said with interest.

"Lips and everything else. It was definitely not a casual kiss. Believe me my only interest in meeting Matt Wells is for information."

Dinah had to get back to grading papers and made me promise to report back to her if I found out anything new.

"I thought of something odd," I said, just before hanging up. "Whoever killed Mary Beth had to know she really liked marzipan. If you're going to lace something with poison, you want to be sure the person will eat it. I wouldn't have eaten any of those almond paste apples sent to me even if I hadn't thought they might be laced with something. Marzipan isn't like chocolate. The killer had to know that she not only liked marzipan, but that she loved it enough to guarantee she would eat the candy apples."

"Good thinking," Dinah said. "It sounds like the kind of information a sister would have. By the way, I checked your box of marzipan yesterday and it was full of ants."

"Dead or alive?" I said feeling my stomach tense.

"The little buggers were very much alive. Can I throw the package away now?"

"Then I was right. The gift was just for shock value. Someone wanted to scare me off the case. I'm glad I didn't show it to Detective Heather." I paused for a moment picturing the ants having a field day on the red candy apples. "You better hang onto it for now. Put it in your garage."

CHAPTER 20

VINCENT HAD SAID MATT WELLS ATE BREAKFAST at Le Grande Fromage every morning, but only after I'd left did I realize he hadn't mentioned a time. I had gone over several possible ways to meet him but had finally decided it would be best to let him arrive first. Then I could casually come up to him.

As a result, the next morning I found myself sitting in the parking lot that served the whole bank of stores, watching every car that drove in. The problem with my car, the green-mobile, was that it stood out. In my peripheral vision, I noticed a black Crown Victoria slide into the spot next to me. I slumped down lower in the seat, willing myself to become invisible. No such luck. There was a knock at the window.

I turned the key so I could open the window. Barry leaned in. A whiff of his cologne blew in with the breeze. His shirt was crisp and he was cleanly shaven. I did my best to ignore how good he looked.

"Loitering isn't allowed," he said, pointing to a sign on the wall of the building that warned cars could be towed for various reasons.

I started to protest that I'd just gotten there, but he tossed it off with a dismissive shake of his head. "This is the second time I've been by. I know you've been sitting here for a while. What are you up to now?"

I was going to make some excuse, but just then I saw a black Jaguar pull in and Matt Wells get out.

"I've got to go. I'm meeting someone," I said. Barry followed my gaze.

"The dancer?" he said with a combination of surprise and irritation.

A few minutes later I walked in the front door of Le Grande Fromage. I had taken my time shutting the window and getting out of the car to give Matt time to get inside the café. Barry had stood next to his car watching me. He started to say something several times but then finally got back in his car, muttering something about poor judgement.

Inside the restaurant most of the tables were empty and Matt had taken one in the back corner. I had been thinking about how to start up a conversation with him. I couldn't very well just sit down and start asking questions about Mary Beth. I needed an icebreaker, and nothing was coming to mind. I did okay when it came to climbing in windows and scoping out places, as I had done at the house in Catalina, but actually going up to someone and starting a conversation—let's just say I didn't have my mother's gifts.

I sucked in a big breath of air, forced my lips to curve upward and moved toward his table. He was looking at what appeared to be the layout for a newspaper ad.

"Hi, you might not remember me." I launched into who I was, how I'd taken a complimentary lesson a few days earlier and that I worked at the bookstore. Then I hit dead air. He looked at me, waiting for me to say more, and I looked at him, hoping he'd pick up the slack. Just when I thought I was going to have to slink out of there in embarrassment, inspiration struck. "I have a proposition," I said quickly, pulling out a chair. "I hope you don't mind if I join you."

Matt regarded me with an amused smile, and I realized I had probably come on a bit too strong.

The waitress brought him his fine herb omelette, warm baguette with sweet butter and fresh marmalade and a glass pot of French-press coffee. She handed me a menu, but I said I just wanted a café au lait with a shot of espresso.

Matt pressed the plunger down in the coffeepot and poured the fresh brew in his cup. "What kind of proposition are we talking about?" There was just a hint of suggestiveness to his voice, and I cringed remembering the hair twirling from the other day.

Between the sparkling gray eyes that seemed to carry a warm smile, the angular chin with the unshaven look and the lithe but definitely masculine build, he probably got lots of propositions from potential dance students.

"A business proposition," I said in what I hoped was a cool professional tone. "Having the dance studio closed and being connected to a murder probably hurt your business. I was thinking maybe we could work something out with a book event we have coming up."

Matt's expression sharpened and he sat up. "That's a great idea. What did you have in mind?"

The ball was back in my court. I had to come up with something fast. "We're having an author in who's written a dance-related book. We could include a drawing for some lessons, maybe even a dance demonstration or something."

"I like it," he said before I had a chance to finish. "The drawing for dance lessons is a great idea. And a little dance demonstration to remind everyone we're open and down the street. Could we do something in the next couple of days? Other than you and your friend there hasn't been any walk-in business, and we've had a lot of refund requests from current students. I know it must seem callous to be concerned with business under the circumstances, but we have to keep on going, don't we?" he said.

It was a rhetorical question, and he went back to pressing me for a date until I said I would check my calendar. I reached in my bag and when I pulled out my notebook, Mary Beth's crochet work came out with it. I tried to snatch the plastic bag back, but Matt got it first.

"Where did you get this?" he demanded. He opened the bag, took out the crochet piece and laid it on the table, staring at it. I heard him swallow a few times. "Mary Beth made this. I've seen enough of her work to recognize it." He ran his finger along the image of the Casino. "Catalina," he muttered.

"Do you know what all this means?" I said, trying to keep the excitement out of my voice. He moved his gaze over each image slowly, and I held my breath in anticipation. It turned out he only recognized the ones I'd already deciphered and had no idea what the rest of them were or what the whole piece might mean.

"How did you get this? Did you know Mary Beth?"

"Sort of," I answered.

"Then you must know she loved doing this kind of work. I could never understand why Lance hated it so much. He said watching the movement of the hook made him nervous." Matt let out a sigh. "The habit of working on it only at Catalina was so ingrained that even when he died, she still didn't keep any of her supplies or finished work at the Tarzana house."

The waitress returned with my coffee, and I regretted the interruption.

"Did we come up with a day yet?" Matt said, pointing toward my notebook. I subtly tried to push it to the side while I picked up my coffee cup.

"Does Roseanne crochet?" I said in an effort to turn the conversation toward the information I was after.

Matt shook his head. "She's too busy trying to run everything and everybody." Finally I had my opportunity. I asked him if the sisters got along.

"I thought you said you knew Mary Beth."

"I only knew her a little bit," I said. He nodded and then started spilling information as though he was glad to have somebody to listen.

Mostly he complained about how difficult Roseanne and Hal were. He said Mary Beth had gotten them the job managing the studio, given them lavish gifts and spoiled their children.

"But it was never enough to please Roseanne. I don't think Roseanne could ever get past being jealous that her sister had the money, status and everything else that went along with being Mrs. Lance Wells Jr.," Matt said. He confirmed what Mason had said about Mary Beth working for a caterer. "She worked all the fancy parties. That's where she met my cousin. He specialized in parties."

I mentioned they'd been married a long time. "They never had any children?"

"I don't think that was the plan. But Lance got the mumps shortly after they were married. I think finding himself sterile was just one more reason for him to drink. They talked about adopting once, but when it came down to it, he backed out."

He ate some of his food, and I waited, hoping he would go back to talking. Instead, he picked up the crochet piece and examined it again. "This reminds me of something I found in the office the other day."

"Is it like this with panels and pictures of things?" I asked. He glanced at the piece again and said it was similar.

"I'd really like to see it," I said.

"Sure. I'll bring it when we do the event. How is Thursday?"

I pretended to check my notebook. It wasn't really a calendar, but I knew Thursday was free. We'd finished all the scheduled events, and Mrs. Shedd had instructed me not to schedule any more until after the *Making Amends* taping. So, I agreed to Thursday and suggested maybe I could stop by sooner and have a look at the crochet piece he had mentioned.

He shook his head. Had he picked up on my plan to cancel once I'd seen it? I drained the last of my coffee and got ready to leave. As an afterthought, I turned back.

"I was trying to remember what Mary Beth's favorite candy was. Do you remember?"

He didn't miss a beat. "Marzipan. Personally, I think it's like eating a pillow, but she adored it."

CHAPTER 21

"PINK, WHAT ARE YOU DOING?" ADELE ASKED, walking into the bookstore office.

"I'm looking for a book about dancing by a local author," I said as I typed key words into the computer.

"I have one." Adele went into the break room off the office. She came back holding a copy of *Margaret and the Dancer*. It looked well read.

"Can I look at it?" I said, reaching for it.

"Not unless you tell me why," Adele said, not letting go. Sometimes I thought working in the children's department brought out the child in her. I had decided not to mention the dance event to Mrs. Shedd, but there was no way to avoid telling Adele.

Her face brightened when she heard the plan for the evening. "Pink, you've finally gotten a good idea."

I tried to be offhand in my remark about not mentioning the evening to Mrs. Shedd.

"Why exactly is it that we're having it then?" she persisted.

Knowing it was probably a mistake, I told her about the crochet piece Matt had said he was going to bring me.

"So it's Nancy Jessica Drew Fletcher Marple in action again." Adele paused for a moment. "You know, I'm taking Marple off of that. She was a knitter."

"Here's another dance-related book," I said, reading the computer screen. "It's a diet book called *Dance Your Way to Size Zero*. That's even better."

Unfortunately, Adele recognized a chip when she had one and basically said if I wanted her silence, I'd have to let her be partners with me on the evening. But this time I was actually glad for the help. It took us both until closing time to get everything set up. Grey Fairchild seemed a little confused about why it had taken us two years to call her about a book signing, but she was excited about doing it nonetheless.

When I finally walked outside, I saw Mason standing in front of the bookstore.

"Burning the midnight oil, aren't you, sunshine?" He stepped toward me and hugged me hello. "I called your house and your father said you were working late."

Adele came out behind me and after locking the door, looked at Mason. "Pink, did you and the cop break up?"

I hardly wanted to start discussing my personal life in the parking lot or with Adele, so I did what politicians do. I didn't answer and instead I said good night to her. She *harrumphed* and then went to her car.

"I thought I'd bring this to you here," Mason said, holding out a shopping bag. "I told one of my associates about the blankets you're making for traumatized children and she was so touched by it, she wanted to donate some yarn."

I took the bag and examined the skeins on top. They were the same kind of soft yarn we were using. I was impressed that he had paid that close attention when I'd been talking about the project. "You could have just dropped it off at my house."

"I'm more of an in-person sort of guy," he said with a friendly smile. He brushed a strand of hair the wind had blown across my face. "So, tell me, has my status changed?"

Adele zoomed past us in her Honda and with a warning beep to the traffic on the side street, zipped out of the parking lot. I knew Mason was wondering if he had moved from an occasional dinner companion into the boyfriend slot. I'd given up fighting the title as nothing else seemed any better.

Since I wasn't sure how to answer him, I did the politician thing with him, too, and simply didn't say anything. But Mason was not one to let it go that easy. "Your mother liked me," he said as though if he racked up enough points, he'd win the prize, which oddly enough, in this case, was me.

I couldn't help but smile. "Don't you know in the rules of relationships that is the kiss of death?"

He chuckled softly. "If I'd known that, I would have worn my motorcycle jacket and told your mother she looked old enough to be your grandmother."

"Well, thanks for the yarn and going to all the trouble to get it to me." I made a move toward my car, but he put his hand on my arm.

"A bag of yarn ought to at least get me a cup of coffee."

"Why not? I'm just going home to rehearsal central. Time is getting short and they're in overdrive."

"Great," he said. We walked to my car and I put the yarn in the trunk. "We could go to Mulligan's," he said, pointing vaguely in the direction of the all-night coffee shop a few blocks down on Ventura. "Or my place. You probably don't know this, but I grind my own beans."

"Mulligan's would be fine." I closed the trunk. Since it was a short distance, we decided to walk. We crossed Ventura and moved in the direction of the coffee shop. I glanced across the street. Most of the stores and restaurants were dark. Then I noticed something odd. When I looked toward the second floor, the lights appeared to be on at the Lance

Wells Dance Studio. There was some kind of coating on the window so you couldn't see in, but I could tell the interior was illuminated.

Mason noticed me staring and followed my gaze. I explained it was the dance studio. "I wonder why the lights are on now?"

Mason linked his arm through mine. "It's after eleven. It's probably just the cleaning crew. Don't worry about it." Then he changed the subject. "You probably missed the news since you were working. They did a little bit on me and Rome O'Brien leaving the courthouse." He didn't have to explain the case. Everyone knew about the actress's DUI, leaving the scene of an accident, having an expired driver's license and the cherry on the sundae: slapping the cop who arrested her.

There was a tone of pride to Mason's voice as he told the outcome of her trial. "Everybody was saying jail time for sure, and none of that serving eighty-three minutes and getting released, either. Once she slapped the cop, she kissed that option good-bye. They were talking months, but I got her off."

"But maybe she should have gone to jail," I offered. "It sounds like she did everything to deserve it."

"That's not for me to judge. My job is to present the best case for my clients," Mason said. "And I did. And to make up for it I'm on the board of directors of every charity," he added with a grin.

While he was talking, I kept my eyes on the dance studio and suddenly I had an idea. "Can I get a rain check on the coffee?"

"It's the lawyer thing, isn't it?" Even in the darkness I could see his expression had deflated. "I'm sorry I'm not a white knight like Greenberg. But just remember who you called when you thought you were going to be arrested."

I told him it wasn't that. I had just remembered something I had to do. As we retraced our steps, he saw me looking up at the dance studio window.

"Does it have anything to do with that?"

I tried not answering, but Mason didn't go for it and continued cross-examining me.

I finally took the fifth.

"As your lawyer, I'm advising you not to do anything unlawful, and I'm suggesting a cup of coffee is a better option." When I politely declined, Mason walked me back to my car.

He told me to stay out of trouble—but if I got in any to be sure and call. Then he leaned in and kissed me. It wasn't just a kiss; it was an extremely persuasive argument not to go. I understood why he won most—but not all—of his cases. I didn't change my mind.

"I'm glad you're not a prosecuter," he said as I got in my car.

CHAPTER 22

"WHY DO YOU NEED A MOP?" DINAH SAID WHEN she sleepily answered the phone. "Another emergency at the bookstore?"

"I have a plan. Are you in?" I asked.

"Am I ever not? Where are you?" she said.

When I told her I was parked in front of her house, she had the front door open before I got out of the car.

She was wide awake by now. She pointed to the pile of essays she'd been grading on the couch. Apparently they had bored her to sleep.

While I explained the plan, we raided her cleaning closet. A few minutes later we were heading out the door, each with a pail filled with a bottle of spray cleaner and rags, along with a mop and a story. We were dance-floor cleaner specialists.

"What cleaning crew is going to turn down help?" I said as we started toward Ventura. Dinah's house was just a couple of blocks away from the dance studio, so even with our supplies, we walked. "Besides, it's not like there's anything valuable they have to worry about up there except maybe some dance charts."

"Why are we doing this again?" Dinah asked. I kept glancing around, noticing that the street seemed very parked up. Everyone around here had a garage and a driveway; there were usually almost no cars on the street at night.

"If I can get a look at the crochet piece that Matt Wells talked about, then I can cancel dance night at the bookstore—even though it does sound like a good idea. But it's so last-minute, and Mrs. Shedd particularly mentioned that we shouldn't schedule anything before the bookstore's TV debut."

Figuring the cleaning crew would come in through the back entrance, we went up the stairs from the parking lot side. There, a glass door opened into a hallway that ran between the corporate offices and the dance studio. I pushed on the door, and my heart rate sped up a few notches when it opened. Dinah clutched my arm with her free hand while hanging onto the mop and pail with her other.

Just as I was about to walk in, a man stepped out of the corner, blocking us. He was about thirty, built like a fireplug and wore an ill-fitting dark suit. He finished off the look with buzz-cut hair and a sour expression.

"What do you want?" he demanded.

The shock of seeing someone so menacing made my voice disappear into my throat. I choked out, "Cleaning crew," and feebly held up my pail.

"Nobody told me anything about a cleaning crew," he said in a deep gruff voice. He looked us over a few times. I was just waiting for him to toss us out, which he looked like he could do with ease. When he shook his head with something that looked like regret, I prepared for the worst.

"It must be tough times for you, huh?" he said as he checked us out again. "A couple of old babes like you working two jobs."

At first I didn't know what he was talking about, but

then I looked down at my outfit and over at Dinah's. Our clothes weren't exactly cleaning-crew wear. All I'd thought about were some props, not wardrobe. I had on my usual khaki pants and a black sweater over a white shirt. Dinah wore black slacks, a turtleneck and a corduroy blazer with a burnt orange scarf swirled around her neck. Her earrings almost brushed her shoulders.

Since he seemed sympathetic, I nodded with a wistful touch of sadness. "I just left my other job. And now this. It's been a long day. . . ." All of which was actually true. I had a hard time with outright lies, but I could live with omissions.

He glanced down the hall as if considering whether he should confer with someone else. "If you have to ask somebody to get an okay, could you do it?" I said, trying to sound like I meant it. "We really need to get going on this so we can get in a little sleep before we have to go to our day jobs." Dinah poked me sharply. Yeah, I was taking a chance, but I was betting that offering him the option would make him not take it. And I was right.

A moment later, he shrugged and gestured for us to go on in. "You two remind me of my aunts. Just stick to the offices, okay?"

"That works for me," I said as we started down the hall. I could feel his eyes on my back as I reached for a door handle and prayed it didn't lead to a closet.

"Whew." I sighed when I saw the inside of an office. Dinah came in and shut the door behind us.

"We better move quickly before he changes his mind," I said. The walls were lined with photos. Some were of Lance Wells Sr. in various movie roles. There was one of him cutting the ribbon on the Lance Wells Dance Studio we were standing in. Then there were photos of other dance studios with captions indicating their location: Dallas, Chicago, Buffalo, among others.

A large desk dominated the room, but there was an emptiness about it. The desktop was too neat, the chair pushed in with finality. There were photos on the front, including a wedding photo of Mary Beth and Lance Jr. She looked as though she'd just won a prize; he looked a little drunk. Another photo showed Mary Beth and Matt laughing and poised to dance on the round porch at the house in Catalina. Obviously, this was Mary Beth's desk, and probably Lance Jr.'s before that and Lance Sr. before that.

Recalling the need for speed, I quickly began opening drawers. In a bottom drawer I found several balls of number 10 thread in white and ecru, along with some size 7 steel hooks. There was a partially completed chart on a piece of graph paper. Attached to it was the cutout of a photocopy of a photograph.

"That's how she did it all," I said, reminding Dinah of all the filet pictures on the wall in the Catalina house. "She took a photo and blew up the size on a copy machine, then drew around it on the graph paper, and then she had a chart of meshes and open spaces to do the filet crochet." I looked at the black-and-white image in the copy. It was a little girl with pigtails. "I wonder who she is." I held it out so Dinah could see.

We were so intent on examining the copy, we didn't hear a door open.

"What are you doing here?" an angry male voice demanded.

When I turned I was looking directly into Hal Klinger's face. Gone was the benignly dull demeanor he'd had at our first meeting. He stood taller now and had a much more domineering expression.

I hadn't noticed the other door before. It was ajar behind him and led directly to the studio. Something was going on in there, but he was blocking my view. I could hear the hum of conversation and a whirring noise and then silence, followed by a clank. Whatever it was, it didn't sound like dancing.

At that moment the security guard, still looking like a fireplug in a suit, pushed the door open wider as he came in behind Hal—and I finally saw what was going on. The whirring was the sound of cards being shuffled, and the clank came from poker chips being anted up. I couldn't see how many tables there were, but they all seemed full. A row of people lined the wall. Were they all waiting for their turn to play?

"You have a poker room here?" I said, noticing a snack bar as well.

"None of your business," Hal said, snapping the door shut. He looked at the open drawer with the contents on the desk. "I should call the cops and report a robbery in progress."

I heard Dinah gasp, and I grabbed her hand, squeezing it in reassurance. The fireplug started explaining our cleaning-crew story until Hal told him to zip it.

I looked Hal right in his beady eyes and said, "I don't think you want to call the cops." I pointed over his shoulder. "Which do you think they would be more interested in—two women with small balls of crochet thread or an illegal card room?"

Dinah was leaning against the desk, no doubt recovering from the adrenaline rush all this had caused, and I felt her nudge me. When I looked she was giving me a thumbs-up.

Hal snorted, clearly not happy with the situation. "Okay, suppose we call it even. I let you go and you keep your mouths shut or my friend in the suit, Grant, will pay you a visit."

It sounded like a good deal to me.

Grant put a beefy hand around my arm and Dinah's. He almost lifted us off the ground as he dragged us down the hall. With a shove we were out the door, and I heard the click of a lock. The cool darkness of the parking lot was a relief. Despite my bravado, I'd been barely breathing; I took a deep swallow of air.

"Hey, we forgot the pails and mops," Dinah said, finally regaining her voice. We looked at each other and shook our heads. We weren't going back. Instead, we walked the distance to Dinah's house in record time and collapsed on her couch.

"What was that?" Dinah said.

"Good question." I leaned back and tried to sort things out. Pieces began to come together and I sat upright. "What if Mary Beth didn't mean the building on Catalina, but the word *casino*. Maybe she found out about Hal's side operation. I bet Roseanne doesn't know, or Matt. It's Hal's own little cash cow." I had taken out my little notebook and wrote down *casino = card room*?

"And Hal killed her to keep her quiet and his business going," Dinah said.

"It's certainly a motive. Too bad I didn't ask Hal if he knew what Mary Beth's favorite candy was."

Dinah laughed. "That would have been a tough segue."

CHAPTER 23

I HAD NO CHOICE BUT TO GO AHEAD WITH DANCE night at the bookstore if I wanted to see the crochet piece Matt Wells had. I hoped it was worth the trouble. Mrs. Shedd was in the dark about the plan. Adele still hadn't told on me. She liked the idea of the dance theme too much.

As I got ready to leave for the bookstore, the She La Las rushed into my current bedroom to get into their costumes. They even had a professional makeup artist to do their faces. They were running a full dress rehearsal for my son Peter. Even though his area at William Morris was television and he had nothing to do with personal appearances, my mother wanted his input anyway.

There was a vibe of excitement. My father had rented a small spotlight and arranged some chairs for the miniaudience—the other two husbands were coming, too. Samuel was dressed in a vintage tux and had a keyboard and some electronic device that he'd programmed to sound like a whole band.

Of course, my mother had ordered in food and pleaded

with me to make my California Noodle Pudding. This struck me as a funny turn of events: a mother asking her daughter to make *her* favorite food. I had complied and it was on the counter in all its buttery noodly richness. Noodle pudding is supposed to be a side dish, but I thought it was great for breakfast or by itself as a meal. With all the eggs, butter and sour cream it was kind of rich, but I liked to think the cottage cheese kind of diluted it. I called my version California Noodle Pudding. Along with the standard ingredients, I added almonds and apricot bits. I don't know why they called it pudding, anyway. It was nothing like that chocolate or vanilla creamy stuff.

I had also taken care of the dogs and shut them in the crochet room with my fingers crossed. Dogs didn't play with yarn, did they? It was either that or take the chance they'd trip up the She La Las during their famous dance number.

As I was about to go out the kitchen door, the doorbell rang. My father answered and I heard voices. I recognized Peter's voice and went to say a quick hello. He wasn't alone.

Mason smiled and waved, and I did a double take. I'd never seen him dressed in anything other than gorgeous suits or elegant casual wear. Not tonight. He was all bad boy, wearing an old beat-up motorcycle jacket over beat-up jeans. He had on boots with spurs and was carrying a helmet. He pointed outside with a naughty grin.

A huge motorcycle was parked at the curb.

I would have loved to stay to see what was going to happen, but I had to go.

ADELE HAD GOTTEN BACK TO THE BOOKSTORE before me and she'd been busy.

"What's all this?" I said as I walked toward the event area.

"You have no sense of pizzaz," Adele groaned. "I just gave the place a little dance-party vibe." Bunches of balloons were tied to bookcases. Bob was setting up a table with punch and cookies for sale. The lights had been turned down, and battery-operated candles surrounded the event area. "Pink, couldn't you have dressed up a little?"

Adele certainly had. I didn't know where she'd gotten her ideas from, and I didn't really want to think about it. She had on a long, purple-sequined dress and a purple turban-style hat emblazoned with a sequined A. Her face looked like a porcelain doll's or a Kabuki mask. Her foundation was thick and almost white, and she had on false eyelashes and bright red lipstick applied to give her a Betty Boop bow-shaped mouth.

At that moment the diet book author came through, looking around at the setup. "What's all this?" she asked in a not too pleasant voice.

"We've made it into a dance evening," Adele said before I could speak.

"No, no," Grey Fairchild said, standing by the punch and cookie table. "That doesn't go with my diet plan." She was tall and thin as a capital *I*, and there was a stiffness about her that made me wonder what her dancing ability was like.

Trouble already. Everybody was trying to run the show, but I was the one responsible. However, I thought it might all be academic since the event was so last-minute, I didn't know if many people would show. For once I didn't really care. I wanted the evening to be over with quickly and without disaster. And more than that, I wanted the crochet piece Matt was bringing.

To my surprise people began to come in, including Camille. "I lost my pattern for the bookmark," she said as she approached me. "Do you have a copy?" She glanced around the bookstore. "What's going on?"

I pointed to the sign explaining dance night and said I'd find a copy for her. When I came back, I noticed she'd worked her way over to the event area.

Then Ali came in with an older woman. Both had coffee

from the café, and as usual Ali looked like an advertisement for the wonders of crochet. I loved her crocheted flower wrist corsage. Ali stopped me and introduced me to the woman, her mother. I mentioned what a wonderful addition to the crochet group Ali was, and they decided to stay.

"Are you going to start soon?" Camille said, stopping me. "This is so much fun. I love the way you decorated the bookstore. Too bad my husband didn't come."

I was getting concerned that Matt hadn't arrived, but I knew we had to begin. To buy time I went to the event area and made an announcement about the drawing for dance lessons. The bowl we used for Halloween candy stood waiting with scraps of paper and pencils next to it.

People were still rushing to get in their chances when I introduced Grey and her dance charts. Finally, just as she got ready to start, Matt Wells came in the entrance.

Adele was handling the music and had put on an uptempo CD. Moving to the beat, Grey began to jump around the chart, demonstrating her diet dance. Matt made his way through the crowd to me. I glanced down and saw that he was empty-handed.

"The crochet piece?" I said, trying to keep the upset out of my voice.

He swept his arm toward the front. "I left it in an envelope with the cashier. You can get it back to me when you're finished looking at it. There's no rush. I don't think anybody but you is interested in all her crochet work."

Unfortunately, once people began to notice Matt, they seemed less interested in Grey and her dance chart. Matt had inherited his uncle's charisma along with his dance skills, and it was almost as if there were a spotlight on him.

Grey finally picked up her chart and moved to the side, allowing Matt to take over the center spot. She appeared a bit testy when she saw the response he got. The audience applauded; Camille gave him a little wave.

"It's wonderful to see you're all so interested in dance. There is nothing quite so romantic as couples in perfect step to slow music," he said. Adele put on his music, which was a classic waltz. He did his pitch about the dance studio as he began to move to the music.

"The Lance Wells Dance Studio has developed the perfect teaching method. At our studio, no one has two left feet." He reached out for a partner to demonstrate with. I could see Adele waving her arm, but he took my hand.

The shock must have shown on my face. No matter what he said about nobody having two left feet, I was going to prove him wrong. Hadn't he seen me get my complimentary lesson?

He began counting in my ear and urged me to do the same and just let go and follow his lead. Did he know what he was getting into? Did he really want bruised toes?

I won't take any of the credit. It was all him and I still don't know how he did it, but all of a sudden I was dancing with nary a stomped toe in sight. He whirled me—as much as you can whirl in a pair of no-wrinkle khaki slacks— around the event area and then twirled me out at the end. Everyone clapped and I curtseyed.

"More demonstrations, more dancing," several people called out.

Matt used the opportunity to mention the special they were running on lessons and that they were located just down the street. So far no one had brought up Mary Beth, so the mood stayed light. Then Matt described the free lessons the winner of the drawing would get.

"Are you going to teach?" Camille said, stepping forward from the crowd.

He diplomatically said something about it depending on his schedule before he reached in the bowl and picked the winner. A woman in the back jumped up, a jubilant expression on her face, while everyone else slumped in disappointment.

There was a rustle in the crowd as two people pushed

their way through it. Roseanne got to the front, her face squeezed into an angry pose. "Have you given away the free lessons yet?" she demanded. Hal was a few steps behind. He had gone back to his semiwimpy manner, but he locked eyes with me and for a moment changed into the man I'd seen the other night.

Roseanne didn't wait for an answer. "You're not authorized to give away free lessons or special deals. I'm the owner now. You have to get my okay first."

A gasp went through the group.

Matt tried to keep his voice low. He said something about that statement being premature and lawyers working things out. Then he turned toward the winner and said for her not to worry, she'd get her lessons. Roseanne started to object, but Matt countered that until things were settled he was in charge. Roseanne didn't seem to care that she was making a scene, and the positive mood of the evening was going downhill fast. Nobody likes to be in the middle of an argument. I stepped in and suggested that Matt do a first dance with the winner and as an aside told them to save their conversation until they were in a private place.

Matt threw a dismissive glance Roseanne's way and took my suggestion. Roseanne stood there for a moment, fuming, then grabbed Hal's hand and pushed through the crowd toward the exit. I was curious about the argument and followed, barely aware that the crowd had started to dance.

It wasn't hard to get Roseanne to talk. All I had to do was ask for her side of the story.

"It only makes sense. My sister Mary Beth inherited her husband's portion of the estate and I'm her only family. Matt keeps saying Mary Beth was in the process of changing things so he'd have a bigger share of the business, but I don't believe it. I am not going to be pushed aside anymore. Matt has always made a point that he's an owner and we're just employees. He has always told us what to do and how to do it. He needs to show me some respect now."

Roseanne left in a huff. Hal followed behind, turning

back just for a moment. He tilted his head toward the front window. I noticed the fireplug in a suit standing outside.

I had been so involved with talking to Roseanne I hadn't noticed the music had changed to hip-hop. Not only that, but everybody had begun dancing beyond the confines of the event area. Couples were gyrating between the book-shelves, and people were spinning alone around the display tables. Matt passed me quickly, giving me a thank-you wave on his way out.

In all her purple-sequin glitter and doll-face makeup, Adele was on top of a table in the window grooving to the music—or trying to. She looked like she was having a fit. Nevertheless, people had gathered around and were mimicking her moves while waving their arms as though she were a dancing goddess.

I pushed through the group and tried to get her down. Above the music I heard a loud rhythmic *thwack* and suddenly the area outside the window was bathed in a blindingly bright spotlight. With lights flashing and sirens on, three cruisers stopped at the curb. I twisted toward the front of the bookstore just as the door flew open and someone on a bullhorn ordered everyone to lay on the floor.

Who knew Mrs. Shedd was going to drive by while Adele was doing her table dance and think she was a masked maniac taking over the bookstore?

As things were getting sorted out, Detective Heather and her partner came out of the café, both holding coffee. She glanced around the bookstore and then looked at me with a disparaging shake of her head.

When Mrs. Shedd finally got the whole story, she turned to me and said, "Molly, why didn't you tell me? I love dancing." She did a little spin. "When Mr. Royal was here, we went dancing all the time." Her voice sounded wistful. All along I'd thought he was a pretend partner. It was the first time I believed he might exist.

Dinah walked in as the last police cruiser pulled away and everyone was streaming out. "Did I miss something?"

In all the commotion, I'd forgotten about the crochet piece. As I was getting ready to leave, I looked under the counter by the cashier stand. There was a large envelope with *Catalina* written across the front. When I opened it, a filet crochet piece slipped out. I spread it out on the counter and shook my head. It was in the same style as the one I had. But the motifs? They were all moons and stars and teddy bears.

This piece had been made for a child's room.

CHAPTER 24

"THAT'S WHAT WE SNUCK INTO THE DANCE STU-
dio for?" Dinah said as we both sat staring at the new piece
spread out on her coffee table. It had been quite an evening
and I needed to decompress. No way could I do that at
home with the She La Las jumping around and running
through their number just one more time. Instead, I had
gone home with Dinah.

She kicked off her shoes and unwound her scarves and
picked up the envelope the new crochet panel piece had
come in.

"Maybe it has something to do with the baby the caretaker and the grocery clerk mentioned," I said.

"Maybe, but I for one am disappointed." Dinah rolled
the piece up and put it back in the envelope. "I hope you
have something better to share."

"Actually I do," I said and told her about the standoff
between Roseanne and Matt. "There's some disagreement
about who gets the dance studios. Roseanne seems to think
they are now hers, which brings up the question of what

lengths she would go to get in this position." I mentioned how jealous Matt had said Roseanne was of her sister.

"I bet Mr. Card Room hopes his wife is right," Dinah said. She had made us some chamomile tea and filled two cups with the sweet-smelling liquid from a pot on the table.

"Okay, if Roseanne is a suspect let's see how she fits in with what we know," Dinah began. "We know Mary Beth was poisoned and poison is supposed to be women's weapon of choice. The poison was in marzipan candy. Whoever did it had to know Mary Beth loved marzipan. If someone gave me a box of that stuff with a diamond ring stuck in one of the candies, I'd never find it. It's cute the way they make little fruits and vegetables out of it, but the taste and texture make me gag."

"Okay, so if somebody wanted to poison you, they'd have to use something else," I said with a chuckle. "Since they were sisters, I have to believe that Roseanne knew Mary Beth's candy of choice. But it isn't a stretch to think Hal would, too. Matt said he knew about the almond-paste candy. Except . . ." I took a sip of tea while a problem circulated through my mind. "How does it fit in with the crochet piece and the diary entry?" I took the original crochet piece out of my bag and laid it out.

"She sure did nice work." Dinah fingered the perfectly even stitches.

"That's not the point." I had my little notebook out and was flipping through the pages. I got to the notes I'd taken in Catalina and looked them over again for the zillionth time. Call it a matter of timing, but my eye went from the list under Purdue Silvers's name to the panel with the vase of flowers and for the first time I made the connection. "Omigod, how could I have been so stupid?" I said, leaning closer.

I showed Dinah the list and the panel with the flowers in the vase. "Name that sounds like a flower and then a vase full of them. I bet there is a connection." We peered closer and then stepped back, trying to get a better perspective.

"The only problem is, what kind of flowers are they supposed to be?" Dinah said. "Maybe droopy tulips? Any way you look at them, they don't look like roses."

"So much for Roseanne in that department." I checked out the motif again. "Yeah, they do look more like drooping tulips."

Dinah yawned and said she was too tired to think anymore. My nerves had settled and I was ready to face my house. I hugged Dinah good night and left.

As I walked out, I saw a black Crown Victoria had pulled behind the greenmobile.

Before I got to my car, the motor cut off and Barry got out. This was awkward. If we weren't friends, what were we? And how was I supposed to act?

"I heard there was some excitement at the bookstore. Something about a masked woman in sequins trying to rob the place." He was trying to sound serious, but who could say that with a straight face?

"Adele just got carried away and Mrs. Shedd overreacted." We were standing facing each other now a few feet apart. Even with the streetlight I couldn't see his expression. He seemed to breathe heavily a few times, as though holding something in.

"I happened to drive by your house. There was a motorcycle parked out front." He left it hanging.

"It's Mason's."

"Oh," he said in an unreadable tone.

"Are you stalking me?" I asked lightly. Barry took a moment to consider before answering.

"It could look that way, couldn't it?" He paused again. "Here's what it is. I got in the habit of checking on you when I was out working. I'd drive by your house to make sure everything looked okay. Or if I saw your car—" He glanced toward the greenmobile. Even in the orange street-light, it stood out. "And if there was a call at the station involving you or your area, somebody always contacted me." He breathed a few times and did the clenching thing with his jaw. "Sorry. Habits are hard to kick. I'll have to make a note that I'm not supposed to care anymore."

He let the words hang in the air for a moment and then continued. "Jeffrey is coming back in a week. Whatever differences we have, it doesn't seem fair for him to lose out on his dog. I'll have him call you, if that's all right, and maybe you could work something out."

My heart squeezed. In all this, I hadn't thought about Jeffrey. Barry was right. Even if we couldn't be friends, his son and I still could. Oh what a complicated web this had become.

When I got home, the She La Las were crowded into the den amidst all the living room furniture that had been moved in there, and were watching themselves on the TV screen.

"Samuel got the idea of videoing us so we could see where we need work," my mother said as I walked in. I had to laugh. She was so completely self-absorbed, she hadn't even said hello. Apparently Peter had also given them some pointers. "No matter what he said about not knowing anything about personal appearances, he did know a lot." She mentioned there was plenty of food left in the kitchen and also that if I didn't want any, it might be a good idea to put it away and take the trash out.

"How many more days before your audition?" I asked, trying to keep the edge out of my voice.

"Not enough. We made so many mistakes. Look right there, Lana. You should have gone right and you went left."

As I turned to go, she mentioned Mason. "What was with him? He was so nice before, but tonight he kept scowling at me. And that outfit." She shook her head with disapproval. "I think you better keep looking."

I stifled a giggle as I walked across the house. Too bad I had to miss that show.

"YOU WERE THERE?" CEECEE SAID TO CAMILLE as the crochet group settled in around the event table. Adele had just told her about dance night. "It's probably just as well I wasn't. They would have had a field day getting photos of me in the middle of a raid."

"There wasn't any press," Camille said. She had her work on the table and was trying hard to be part of the group. "It was my first book event, but it won't be my last. We had everything: music, dancing, drama and police action. I couldn't wait to tell Hunnie about it."

CeeCee appeared worried. "Did you tell him I wasn't there?" Camille shook her head and seemed confused by the question. I knew CeeCee was still convinced Camille was spying on her because of the contract negotiations.

"My mother was pretty surprised by all the excitement," Ali said. "I tried to talk her into joining the crochet group, but she's really busy with her cactus nursery." Ali held up another crochet cactus she'd made. "She's going to start selling these, too."

Sheila picked it up and admired it. "I'm okay with missing last night. It sounds kind of tense." She turned toward me. "Have you had any luck figuring out more of the filet crochet piece? The woman at the gym with all the police information said they had decided Mary Beth's sister was a person of interest. And the poison was in the candy apples, just like you said."

"Wow," I said, turning to Dinah.

Camille obviously wasn't listening. She was ruffling through her designer bag du jour and after a moment pulled out a newspaper page and held it up. "I don't know if you saw this." There was a photo of a patrol officer walking a child to a cruiser. Their backs were to the camera, but it was clear what the child was holding. More than holding, he was really cuddling it.

"That's the blanket you made," I said to CeeCee.

"Dear, you're right." CeeCee looked closely at the picture. It was something to see one of our blankets actually providing a little comfort.

Camille stood up. "I am so proud of working with you all. This is so different than just planning charity dinners and having to make sure I don't wear the same dress twice. This is real. It is direct to a person in need. Thank you."

Adele rolled her eyes. Maybe Camille was laying it on a little thick, but after all her years of living like a princess the experience of tangibly helping someone in need had to be new to her, and in its own way, probably wonderful.

"Pink, give us an update. Have you found out Mary Beth Wells's secret or who killed her? You've had enough time."

"Actually, I'd like your opinion," I said, bringing out the original panel piece.

"More about the mystery," Camille said in an excited whisper. "I can't wait to e-mail my kids about this. They think I'm such a joke—that all I do is get dressed up to have lunch with a bunch of women. I want them to know I'm doing something real." Camille put up her hands. "It used to be you wanted to make your parents proud. Now, you have to impress your kids."

I remembered the photo Dinah had shown me of Camille in the background the day we found the bag. Okay, she was sitting there and her name sounded sort of like a flower. It seemed like the perfect time to ask her about it.

I pulled out the print Dinah had made and slid it in front of Camille. "Do you want to tell me about this?"

Camille kept her face down as she stared at the photo. Trying to help her along, I pointed out Mary Beth. "I thought you didn't know her. But it's obvious you're looking right at her."

CeeCee's eyes grew wide with horror, and she started

waving at me from across the table. I knew she was trying to stop me, but I wouldn't look up. Finally, CeeCee came around the table and snatched the picture away.

"Molly, what are you trying to say? That Camille had anything to do with what happened to Mary Beth Wells. Don't be ridiculous."

Camille glanced at the print now in CeeCee's hand. "So that's Mary Beth Wells. I only talked to her on the phone." Camille didn't seem offended. If anything, she seemed kind of excited that someone thought she was a murder suspect.

I pointed to the panel of the vase of flowers and said that someone had mentioned a woman who was connected with Mary Beth had a name that sounded like a flower. "I think this panel might refer to that woman, but Dinah and I can't figure out what kind of flowers they are supposed to be. I wanted to see what the rest of you think."

"Let me look, Pink," Adele said, taking the piece and studying it intently. A moment later she shrugged and pushed it away. "I don't know, maybe snapdragons."

"It can't be snapdragons. It has to be a flower that also sounds like a name," I said.

Sheila suggested they looked like sad tulips.

Ali pulled it toward her. "A flower that is also a name. There are lots: *Rose, Daisy—Camille* sounds almost like a flower," she said, nodding at Camille.

"I think it looks like an iris," CeeCee said finally.

"Iris," Ali repeated with a laugh. "How could I forget to mention Iris? That's my mother's name."

"It is?" I said, forgetting the crochet piece for the moment and giving her all my attention.

"I guess when I introduced her the other night I just said she was my mother." Ali rolled her eyes. "What was I thinking?"

As I looked at her, an idea began to roll around in my mind. In all my thinking about a baby being involved in the secret, I'd forgotten one thing: The baby wouldn't be a baby anymore. The baby would be a twenty-something adult. And there was a twenty-something adult before me with a mother whose name matched the flowers in the filet panel. Could it be that part of the puzzle had been right in front of me all the time? I was almost afraid to ask, but finally I swallowed and spoke.

"How old are you?" I said. She looked at me oddly, and I realized my question must have seemed out of place. I quickly said something about her being about my son's age and wondered if they'd gone to school together. "He's twenty-three and went to Wilbur Avenue Elementary."

"Me, too, on both counts," she said. She thought about it for a minute and asked if his name was Samuel. When I said yes, she made a comment about having a crush on him in second grade.

So she was the same age the baby would be, and her mother's name was the same as the flowers in the crochet piece. My next question would tip the scale.

"When's your birthday?" I asked, holding my breath.

"Pink, what's with all the questions?" Adele interrupted. "We're here to crochet." I wanted to tell Adele to put a sock in it. But it was too late; Ali was already gathering up her things.

"Oh no, I'm late for my dentist's appointment." She was gone in a flash.

Sheila shook her head. "Doesn't she see the pattern? She gets here late and has to leave early because she's late somewhere else."

"Ladies, Ali will have to work out her own time issues. Meanwhile, we're wasting ours," CeeCee said. "Adele, show them your bookmark." Adele displayed the one she'd just finished. Even though she'd ruined my questioning, I couldn't help but be impressed. Her work was beautiful. The bookmark was white filet with a checkerboard pattern. She explained how she'd sprayed it with starch and attached it to a piece of cardboard to block it. CeeCee took out a handful of bookmarks she'd made and showed them off. She went on talking about what a hit they'd be at the next library sale. I wasn't listening. All I could think of was that I had to talk to Ali's mother.

CHAPTER 25

IRIS STEWART RAN THE CACTUS AND SUCCULENT nursery out of her house. It was on one of the big plots of land north of the 101 Freeway. I'd passed it often, though I had never stopped there before. A sign across the front fence beckoned customers: Exotic Cacti and Succulents Nursery. Check us out.

I parked on the street and walked up the driveway. The whole front yard was devoted to cacti and succulents of different sizes and shapes. Most were in pots or some other transportable container, but quite a few were in the ground as part of the landscape. It was a far cry from the lush lawn of the next-door neighbor.

The house was an old one-story white stucco from the time when Tarzana was out in the sticks. Bougainvillea made a roof over the patio across the front. As I reached the house, the front door opened and a man walked out.

"Hi," he said in a friendly tone. He introduced himself as Paul Stewart and explained he was just the advance man. His wife would be out shortly. Although I'd never met him before and had nothing to compare with, his appearance made me think he'd been sick—very sick. His hair was lackluster and his complexion too pale, but mostly it was the way his shirt collar seemed too big for his neck.

As he went back inside, I noticed there was some effort in his walk. Iris almost passed him in the doorway. I had barely noticed her when Ali introduced me to her at the bookstore. Not that saying, "This is my mother," exactly qualified as an introduction.

She was a tall, pretty woman, with shiny brown hair pulled back in a ponytail. She was wearing jeans and a tee shirt with a green plaid flannel shirt on top and had some gardening gloves stuffed in her pocket.

"Are you looking for anything in particular?" she asked in a pleasant voice. When she got closer a flash of recognition crossed her face. "You're Molly from the bookstore. Ali just loves being in the crochet group." She laughed. "Though knowing my daughter, she is probably not too punctual."

We made a little small talk, and I told her how much we all liked Ali. "She's so much fun, and she's stretched our ideas about crochet." I pointed toward the crocheted cactus sitting on the patio table.

"She's a good kid," Iris said. "Things have been a little rough around here, and she moved back home to help me."

I took a deep breath and prepared to proceed. I had no authority to demand information. My best bet was to try friendly conversation.

"I'm thinking of landscaping part of my yard with succulents. I saw something I like at the home of an acquaintance of mine. She said she got her plants here. I don't know if you remember her—Mary Beth Wells?" I watched Iris's face to gauge her reaction to the name. There was a flicker that was quickly replaced by confusion.

"She must have gotten them somewhere else. I don't recall the name," Iris said too quickly to be believable.

I persisted. "I'm sure this is where she said she got them. Maybe you don't remember her. She was tall with golden blond hair."

But Iris dismissed the comment and gestured toward the front yard. "Why don't you look around at what I have and maybe you'll see what you're looking for." She followed me as I began to walk through the rows of plants.

A car pulled into the driveway and two teenage girls got out. They waved and headed inside.

"Are those Ali's sisters?" I asked.

When she said they were, I commented that they were quite a bit younger than Ali.

"And your point is?" Iris replied with the beginning of an edge in her voice.

"No point, just an observation." I stopped at a pot filled with low-growing fleshy rosettes that had a reddish color. "I think this is it. Mary Beth had one in a pot in her house on Catalina." Glad that I was wearing sunglasses, I again watched Iris for her reaction. She showed none.

"I hear it's very nice there." Iris picked up the pot. "Did you want to get sempervivum?"

Another car drove into the driveway. This time Ali got out. As soon as she saw me, she came to join us. "You came to the right place. My mother's plants are the best."

But her willingness to talk left a lot to be desired. So far I'd gotten nothing but the name of the plant I was holding. Sure, it was obvious Iris knew Mary Beth, but as long as she denied it what could I do?

"I forgot to ask you earlier," I said to Ali, trying another tactic. "We have a thing at the bookstore for people's birthdays. We send out discount coupons. If you tell me yours, I can add it to my file."

"That's so nice," Ali said. She sounded so genuine I felt bad about deceiving her and decided right then to actually start a birthday-discount program. "My birthday is December 19," she said. "I'm just barely a Sagittarius."

Ali's birthdate was in sync with the diary entry. I decided to push the envelope and ask one more question. "Were you born here in Tarzana?"

"Actually, I was born on Catalina."

Iris appeared more uncomfortable but said nothing. Ali spoke for her. "Ali is just my nickname. It's short for Catalina. Get it—Cat-*ali*-na?"

"I'm sure you're in a hurry," Iris said, taking the pot and heading for the patio. "Let me just write this up." She looked for me to follow her, but Ali intervened.

"While you write it up, I want to show Molly the afghan I'm making."

Before Iris could stop her, Ali had taken me inside. It was dark after the bright sun of the front yard. Paul was sitting in a recliner watching television. Ali led me to a small bedroom that looked out on the backyard. While I was trying to think of something brilliant to ask her, Ali brought out her work. It was beautiful. She'd made multiple creamy off-white squares, each with the pattern of an angel in the center. She was in the process of joining all the squares.

"It's for my mom and the most traditional thing I've ever made," Ali said, holding some of the squares together so I could see how the completed project would look.

"You have to bring that to show the group," I said.

As we were walking back through the living room, I noticed a glass-fronted frame hanging on the wall. When I stepped closer, I smiled and took it down. Ali gave me an odd look as we went outside.

I stepped up to Iris and held out the frame. "I know you know Mary Beth, and no doubt quite well since she made this for you." Confused, Ali turned to Iris, who reached out and angrily grabbed the frame from me, muttering something about how she'd forgotten all about it. Behind the glass was a filet picture of a cactus in a pot with a tiny *MB* embedded in the bottom of the cactus. The wishing well in the panel piece was signed the very same way, I was sure it was Mary Beth's artistic signature.

"I think you better take your succulent shopping some-where else," Iris said, giving me a shove as she held my arm and walked me to the gate.

CHAPTER 26

"SHE THREW YOU OUT?" MASON SAID. FOR SOME reason he found that amusing, then he apologized. "I know this is serious, but I can't imagine you pushing the Stewart woman so far she'd toss you out."

"Believe me, I did and she did. I caught her in a lie and I showed her."

Mason and I were on the way to a dinner for the Entertainment Fund for Kids Kamp USA. I'd called him shortly after my run-in with Iris and asked him if he could get some background information on Iris Stewart and anything more on Matt Wells. He'd dangled getting it in exchange for my going to the dinner with him.

"If you come it'll be fun instead of a duty," he'd said. How could I turn down a compliment like that? Besides, I really wanted the information. After a brief stop at home to change, I drove to Mason's and waited while he fed Spike and took him for a walk. Then we drove into the city in his car. I hadn't been over the hill for awhile.

In the old days, it was a long trip because of the poor roads. Now it was a long trip because of the traffic.

"You can tell me now," I said, referring to the information I'd asked for.

"Patience, patience," Mason said, steering his car through a twisty canyon.

"What? Are you afraid if you tell me now, I'll jump out of the car?" I asked, laughing.

"It would be a long walk home," Mason teased. "Does this make me your assistant?" Mason chuckled. "I haven't had so much fun in a long time. First, I get to be a bad boy and antagonize my girlfriend's mother, and then I get to be her secret information source."

Girlfriend? I swallowed. Then I just let it go. Why make an issue out of a word I wasn't sure applied. I was having fun, too.

"I think I might just have to wait until the way home to share what I found out. Or even better, save it for drinks at my place." Mason was joking, but he was also seriously trying to lure me into his house.

"The ride home is as far as I'm going to go," I said. My voice was light, but there was just a touch of seriousness and he knew what I meant: *Not yet.*

We pulled into the driveway of the Beverly Hilton, and a valet whisked the car away.

Mason took my arm and led me down the walkway to the main ballroom. As we entered, we passed through the area set aside for the silent auction tables.

The ballroom was filled with well-dressed people mingling over cocktails. Among the crowd I noticed several familiar faces, people I hadn't seen since Charlie's funeral. I met the gaze of one man and started to smile, but he quickly looked away. I'd lost my status when Charlie died— but apparently not permanently. I almost laughed when the same person looked back and saw who I was with. He and his wife came over and gushed about how nice it was to see me again. Ah, the awkwardness of being a widow.

Mason grabbed my hand. "Let's get a drink."

We changed direction and squeezed around a clump of people. I felt someone touch my arm.

"Welcome to my world," Camille said. "Hunnie, look who's here." She nudged her husband and he turned toward me.

"It's the bookstore lady," he said with barely a glance. But when he saw who I was with, his demeanor changed. Clearly, being with Mason made me somebody who mattered, at least to these people.

Mason picked up on what was happening. "Don't take it personally," Nodding toward Hunter and Camille, who were standing by their table greeting all who approached, he said, "Let me give you a refresher course in the politics of power." He pointed out a couple and explained the guy was a William Morris agent like my son. He and his girlfriend were moving around. They'd stop, say a few words and move on. They were working the room. Then Mason pointed to Camille and Hunter. Sure enough, they stayed put and a continuing line of people came up to them.

"There's lots of congratulating," Mason said. "It's been a long haul for him, but Hunter finally got the brass ring. Next week, he's officially being made president of Rhead Productions. Everybody wants to be on his good side."

Statuswise, Mason seemed to be somewhere in the middle. Some people approached him, and some people he approached. After we got our drinks, he continued socializing while I went to check out the silent auction. It was the usual things: a walk-on part on a sitcom, signed scripts of popular shows and a lot of spa days and golf vacations. One item surprised me: a small crocheted scarf donated by Camille. The uneven stitches and wavy edges showed it was very much a beginner's first project. And yet the list of bidders had already filled the page. Yes, there was plenty of power politics going on.

Camille caught up with me. She was just checking on her scarf. "You don't know what this means to me. This is the first time I've ever donated something I made. It makes me fee so authentic."

I glanced at her dress. Like an actress at the Academy Awards, she was wearing a gown from the "Who are you wearing?" category. I looked down at my dress. Nobody was likely to ask me who I was wearing. More likely they'd ask, "*What* are you wearing?" in a tone that made clear it wasn't a compliment. It was my standby black dress, which I now realized was dated. If I was going to go to more of these, I'd have to buy some new clothes. I stopped myself. If I was thinking about going to more evenings like this, then I was thinking seriously about Mason's remark. Did I want to be his girlfriend?

The jury was still out when the evening ended. As we drove back to Tarzana, I turned my attention away from my future social life and refocused it on the information I'd asked Mason to get. He played his game again, trying to withold it until we went to his house, but I held strong and he backed down.

"Okay, here is what I found out. The property where Iris Stewart has her home and business is in the name Iris Woods, and she's owned it for almost twenty-three years. Iris married Paul Stewart twenty-one years ago. Adoption papers were filed and Catalina Woods became Catalina Stewart."

I was rushing to write down what he said. We were standing outside my car parked in his driveway. "It's kind of cold out here. You must be freezing," he said, looking at the lacy mohair shawl draped around my shoulders. "Wouldn't you rather be doing that in front of a nice fire?" He tilted his head toward his house. Okay, maybe he had backed down, but he hadn't given up. When I asked about Matt Wells, Mason shivered and said he was getting cold. I offered him the inside of my car, but he laughed and declined.

Mason gave in and repeated Matt Wells had been married three times and was currently single. He had four kids ranging from elementary-school age to late teens. "Which amounts to a lot of child support," Mason said. "He's currently living in a luxury condo in Encino, and his credit rating is kind of shaky."

"In other words, he really needs a bigger piece of the dance studios," I said. Mason nodded in agreement.

"Well," I said, looking toward my car. "Thanks for all the info."

"My pleasure," he said, taking me into a warm embrace. Sharing his body heat felt good. Too good, and I knew staying wrapped in his arms was only going to lead to trouble, so I pulled away and said good night.

"You let Mason be your sleuthing partner again," Dinah wailed. "I thought that was strictly my job." She paused for only a second, then said the least I could do was fill her in on everything. I had driven to her house after leaving Mason.

On the coffee table Dinah had the usual stack of papers waiting to be graded, but there was something else.

"Yay, you've gotten past the kids leaving," I said, holding up the form from Date-A-Lot. "You're ready to work on your social life. Good for you!"

She deflected the comment by asking about Mason and me. I told her the truth. "He's fun to be with, and the fact he doesn't want to turn it into anything too serious is appealing."

"And the downside?" Dinah prompted.

"I'm still getting over Barry. And it's messy because of the dog and his son Jeffrey. Jeffrey leaves and we're a couple, and he comes back and we're not even friends. I did tell you he rejected the friend idea and even gave me back his key, didn't I?"

"Several times," Dinah said. "Okay, so what do you think the information Mason gave you means?"

"The most obvious is that Paul Stewart isn't Ali's father,"

I said. "And somehow Iris had the money to buy the house for the nursery. Things were cheaper back then, but that was still a sizeable investment for someone so young."

"Do you think she was blackmailing Mary Beth? Maybe that's it. Mary Beth decided to go public so she couldn't be blackmailed anymore."

"I considered that, but Iris doesn't seem the blackmailing type." I wasn't sure what the blackmailing type was, but I doubted that the hard-working owner of a plant nursery fell into the category. "Maybe Mary Beth gave her the money for the down payment."

"That's a lot of money to give," Dinah said. "There must have been something she wanted in return."

We went back and forth, getting nowhere. I had no choice but to go home and face the She La Las. Did those women ever stop practicing?

The weather had turned cold and damp by the time I drove home. I had narrowed things down a little. There wasn't a doubt in my mind that the secret Mary Beth had wanted to settle focused on Ali. I was also sure Ali didn't know what it was, but her mother did. How far would her mother go to keep the lid on it?

At home, I checked my phone messages. The third one made the hair on my neck stand up. I couldn't tell if it was a man or woman. Just a harsh whisper telling me I was asking for trouble.

My father came in and handed me a large padded envelope with my name written in red. He said it had been on the front porch when Lana and Bunny arrived.

I ripped back the top with shaking hands. Something slid out and hit the ground.

When I looked down, I screamed. A big dead fish with a marzipan apple in its mouth had landed on my foot.

CHAPTER 27

"PINK, WHAT DID YOU DO?" ADELE DEMANDED, rushing up to the event table as I was setting up for the group. I stopped what I was doing and fortified myself with a big sip of my red eye.

I was still recovering from the previous night. It hadn't been pretty. My father kept asking about the dead fish, and I didn't have a good answer. Telling him it was some kind of joke didn't work, partly because my son Samuel had told him I'd gotten involved in a couple of murder investigations.

"Molly," he'd said, shaking his head. "I know you've had to make a lot of adjustments since Charlie died, but what are you doing getting mixed up with murder?" He shook his head again. "I'm not going to tell your mother."

I had refrained from voicing my thought that she probably wouldn't pay attention anyway. If it didn't have to do with the She La Las and their upcoming audition, she wasn't interested. Then I had told my father not to worry and that I had the business with the fish under control.

"Well," Adele said, glaring at me from across the table.

"What are you talking about?" I said, putting the box of yarn out. Sheila arrived and took off the jacket of her black suit before stretching her arms and sitting down.

"I'm talking about Ali quitting the group. She wouldn't give any details. She said you would explain." Adele dropped into a chair. CeeCee put her things on the table and stared at Adele.

"What? Ali quit the group? She was such a nice addition. What happened?"

"Ask Pink," Adele said with irritation.

"What's going on?" Dinah asked as she set down her things and checked out Adele's stormy expression. "Did somebody call us a knit group?" Dinah said, smiling. Adele glared in response.

CeeCee was used to people coming and going in the group and recovered immediately. She glanced up and down the table. "Camille's not here, huh?" Letting out a sigh of relief, she announced, "I think I'll go and get some of Bob's special cookies and a latte with whole milk. Anybody else want anything?" When no one responded, Cee-Cee stayed put. All eyes were on me. They were waiting for an explanation.

"You remember how Ali mentioned that her mother's name was Iris like the flowers in Mary Beth's crochet piece?" Everyone nodded but Dinah. She already knew where I was headed. "I thought it might be just a coincidence, but I decided to talk to her mother."

I described my visit to the cactus nursery and my conversation with Iris. "She denied knowing Mary Beth Wells and I proved she was lying."

"Ouch," CeeCee said. "Dear, that sort of thing never goes over well. I remember a role I had in *The Devil's Mistress.*" She looked at us for recognition of the title and continued. "It was a period piece, all bustles and rustling dresses. Thank God that fashion hasn't made a comeback. I played the sweet sister who got killed for doing exactly what Molly did. My sister in the movie kept saying she'd never met the grand duke, and my character found a letter the sister had gotten from him that proved she was lying. She smothered my character with a pillow."

All eyes were back on me. "No pillows on my face last night, just a creepy whispering phone call and a dead fish with a marzipan apple in its mouth."

That information elicited a couple of *ewws*. Sheila was the only one looking away. She was intent on her blanket, and I could see her stitches getting tighter with each movement of her hook. Suddenly she set it down, rushed over and started hugging me. Tears were streaming down her cheeks. "You have to drop it, Molly. I don't want anything to happen to you. I can't let anything happen to you."

I hugged her back and told her not to worry. With her grandmother dead, Sheila was alone in the world and overburdened by work, school and an unpleasant living situation. The group was her family, and I was the one she felt closest to.

I could feel Dinah's eyes on me. She'd known about everything except the dead fish and the phone call.

"That's why I don't get involved when people drop things like this on me. Just because I'm on a show about solving problems doesn't mean it's my job to solve them," CeeCee said.

"I don't think Mary Beth left it for you to figure out. From what I've found out, Ali is at the center of whatever Mary Beth was trying to fix. I think she left that panel piece with us because she saw Ali was in our group," I said.

"*Was in our group* is the operative phrase, Pink," Adele added. "It sounds like you've made a mess of everything. Let's see. We lost a wonderful member of the group, you insulted her mother, someone is dropping off dead things at your house—and you still haven't figured out what the crochet piece means."

Sheila was still hugging me when Camille showed up. She was breathless and either ignored that she had arrived in the middle of something or didn't notice. I was voting for the latter since she immediately launched into a speech telling everyone how much her scarf had gone for at the silent auction.

When they heard the amount, the group wanted details on the scarf, apparently thinking the quality and design had determined the high price.

CeeCee and I looked at each other over the table. We knew the scarf would have sold even if it had been made of knotted string. Camille's name was the attraction, not the scarf.

Camille described how the person with the winning bid had come over to her and complimented her on her crochet work. Then she pulled out some photos and passed them around. An ambitious-looking dark-haired man was wearing the scarf and standing between Camille and her husband. The scarf guy's eyes were on Hunter. "It was truly rewarding to feel something I'd made could do so much good," Camille said, finishing her story.

"Weren't you going to the café?" Dinah asked CeeCee. CeeCee glanced toward Camille and said something about having changed her mind.

Eduardo came in later and apologized all around for being MIA. But he hadn't been idle. He had two of the blankets finished and lots of bookmarks. I was amazed how with his big hands he could maneuver the tiny hook and thin thread.

Dinah pulled her chair close to me. "What are you going to do?"

I sighed and told her I didn't know. "The worst of it is, much as I hate to admit it, Adele's right. I have made a mess of everything and gotten nowhere."

Dinah tried to make me feel better and regretted she couldn't hang around after, but she had office hours to get to. We promised to catch up later.

After the group left, I cleared away our table and chairs and then kept busy around the bookstore. While I was putting out copies of the newsletter I'd written I noticed Mrs.

Shedd was in. Ever since the television show had arranged to film there, Mrs. Shedd had been around much more. In the past, she usually came in before we opened and after we closed.

I walked over to her as she was supervising the removal of all the easy chairs we had spread around the store. "They're being upholstered," she said, showing me a swatch. She'd changed the artwork, too. Before there had been some prints that I had barely noticed. Now there were framed photos of the store, some customers, Bob and his cookies and the transformation of the street over the years. I had to agree with her thinking. The local photographs made the bookstore feel more personal.

The one good part of having my parents staying with me was that my father was happy to take care of the dogs. So, I had no reason to rush home. I stayed until the bookstore closed.

It was dark and cold when I drove up my driveway. I felt a certain apprehension as I walked across the backyard. Would there be another phone call or gift on my doorstep?

The house was quiet when I walked in. All the take-out food had been put away. I peeked in the living room, wondering if the She La Las had fallen asleep in midpractice. I wasn't ready for who I saw.

The couches, tables and chairs were still piled in the den. The only seating available in the living room was a bunch of folding chairs up against the wall. My parents were in two of them, and Barry was in a third with Cosmo draped over his lap.

"What?" I said, walking in. My gaze stayed on Barry, and I supposed my expression wasn't exactly welcoming.

"They called me," he explained. He looked exhausted, his tie was off and his shirt open at the collar. His eyes were heavy and his beard overgrown. The black eye my father had inadvertently given him was fading but still visible.

"I was on my way home. Thirty-six hours straight." His eyes met mine. My immediate thought was sympathy, but then I reminded myself that had we still been seeing each other, I would have been wondering where he was and probably worried. And, I also reminded myself, he had left out a huge chunk of his life.

My father got up, went to the kitchen and came back with a freezer bag. As he passed I saw the silvery dead fish with the marzipan apple still in its mouth. He showed it to Barry.

"I heard the phone message," my mother said. "We were worried, so we called him."

Barry blew out some air and looked at me. "What have you gotten yourself in the middle of this time?"

"She's gotten in trouble before?" my mother said.

First, I was surprised and maybe a little pleased that my mother seemed so concerned. She'd always been self-absorbed, but with the She La Las rehearsals she'd gone over the top even for her. Then I was upset. I didn't want my parents to worry, and it was embarrassing to have them call my ex-boyfriend about a dead fish with some almond-paste fruit stuck in its mouth.

I gave Barry a little shake of my head, hoping he wouldn't start giving details.

"Didn't you at least offer him some food?" I said, trying to change the subject.

Barry looked at the dead fish and made a face. "If that's what you had in mind, no thanks."

"Okay, intervention over," I said to my parents. "I'll tell Barry about it myself."

They looked relieved and went into the bedroom. My father came back a minute later and pressed a tube of something in Barry's hand.

"It's moisturizer with a little color. It ought to camouflage your eye."

"Makeup?" Barry said, eying the tube with discomfort.

"It's not makeup," my father insisted.

I took Barry into the kitchen. He was still holding the now-frozen dead fish and the makeup, and I wasn't sure which one upset him more.

I pointed toward the trash, but he suggested I might want to hang onto it for now in case it turned out to be evidence. Then he opened the freezer and popped it back in, before putting the makeup on the counter and leaning against it. Cosmo had followed us into the kitchen and parked himself next to Barry's leg.

I made him a plate of the leftover take-out food and then heated up a square of the noodle pudding. The buttery smell filled the kitchen.

He nodded when I handed it to him. "Looks homemade. Your mother?"

I laughed. "No. Me."

We sat down at the kitchen table, and he began to eat ravenously. I noticed he went for my noodle pudding first. He nodded as he chewed and sighed with pleasure. Then he went back to his tough expression. "I am not going to ask you what's going on. I know that you're still mucking around in the Mary Beth Wells case. The fish is a warning. Drop it."

I nodded. I had my pride and wasn't about to let on that the whole case was a disaster anyway.

Barry finished the noodle dish and moved on to the corned beef sandwich, potato salad and coleslaw I'd given him. I offered him something to drink. "I can help myself," he replied, getting up. This was all too weird. So familiar and strange at the same time. He opened the refrigerator, and I saw him do a double take.

"Who's the beer for? Your new boyfriend."

"No, it's for my father. He likes to drink a bottle at night. It helps him sleep. Feel free to have some."

"How's it going with the dancer?" There was an edge to Barry's voice as he came back to the table with the amber bottle. Cosmo was following his every move.

"I'm not going out with the dancer," I said, hoping to end it.

"Who then?" Barry was looking directly at me. He was Mr. Detective now, interrogating and confrontational.

"You don't want to know," I said, breaking eye contact and looking down.

Barry put down the sandwich. He didn't have to say the name for me to realize he knew it was Mason. When he had finished eating and drank most of the beer, he looked down at the black mutt and ruffled his fur. His face softened for a moment, but it was back to tough cop when he looked at me. "Do you have any idea who the caller was or who might have left the gift?"

I groaned. There were so many possibilities.

"Just spread the word that you gave up," he said, rising to leave.

There was an awkward moment while we stood facing each other and his gaze held mine. "I don't know if it matters to you, but I contacted my daughter."

He thanked me for the food and went to the kitchen door. Cosmo tried to follow, but Barry stepped out quickly, closing the door before the dog could get out. Then Cosmo sat down in front of the glass door and whined.

CHAPTER 28

THE PHONE CALLS, THE FISH AND MY PARENTS
concern had gotten to me. Maybe it was time to drop it. So
I did as Barry suggested; I told everyone I was stumped by
Mary Beth Wells's secret and who killed her and I was
giving up. Only Dinah asked me if I was sure. Nobody
even mentioned the crochet piece the next time the group
got together. For once all we did was work with yarn and
make small talk.

When I got home that evening, my mother was at the
kitchen table drinking her hot water, lemon juice and honey.
Her hair looked newly done and her nails manicured.

"Sit, sit," she said after I'd taken care of the dogs.

I listened and the house was quiet.

"No one's here," she said. "We've practiced as much as
we can. We're as good as we're going to get. Now we need
to rest our voices and our feet so we'll be fresh for the audition."

I sat down on the bench across from her. She was nurs-
ing her drink and explained my father had gone out.

"I know our visit has been a little disruptive to your house, and I wanted to thank you," my mother said.

I said the usual baloney about it not being any trouble, and she shocked me by telling me what a good daughter I was. I never knew she noticed.

"So fill me in about these murders you've been involved with," she said, setting her cup down.

"You really want to know?" I asked.

"I wouldn't ask if I didn't want to know," she answered matter-of-factly. Apparently she had never noticed that we hadn't had a lot of mother-daughter moments. I told her I'd been in the middle of a couple of murder investigations and solved both cases.

My mother's face brightened into a laugh. "Who'd ever figure you'd end up as an amateur detective?"

I shrugged.

"Did you ever get sent a dead fish before?"

"No. This was a first." I kept waiting for her to turn the conversation around to herself, but she seemed genuinely curious and asked for the details of what had led up to the special delivery. "Are you sure you really want to know?" I asked again. She rolled her eyes and nodded in response. I went into my work room and got the package with the crochet piece and the notes. I had stopped carrying it with me. What was the point? When I laid everything out on the table, she leaned closer for a better view.

"Oh, I remember this thing. That's the Casino Building." She examined the first panel and then glanced over the rest of them. "What about the others? What are they supposed to be?"

I started going over the filet crochet designs one by one. I pointed out the odd house with the cone-shaped roof and the three panels around it, all with cats. "I found this house a short distance from the Casino and there were cats everywhere." I indicated what I'd first thought to be the Arc de Triomphe. "This fireplace is inside that house and now

I'm pretty sure the mantelpiece has a secret compartment with something hidden in it."

My mother's fascination was obvious as I continued on. I explained I thought the motif of the figure with the bow and arrow was meant to signify Sagittarius and referred to a baby's birth sign. "And I know this vase appears to be filled with drooping tulips, but they are supposed to be Irises and are a clue to the baby's mother's name."

I turned the piece around so the wishing well in the adjacent panel was recognizable. "See the *S* hanging from the roof. If you add that onto well you get Wells, which is the last name of the person who made this."

My mother found the *MB* and nodded with enthusiasm. "I get it. This was like her signature. Very clever of you to figure that all out," she said. Had my mother just given me a compliment? I told her the rest of it—how the baby turned out to be somebody in the crochet group.

"And I thought your only problems had to do with dating," my mother said when I had finished.

My mother fingered the stitches on the piece. "This is really crochet? I thought crochet was just used to make those multicolored squares and shawls."

She picked up the diary entry and read it over:

The island is decorated for Christmas. All the colorful lights brighten up the short cold days, but it doesn't help me feel any less sad. I hate to have to say goodbye even for a short time. I know things will work out and we will be back together again for keeps. Tomorrow I go back as if nothing has changed. I know I am doing the right thing.

"This is about heartbreak and hope," she said. I must have given her an odd look. "Molly, it's like when somebody gives me lyrics to a song. I read over the whole thing to see what it's about before I worry about each line. Then when I go back it's easier to get the meaning. The person writing this is sad about having to say good-bye to someone." My mother flipped the page and read the line on the back. "Oh, she's saying she's going to miss the baby."

"What?" I said, and my mother pointed to the line on the back: *Catalina, I'm going to miss you.*

Dinah and I had taken that line to mean the island.

"You said that's what the baby's name was, didn't you? But she has hope they'll be reunited," my mother said and then appeared confused. "If it's her baby, why is she having to say good-bye anyway?" Before I could tell her that Mary Beth wasn't the mother, my mother looked at the crochet piece again.

"What about these other panels?" Her hand brushed the square with the plain ring and then the divided circle before moving on to the double-sized panel with the aqua rectangle. Her finger traced the open area in the middle.

I raised my hands, palms upward, in the universal I-don't-know sign.

My mother continued to study the panels and then scrunched her face in disapproval. "Why would somebody put a switch in with all this other stuff?"

Just as I got out a "huh?" my mother held the panel up next to the light switch in the kitchen. It took a moment of my eye going back and forth, but then I saw that the panel image and the light switch were an exact match. How could I have missed it? "Mother, you're a genius," I said, kissing her cheek.

"I have my moments," she said with a pleased smile. "As long as we're playing detective—I think your father is having an affair with Belle Gladner." When she got through laying out the facts, they were so ridiculous, I had a hard time not laughing. Her evidence: My father had gone shopping for a shirt without her and mentioned running into their former neighbor at the drugstore and noticing that her skin looked very good. My mother was back to thinking the world revolved around her.

DINAH MET ME AT CAITLIN'S CUPCAKES IN THE morning. "Think about it," I said, discussing the crochet panel. "Switch. Like maybe switch Iris and Mary Beth and—"

"Ali's mother is really Mary Beth," Dinah said, finishing my thought. We were sitting at the counter that ran along the window.

"I think that's Mary Beth's secret," I said.

"But there's no way to prove it," Dinah said. I looked out the window and down the street. I saw Ali and Iris heading toward the bookstore.

"Maybe there isn't a way to prove it, but there is a way to prove Iris isn't her mother." I got off my stool. "I have a plan."

"I guess that means you're back on the case," Dinah said, rushing after me.

It took some fast action, but when we got to the café at the bookstore I got Bob to make up a tray of iced tea samples. Then I got our head cashier, Rayaad, to carry the tray around the bookstore.

Ali and Iris were in the nature section, and I slipped behind a bookcase. As Rayaad headed in their direction, she glanced over her shoulder at me. I gave her the nod. I watched from my hiding place as our cashier stopped next to them and offered the samples. Other people came out of nowhere and took some of the small cups, but Ali and Iris shook their head. Rayaad looked back at me and I waved her back at them. She offered again, and persisted. They finally each took a cup and then walked away.

Dinah was right behind me as we shadowed them from the other side of the row of bookcases. We kept catching glimpses of them whenever we passed an aisle. They were drinking. Finally, they appeared to drain the contents and be looking around for someplace to discard the cups.

Before I could get Rayaad to swing by and pick them up, Iris found a trash can. Oh no. There went my plan. I'd never be able to pick out their cups from all the other trash. Iris pushed on the small metal door, but it didn't move.

Hallelujah, somebody had forgotten to empty the can. With a shrug, Iris set her cup on top and then Ali did the same. I forced myself to count to ten before I made my move to get the cups.

But ten wasn't enough. Iris turned back just as I snatched them.

"Sorry," she said in a pleasant voice, and then she realized who I was. "Give them to me and I'll throw them somewhere else," she said, walking back to me. Her face had settled into concern.

"I have it covered," I said, putting my hands behind my back and hoping there was enough saliva on them to do a DNA test. I even knew where to send them thanks to the dog DNA author's event we'd held.

"But I insist," she said. All pretense of pleasantness had drained from her voice. Our eyes locked and I knew she knew there was more than garbage at stake.

"Give them to me or I'll make a scene. I'll say you stole them from me." She sounded shrill and panicky.

"I'll call the cops for you," I said. "When you throw something away, it's no longer yours. And I have a witness." At that, Dinah stepped out from behind the bookcase and waved.

"I need to talk to you," Iris said, finally relenting. Ali had been watching the whole interchange and regarded her mother with concern. Iris told her it was okay and then urged her to go on to another department and said she'd catch up with her in a few minutes.

I took Iris to the bookstore office so we'd have some privacy. "Mary Beth is her mother, isn't she?"

Iris sat down and put her face in her hands. I borrowed one of Barry's interrogation lines. "Do you want to tell me what happened?"

Iris looked up; the color had drained from her face. "You have to promise you won't tell Ali."

I nodded in agreement. It took her a few moments to collect herself, but then she took a couple of deep breaths and started to talk. "It was not supposed to turn out this way. . . . I was Mary Beth's assistant. I did whatever she needed whether it was handling an RSVP for a party or going with her to Catalina. If I had known—" She glanced out toward the bookstore. Ali was standing by the magazines. "No matter what, I love that girl as if she were mine. And as far as I'm concerned, she is my daughter."

The story went that Mary Beth hadn't told Iris she was pregnant until she was in her seventh month. "She was one of those women who barely show. She wore loose clothes, and not even her husband figured it out. She never gave me details, but I think she planned to leave Lance and go off with the baby's father, and then something happened with him. She got panicky. Her husband couldn't have kids, so there was no way she could pass the baby off as his. She came up with this plan. We'd spend her last month on Catalina and she'd have the baby there, only she would tell the doctor that she was me."

Iris examined her hands. "You have to understand, I was broke. Just out of college with student loans and I wanted to start a business." Her breath caught. "I'm so embarrassed I did it for the money.

"It wasn't that hard to pull off. Mary Beth had dark hair in those days, and we both wore ours long and loose. We both wore baggy clothes and were always together. The local doctor delivered the baby. He didn't know either of us, so he didn't question it when Mary Beth gave him my name." Iris had to stop for a moment, then went on.

"She had already gotten Lance to agree to adopting. I was going to take Ali home with me, and then we'd arrange a private adoption. But Lance flew into some kind of rage and said he'd changed his mind. At first Mary Beth thought she'd get him to change his mind back, but he completely refused. She stayed involved with us, but then we had this big blowup. She wanted to run things, but by then I'd fallen in love with the baby. For better or worse she was mine." Iris had been staring at some spot on the floor as she talked. Finally she looked at me directly; her face was wet with tears.

"There was no reason ever to tell Ali. My name is on her birth certificate. And then out of nowhere Mary Beth contacted me. She told me it had been bothering her all these years and now that her husband was dead, she wanted to come clean and claim her daughter."

"And you killed her to keep it quiet," I said. Iris's expression went from distraught to angry.

"Killed her? Don't be ridiculous." Iris got up to leave. She turned back at the door. "If you want to know who killed her, why don't you look for Ali's father? Mary Beth said she wanted Ali to know who both of her parents were." She glared at me. "And no, I don't know who he is."

"I HAVE TO GO BACK TO CATALINA," I SAID TO Dinah when I found her in the bookstore. My comment didn't sit well with her even when I repeated Iris's story.

"Molly, you can't go back there. You'll get arrested. That deputy will nab you as soon as you set one foot off the boat."

"I have to see what's hidden in the fireplace. I bet it points to Ali's father," I said.

"Who probably killed Mary Beth," Dinah said softly. "And once someone has killed someone it's not that hard to kill someone else, if you get my meaning."

I didn't say anything and Dinah nudged me impatiently. "Did you hear what I said? You go back there and you'll be in double jeopardy—from the deputy and from Ali's father."

"Will you come with?" I asked.

Dinah said yes, then changed her answer when I told her I planned to go the next day. She had an in-class essay and had to be there. Then Dinah surprised me by suggesting I talk to Detective Heather.

"Is your scarf pulled too tight?" I said, looking at the pale pink and burnt orange combo of scarves she had wound around her neck. "I want you to stop for a minute and consider the details. She already laughed off the crochet piece. If I start telling her about people switching identities and secret fathers—"

"I see your point. It might sound a little like a soap opera plot," Dinah conceded.

"My plan is simple. I'll wear a hat, dark glasses and a hoodie over some jeans. I'll blend right in with everybody else. The deputy won't recognize me, and there's no way for whoever Ali's father is to know what I'm doing. I'm not going to tell anybody else about the trip."

"But Molly, if you get caught breaking and entering, you won't get off with a warning," Dinah cautioned.

"No breaking and entering. There might be a key." Dinah gave me a quizzical look and I explained. "Before Iris left the bookstore I asked her if she knew anything about a secret compartment in the fireplace. She said the only hiding place she knew about was the flower pot on the front porch where a key was buried."

"But that was a long time ago," Dinah said.

"I've been keeping my spare key in the same place since we moved into our house," I said. "I'm betting it's still there."

Bob interrupted and asked if I wanted him to make up more iced tea samples. I told him my need for them was done. As he prepared to go back to the café, he asked me if I'd heard any more about who was to be the subject for

Making Amends. It took me a moment to remember what he was talking about.

PANDEMONIUM WAS WAITING WHEN I ARRIVED home. The She La Las and their spouses had gathered for a pep evening before the audition. All three women were drinking hot water, lemon juice and honey spiked with vodka. My father was trying to calm the women down by telling them they were a sure thing. The other two husbands looked exhausted by the ordeal.

My mother saw me trying to slip down the hall and rushed over. "Wish me luck, honey, wish me luck," she squealed as she held me tight. "Tomorrow's the big day."

I smiled and agreed it was a big day. *For all of us.*

THE DOGS FOLLOWED ME INTO SAMUEL'S ROOM and I shut the door. I was looking through his old hooded sweatshirts when the phone rang.

"Hi, sunshine," Mason said, sounding fresh and upbeat. As soon as he heard the tension in my voice, he offered to come rescue me from Camp She La La. I was too focused on getting ready for my Catalina trip and without giving details, passed.

"How about tomorrow night?" Mason offered.

I gave him a pass on that, too. I didn't want him to take it personally and I also didn't want to explain about my trip, so I suggested Saturday. He made some comment about checking his calendar.

"It's my grandson's birthday. Ever since my son moved back in the area, birthdays have become an all-day affair. The whole family shows, and there's a magician for the kids and a pitcher of sangria for the adults."

"I could do that," I said. "It's been a long time since I've been to a kid's party. It would be fun."

There was such a long pause on his end, I thought we'd been cut off. "Mason, are you still there?" I said finally.

"Molly, about Saturday," he said with an ominous catch in his voice. "I never take my girlfriends to family things."

Now the silence was on my end. I didn't know what I was more upset about. The *s* on the end of *girlfriend* or being put off.

"Girlfriends," I said finally with a huge emphasis on the *s*.

I heard Mason groan. "It was an unfortunate use of the plural. I meant I never take my current girlfriend to family events. There, is that better?"

"No." The word slipped out before I really thought it out. All he was doing was offering me exactly what I'd said I wanted. Something casual with no strings, no commitments and no future. He didn't bring any of his girlfriends to family things because they were just temporary players. I didn't like being relegated to a list, and I didn't like knowing the ending when we'd barely begun. "I'm sorry, Mason, that doesn't work for me. I'm an all-access sort of person, like you've had with my family."

"It's different with your family. I knew your son first." Mason made regretful noises. "Molly, lets just erase everything I said and start over."

"Can't. I have to go," I said quickly and hung up. *Good work, Molly, from too many men to none.* I wondered if Mason would still bail me out if things went badly on my trip.

CHAPTER 29

I STOPPED AT LE GRANDE FROMAGE IN THE morning for a red eye before driving to Long Beach to catch the boat. There was too much hysteria at my house to even attempt to make a pot of coffee. I wished my mother good luck and left as she was yelling "Irv, I can't find my shoes." Nobody asked where I was going, and I didn't volunteer the information.

Everyone in Tarzana seemed to have stopped there for coffee, and I joined the crowd at the counter. Adele found me in line. "Pink, why are you taking the day off?" Adele had a naturally loud voice, and several people turned to see what the noise was about. I tried to give Adele a vague answer, but she saw the printout of my Catalina reservation sticking out of my tote bag. She stared at my outfit—the baggy hooded sweatshirt over jeans, my hair hidden under a baseball cap.

"I get it, you're going to Catalina incognito. But Pink, consider this: I knew it was you right away. It's the mystery thing with that crochet piece again, isn't it?" she said.

"Could you keep your voice down," I said in a loud

whisper. I glanced over the line behind me and saw several familiar faces. Hal was back there and just behind him, Camille. I wondered if they had heard. Then I noticed Matt was at his usual table poring over something as he ate his breakfast.

"I thought you gave that up," she said, sticking to me like glue.

I merely smiled at her and said nothing, but it didn't help. "Pink, you have to let me come with you. You need someone to watch your back. Please." At that she hugged me and hung on to me. "You and Dinah have all the adventures. Let me be your sidekick this time."

I hated to admit that she had a point. Even with Mason's number already punched in my phone ready for the send button, it would be better not to go alone. But Adele? She seemed to have forgotten that not too long ago she'd been telling me what a mess I'd made of everything. Now she was acting as though we were almost best friends or at the very least, crochet sisters. Hoping I wouldn't regret it, I said she could come.

Never the subtle one, Adele started jumping up and down and saying I was going to be glad she came with me.

There were no dolphins on the trip over this time and not much sun. Just a white sky and me trying to will the boat to go faster and Adele trying to grill me about what I was going to do on the island. I told her it was better for her if she didn't know.

I pulled the hat down as we got off the boat. I glanced ahead to the business area and was relieved not to see Deputy Daniels. When we got to the green pier, Adele and I separated. She went to play miniature golf, and I followed the curved road along the shore. We'd agreed that we would meet back at the boat dock and take the next boat back. And if I didn't show up, she should call Dinah.

My heart rate kicked up as I passed the Casino Building and went around the bend.

The cats looked up as I approached the house, but other

than that it was deserted. The trees shaded the area into gloominess. When I reached the house, I tripped up the stairs with nervous clumsiness. There were two pots of impatiens on the top step. I made a move toward the pot on the left. Hoping Mary Beth had been as much of a creature of habit as I had been, I stuck my hand in the dirt. I dug around, but after a few moments felt nothing but roots. I shook the grit off my hand and my heart rate kicked up as I moved to the pot on the right.

If I didn't find a key in there I was in big trouble. I rummaged through the dirt feeling more and more frantic. Something crawled up my arm and I started to jerk away. But just then my finger brushed something metal. I grabbed onto it and pulled my hand away from the pot, while frantically brushing the insect off my inner arm. When I opened my hand I saw the key. It was old and crusted with gunk and I wondered if it would still work.

I checked the area again and saw no one. Even so, I stayed low as I tried to put the key in the lock. After some maneuvering, the key slid in and then I had to jiggle it back and forth before it turned and I heard the bolt move.

I opened the door and went inside quickly.

The faster I was out of there, the better. There was always the chance the deputy would come by and see movement in the house or that the caretaker would come by to feed the cats. I walked across the living room directly to the fireplace. As I stood in front of it, examining the tiles and the mantelpiece, I realized I had a problem. While I might be confident a secret compartment existed, I had no idea where or how to find it. Wasn't that the thing about a secret compartment? They were *secret*, invisible.

The tension was making me light-headed, and I had to remind myself to take some deep breaths. Even so, my heart was pounding as though it would beat itself right out of my chest.

I ran my hands over the front of the fireplace and then along the mantel between the two metal candleholders.

Nothing. I lifted each photo along the top and felt the space underneath for some kind of button or lever. Still nothing.

The tension was turning into panic. In desperation, I pulled Mary Beth's filet piece out of my tote bag and looked at the fireplace motif for a clue. Was that a mark on the right side of the mantel or just an extra double crochet in a space? Maybe here was something under the candleholder. I grabbed it to pick it up, but it didn't move. Then I pushed and it slid, and as it did, I heard just the slightest click. When I looked at the front, one of the tiles was sticking out a fraction ahead of the others. When I pushed on it, it popped out and slid to the side revealing a box-shaped hiding place. My hand was shaking when I reached in. There were several old Polaroid photos. I looked them over and glanced at the crochet piece in my hand. And suddenly I got it. How could I have missed it? The answer was right in front of me all the time.

The several panels of cats didn't refer to the four-legged variety hanging around the house. I'd needed to change the spelling to *Katz*. And the figure I had taken to indicate Sagittarius wasn't really meant to mean an archer. The figure was a hunter. The first photo showed Mary Beth holding a baby and gazing down at it. But in the second, the baby was held by Hunter. He was looking away, as though he wanted to drop the bundle and run.

I put the crochet piece and the photos in my bag, closed up the panel, reburied the key and left quickly while the truth rolled around in my head. And the question of what to do with it.

I retraced my steps. My plan was to go back to the boat dock and wait there for Adele. The less wandering through town, the lower the chance of being noticed. As I got back into the main shopping area and was passing the green pier, I glanced out at the boats. I did a double take when I saw the name across the back of the one in the closest slip. *Camille* in gold block lettering. Coincidence or had Hunter followed me? I saw Hunter tying his dinghy to the dock just below the green pier. I ducked behind a palm tree and watched as he climbed the steps to the pier and walked down it toward the beach. I moved around the tree as he passed. He was so close I could see he hadn't shaved. He stopped when he got to the walkway in front of the business area and looked in both directions. Then he went toward the Casino Building.

A plan formed in my mind as I glanced out toward the boat. I still had the cups from the encounter with Iris and Ali. If I could get something with Hunter's saliva, I could prove he was Ali's father. Surely there was something on the boat—a discarded paper cup or even a straw. I could be on the boat and off in a flash.

I raced-walked up the pier and down the stairs. I chose the closest dinghy and got in. I put on the life jacket sitting on the seat, untied the dinghy and began to row. At first the boat went in circles, but then I got the hang of it. A few moments later, the dinghy bumped against the side of the *Camille*. I tied it up, climbed the ladder and went aboard the boat.

I called hello a few times but no one answered. I rushed past the table and chairs set up on the open back deck. I half tumbled down the stairs to the galley and began fumbling through the small trash can. I pulled out a paper cup from Le Grande Fromage and stuck it in my bag. I was up the stairs and halfway across the deck when Hunter's head appeared above the side.

CHAPTER 30

"IT'S MOLLY FROM THE BOOKSTORE, ISN'T IT?" he said in a friendly tone as he climbed the rest of the way and stepped onto the boat. "People don't appreciate it when you borrow their dinghy," he chided.

Stay calm, I told myself. Still, my heart was in my throat. "I was walking down Crescent and I saw your boat. I thought Camille was here and came to say hello."

He was all friendly charm. With the slightly shaggy black hair streaked with gray and the rimless glasses, he looked like a nice guy. "She didn't come. I decided to play hooky and take the boat out."

"Well, now that I know she's not here, I'll just go. I want to get the dinghy back before the owner misses it." I made a move for the side of the boat, but Hunter put his hand on my arm, stopping me.

"I don't know how to thank you for letting Camille join your group. I've never seen her so happy. I was just going to open a bottle of wine. We Tarzana expatriates have to stick together. Stay and have a glass."

I made a comment about not wanting to miss my boat

back, and he glanced toward the empty spot by the dock. "You have plenty of time. It hasn't even arrived from the mainland yet." His gaze rested on my tote bag and purse. "What kind of host am I?" he said, taking both items from my arm before I could stop him. "I'll put this down below until you're ready to leave." He tried to unhook the life jacket and take it as well, but I managed to pull away.

He disappeared down the stairway with my stuff. All my proof was in the tote bag and I wasn't leaving without it. I considered following him down below and taking my things back, but he was already on his way up with two glasses of wine. He put the glasses on a round filagree doily set in the middle of a small round table.

"I hope you like pinot noir," he said, picking up the glass closest to him and taking a sip. He went on about how it came from a small winery near Santa Barbara. "I'd like your opinion on it. I'm thinking of ordering a case." He gestured toward my glass. I stalled, examining the doily. It was perfect except for a tiny loose stitch next to the glass.

Although he was completely pleasant, I was sure he had followed me to the island.

I took a step back from the table and stumbled. He set his glass down quickly and grabbed my arm to steady me. "I'm sure the wine is delicious," I said. "I just need a minute to get my sea legs."

He suggested I sit, but instead I walked to the side of the boat. He was like my shadow he stayed so close.

His voice had just a hint of impatience as he suggested we go back to our wine. "I don't want you to miss your boat," he said. "Or the chance to try the pinot."

He again suggested I sit down or at least take off the life jacket. I glanced at the table and told him I was okay.

"I think I have the hang of standing on the boat now." I went to take one of the glasses, but he reached first and picked up the one on his right. "Cheers," I said, taking the other. I just held it, though, and he pressed me to taste it, his tone growing more impatient. I had the feeling if I didn't start drinking, he was going to pour it down my throat.

His eyes were locked on the wine as I lifted the glass and took a swallow. I heard him release his breath as he held up his glass. "Cheers." He drank a large sip of the deep red liquid.

He watched as I continued tipping the glass to my lips and the amount in the glass diminished. Suddenly, he let down the act.

"You found the photo, didn't you?" he said. When I nodded, he wanted to know where it had been, and he appeared angry and frustrated when I described the hiding place that he obviously had missed.

"You could have made it so much easier on yourself if you had just listened when I left the messages and the gifts." He ran his fingers through his hair. "What was with Mary Beth? Suddenly after all those years, she wants to turn everybody's life upside down. The kid was happy with the cactus people. Why couldn't Mary Beth have left things as they were?" He peered at me. "You didn't know her, did you?"

I shook my head and he continued. "She married Lance for the package that came with him—he wasn't the star his father was, but he had control of the estate. They were on the A-list for invitations everywhere. I met Mary Beth at some action actor's Christmas party in Malibu. Camille and I'd been married for a couple of years." Hunter ran his finger along the stem of his wineglass. "While I guess Mary Beth liked all the charge accounts, she was getting a little tired of what went with it. Lance had an alcohol problem and an angry disposition. As for me—Mary Beth was hot and I needed some recreation after all the bowing and scraping I had to do for the Rhead family.

"When Mary Beth got pregnant, I think it made her loopy in the brain. Where she got the idea I would leave Camille and go off with her—" He shook his head with disbelief. "I had the beginnings of a glorious future. Why would I give that up to go off and live in poorsville? She figured it out eventually and went into the save-her-marriage mode." His voice rose in intensity. "And now, just as I was about to take over for Alexander Rhead, Mary Beth wanted to ruin everything." He glared at me. "Right, suddenly I'm going to claim the love child I had twenty-something years ago. Even if Camille was willing to forgive me, Alexander Rhead never would. He'd insist she divorce me. He certainly wouldn't turn over the production company. He's a vindictive man, and I have no doubt that he'd put the word out and make sure my career was in ashes. And for what? So some girl who has been okay with who her parents are suddenly gets her world flipped upside down."

He glared at me again. "And you. What is any of this to you?" He didn't wait for answer, but went back to talking about Mary Beth. "When she told me what she was planning to do, I asked her for some time to tell my family first. I gave her every indication I was going along with it completely. It really perturbed me when she left that package with your group."

When I looked surprised, he explained. "Yes, we were at the rinky-dink charity sale at that park. Part of my wife's effort to be a regular person." He made a few disparaging remarks about Camille's "life coach" and went back to talking about Mary Beth. "We had dinner a few times to discuss how to make the announcement. We met at her place, and I offered to help with the cooking. I tried lacing her food with arsenic, but all it did was make her sick. The last night I brought her the box of marzipan apples laced with cyanide. She loved that stuff, and I knew she wouldn't be able to turn it down even if her stomach was queasy. There was no way anyone would have linked us if it hadn't been for you and that stupid crochet group. Every time Camille mentioned that thing with the pictures that Mary Beth made—" His face grew angry. "Mary Beth showed it to me and said it was an expression of the anguish she'd been going through all those years. My mistake was not to have gotten it from her."

"Then you know what all the motifs mean?" He looked confused by the word *motifs* so I changed it to *images*, and then he nodded. "What about the strange circles?"

"She was trying to say *not* with the split one. You know, like those warning signs showing a picture in a circle with a line across it—no smoking, no swimming, no skating. And the plain circle was supposed to mean *yes* or *is*. She was trying to say 'not Iris, is Mary Beth.'" He threw up his hands. "What's the difference? That piece is never going to see the light of day again." He drained his glass and put it on the table with a soft thud.

I set my almost-empty glass down and leaned against the table, appearing to lose my footing for a second.

"Don't worry," he said, watching me intently. "It's just the sleeping pills kicking in. They're quite potent when mixed with alcohol." His lips curved into a smirk. "We'll be pushing off in a few minutes. I want to get out into the channel before I dump you overboard. You won't be needing this." He leaned forward to unhook the orange life jacket, but his features suddenly seemed to melt and he sagged against the table.

"Don't worry," I said. "It's just the sleeping pills kicking in." He tried to fight the growing grogginess, but his legs buckled and he collapsed on the deck. I reached in my pocket for my cell phone, but before I could dial, a boat approached and I heard a voice through a bullhorn.

"Put your hands on your head, Mrs. Pink." Adele and Deputy Daniels were in the front as it pulled alongside the *Camille*. He looked at me and then saw Hunter crumpled on the deck. Before he even climbed aboard, Deputy Daniels was already taking out his handcuffs.

CHAPTER 31

"SEE, PINK, AREN'T YOU GLAD I CAME WITH," Adele said as I sat behind the counter in handcuffs and she stood in the lobby watching. "I saw you on the boat and knew you were in trouble. Pretty clever on my part that I told him I thought you were stealing it. As soon as I mentioned your name, he double-timed it."

A moment later Deputy Daniels came out of a tiny back office holding the keys. Mason followed him out and gave me a thumbs-up. When my hands were released, I shook them out gratefully. Mason took my arm, and the deputy unlocked the door and let us out. Adele came out through the lobby, and the three of us made our way through the crowd. Everyone was talking about what had happened and pointing at me. I had become the center of the island story of the year.

"Free again," I said, taking a deep breath of the fresh air as we walked toward the water. "How did you get him to let me go?" Even though our relationship seemed to have faltered, Mason came over by helicopter when I called him.

"Good lawyering," Mason answered with a smile. "And my cell phone." He held it up to demonstrate. "And good work on your part."

"More like a lucky break," I said, shaking my hands again to make sure they were free. I had been so concerned about bumping into the deputy, I had punched Mason's number into my cell phone just in case. In the midst of the episode with Hunter, I'd pushed the send button without even knowing it. Mason's voice mail had answered and had recorded Hunter's whole confession. When Mason played it for the deputy, he finally realized who the bad guy really was.

I knew that Hunter had already been flown by medevac helicopter to the hospital at Long Beach. But Mason added that when he came to, he was going to be arrested.

When we got to the dock, Mason stopped. "How did you manage not to drink the wine laced with sleeping pills?"

"Yeah, Pink, how did you manage that?" Adele piped in. I told him the story of how Dinah and I had reversed our drinks by mistake during our first trip to the island. "We didn't realize it, but we had gone to the other side of the round table and what had been on my right was now on my left and vice versa. I noticed the imperfection on the doily next to the glass Hunter had prepared for me. When he set down his glass to grab me and followed me to the edge of the boat, I went back to the other side of the table. He was so intent on watching me, he didn't notice that the drink on his right was now the one he'd made special for me."

Adele was speechless. I noticed the *Catalina Express* was getting ready to load. "That's us," I said.

"Are you sure you won't come with me? There's room on the helicopter," Mason said, loosely gesturing toward the heliport just around the bend. I'd had enough heart-stopping action for one day and passed.

"How can I thank you?" I said to Mason.

"I can think of a few ways," he said with a warm smile.

"Beginning with giving me a do-over of yesterday." I knew he meant the phone conversation when he'd mentioned his grandson's birthday party. But I also knew the do-over was more about phrasing than changing his girlfriend-family policy. "It was fun playing the white-knight rescuer flying in on my trusty-steed helicopter. Life is never dull around you." He kissed me softly on the cheek.

"C'mon, Pink, we're going to miss the boat." Adele started walking. Mason squeezed my hand and let go, and I rushed after Adele. When we got on the boat, I looked back toward the dock. Mason had gotten into the golf cart cab and was driving away.

"THANK YOU FOR EVERYTHING, HONEY," my mother said as I walked my parents out to their SUV. The bags were already in and they were ready to head back to Santa Fe—for a short time, anyway. The She La Las had aced the audition. Not only would they get to do their famous "My Man Dan," but they would also be doing covers of "Hug Me, Kiss Me, Love Me" and "From One Night to Forever" because the Nonpareilles and the Peaches and Creams didn't want to leave their retirement communities. The ten-city Nostalgia Tour was culminating in a stop at Carnegie Hall—my mother's dream come true. And my son Samuel was going along as their musical director.

"You'll come to New York, won't you?" my mother said, stopping at the curb.

"Miss my mother's debut Carnegie Hall appearance? Are you kidding? I'll be in the first row." My father hugged me and pressed another tube of sunscreen in my hand before he climbed into the driver's seat. "My daughter the detective. Who would have thought?"

My mother hugged me for a long time and thanked me again for the cooler with a whole noodle pudding. She started to climb in the SUV but came back. She slipped off one of her silver and turquoise bracelets and put it on my arm. "Honey, you need a little color." Then she got in and a moment later they drove off. Good-byes were always hard for me, I started to tear up as I walked back to the house.

As EXPECTED, HUNTER WAS CHARGED WITH Mary Beth's murder and an attempt on me. Alexander Rhead sent out a press release announcing that he was staying on as president and that Hunter was taking an extended leave of absence. Camille stuck by Hunter long enough to handle bail, organize a legal team and set him up in a condo before filing for divorce.

Alexander Rhead appreciated his daughter's abilities for the first time and was so impressed at how Camille took charge of everything, he offered her the position of coproducer of Rhead Productions' new show *Couples Stranded in Paradise*.

"I want to thank you for my first experience being part of a regular group," Camille said when she came to her last group meeting. She dropped off a slightly crooked blanket for our project and apologized for not having made a bookmark but the thread crochet just wasn't her thing. "I'm afraid with my new job, I just won't have time now. I do plan to keep crocheting, though." She produced a ball of yarn and the beginning of a scarf. She had thanked us for the support during her ordeal. She turned to CeeCee. "By the way, it was Hunter who wanted to replace you. I told my father that you are the show, and A. R. said he'd make sure your contract was straightened out before they tape the season opener here at the bookstore." When Camille left, Cee-Cee looked around the table.

"I told you she was a spy. But, thank heavens, one with good sense."

ALTHOUGH I HAD PROMISED IRIS I WOULDN'T tell Ali who her parents really were, after everything that

had happened it didn't stay a secret. When she was faced
with the DNA tests that confirmed her parents were Mary
Beth and Hunter, Ali was shocked, particularly when she
heard Mary Beth's original plan to adopt her. Iris stood by
her and helped her get through it. I made sure she got the
filet piece that Matt Wells had given me, since it had her
name on the envelope. Ali didn't know how to feel about it,
but I noticed that she didn't turn it down. She didn't want
to see Hunter even if he was her father.

Roseanne and Hal weren't pleased to find out they had a
new niece because as Mary Beth's closest blood relative
Ali inherited her real mother's share of the Lance Wells
estate. Matt Wells took it fine, however. Ali was much nicer
to work with than Mary Beth's sister and her husband, and
Ali was okay with him running things.

Someone snitched on Hal's card room—not me—and
he had to shut down. Last time I saw the fireplug in a suit,
he was taking a dance lesson and was amazingly light on
his feet.

No matter who her biological parents were, Ali was
clear her real parents were Iris and Paul, and she was glad
to help them out with her newly inherited income.

She promised to rejoin the crochet group soon.

THE SAYING THAT THE SHOW MUST GO ON WAS
true. Despite all the upheaval, CeeCee got her contract,
and the *Making Amends* film crew did their setup at the
bookstore on the appointed day. The director wanted the
store to appear real, so Bob was at his station in the café
and Adele, Sheila, Dinah and I were gathered around the
event table with our crochet work out. William aka Koo
Koo was in the children's area showing off his book to a
couple of kids Adele had rounded up. Even Rayaad was at
the cashier station. Mrs. Shedd had gotten her hair done
and was hanging by the front counter as taping began and
CeeCee started to read from the teleprompter.

"We're here at Shedd & Royal Books and More in Tarzana, California, to let you the audience be the witness to the righting of an old wrong."

They stopped taping and the director said a photo essay of the subject's story would be inserted for the real show.

"And now we have the resolution. The moment we've all been waiting for," CeeCee read when the taping resumed.

Everyone in the bookstore looked around as music came up. With a theatrical flourish, the front door of the bookstore was opened by two men in tuxedos, and a red carpet was rolled out.

A man walked in and glanced around. His silver hair accentuated his tan face. His features had the character that only comes from having lived an interesting life. The tuxedo was no doubt provided by the show, but he appeared at home in it. But who was he?

Mrs. Shedd gasped and leaned against the counter, appearing almost faint.

"Joshua Royal is co-owner of the bookstore with Pamela Shedd," CeeCee read. "He was single, she was a widow and their business relationship became personal. But Joshua had places to go and adventures to have and left without a word. But all the while he was working on the freighter, as a cook in Antarctica, in the monastery in Tibet and the ride operator at Tivoli Gardens in Copenhagen, he never forgot Pamela or stopped thinking that someday he'd come back."

The music swelled. Mr. Royal took long strides toward Mrs. Shedd and à la *An Officer and a Gentleman* scooped her up in his arms and amidst all of our cheering, carried her out. Only Adele looked disappointed.

It was past midnight by the time everything was packed up and I went home to a quiet house. Tomorrow a crew would come to put the bookstore back in order.

As usual the dogs ran out when I opened the door. The photo was still sitting on the kitchen table. I had found it slipped under the door a few days earlier. It was of Barry and a young woman who resembled him around the eyes. On the back he'd written simply, *Thank you.*

Cosmo and Blondie ran around the yard a few times and rushed back inside. The dog situation had stayed as is, though now that Jeffrey was back, he'd come by several times. He would always deliver a message from his father that he sent his best.

I'd heard from Mason a few times, reminding me that I owed him another chance and that his girlfriend-and-family rule wasn't written in stone. So far I'd been putting him off. The problem wasn't him. It was me. What did I really want? Was I after pleasant companionship without real involvement. Or did I want something with all the complications that went with intertwined lives?

The night sky was heavy with clouds. The weather guys had predicted rain, and in the typical Southern California style of feast or famine in the precipitation department a heavy steady rain began to fall.

I curled up in my own bed with Cosmo snuggled next to me. Blondie as always took her chair.

A noise in the corner disturbed me. At first it was a drip, but it quickly turned into a steady gush, like water being poured from a pitcher. I realized the old leak in the roof over the bedroom was back.

I picked up the phone and hesitated. I knew he would come, but did I want what came with him?

Filet Bookmark

EASY TO MAKE

Materials: 1 ball of bedspread-weight cotton thread (number 10). It is enough for a number of bookmarks. Steel hook size 9 (1.40 cm) or size needed for gauge

Finished size: About 1¾ by 8 inches

Gauge: 4 blocks = 1¼ inches
9 rows = 2 inches

Stitches: Single crochet
Double crochet

Attach thread to hook with a slipknot and chain 15.

Row 1: Double crochet in the fourth chain from hook, double crochet in the next 2 chains, chain 2 and skip the next 2 chains, double crochet in the next 4 chains; chain 2 and skip the next 2 chains and double crochet in the last chain. (4 blocks made: 2 are solid and 2 are empty.)

Row 2: Chain 3 (counts as double crochet), turn work, double crochet in the next 3 stitches, chain 2 and skip the next 2 stitches, double crochet in the next 4 stitches, chain 2 and skip the next 2 stitches, double crochet in the last stitch.

Repeat Row 2 twenty-eight times. Do not finish off.

BORDER

Round 1: Chain 1, do not turn work, make a row of single crochets around with 3 single crochets in each corner. Join with a slip stitch to the first single crochet.

Round 2: Chain 1 and make a single crochet in the same stitch, chain 1, *single crochet in the next single crochet, chain 1*. Repeat from * to * around. Join with a slip stitch to first single crochet, finish off.

BLOCKING

Dip in liquid starch and squeeze out excess. Shape on a piece of cardboard covered with a sheet of waxed paper. Hold in place with rustproof pushpins. Let dry.

Chart for Filet Bookmark

Cuddle Blanket

EASY TO MAKE

Materials: Super bulky soft yarn such as Red Heart Baby Clouds

About 284 yards of color A

About 284 yards of color B

Size P (11.50 mm) hook for body of blanket, size N (9.00 mm) for border

Finished size: About 42 by 48 inches

Attach color A with a slipknot to size P hook and chain 54.

Foundation row: Single crochet across. (53 single crochets made.)

Row 1: Chain 1, turn and single crochet across.

Row 2: Chain 3 (counts as double crochet), turn and double crochet across.

Row 3: Chain 1, turn and single crochet across.

Row 4: Chain 3 (counts as double crochet), turn and double crochet across.

Row 5: Chain 1, turn and single crochet across.

Row 6: Chain 3 (counts as double crochet), turn and double crochet across.

Row 7: Chain 1, turn and single crochet across; fasten off.

Attach color B to last stitch of row 7. Repeat rows 1 through 7 with color B; fasten off.

Attach color A to last stitch of row 7. Repeat rows 1 through 7 with color A.

Attach color B to last stitch of row 7. Repeat rows 1 through 7; fasten off.

Attach color A to last stitch of row 7. Repeat rows 1 through 7; fasten off.

Attach color B to last stitch of row 7. Repeat rows 1 through 7; fasten off.

Attach color A to last stitch of row 7. Repeat rows 1 through 7; Repeat row 1 and fasten off.

The blanket will begin and end with color A. There will be 3 stripes of color B and 4 stripes of color A.

BORDER

Round 1: Change to size N hook and attach color B with right side facing, single crochet around the body, increasing at the corners; join to first single crochet with a slip stitch. Turn.

Round 2: Chain 3 (counts as double crochet), skip first single crochet, double crochet in each single crochet around increasing at corners; join with a slip stitch to the top of the chain 3. Do not turn.

Round 3: Chain 1, single crochet in each stitch around, increasing at corners; join to chain 1 with a slip stitch and fasten off. Finish off by weaving in yarn tails.

California Noodle Pudding

SERVES 12

*16 ounces wide egg noodles,
cooked and drained
4 ounces of butter, cut in
small pieces
1 pint sour cream
1 pound cottage cheese*

*6 eggs, lightly beaten
1 teaspoon vanilla
2 tablespoons sugar
6 ounces of dried apricots,
cut in small pieces
1/4 cup slivered almonds*

Pour cooked noodles in a bowl and mix in butter pieces. In a separate bowl mix the sour cream and cottage cheese. Add the beaten eggs and mix until blended. Mix in vanilla and sugar. Mix in the apricot pieces. Combine mixture with the noodles. Pour into a greased 9-by-13-inch pan.

Bake at 400° for 15 minutes. Lower oven temperature to 350° and bake 1 hour.

Can be eaten hot or cold.